THE BURNING

THE BURNING

LAURA BATES

sourcebooks
fire

Published by Sourcebooks Fire, an imprint of Sourcebooks
P.O. Box 4410, Naperville, Illinois 60567-4410
(630) 961-3900
sourcebooks.com

Originally published in 2019 in Great Britain by Simon &
Schuster, an imprint of Simon & Schuster UK Ltd.

Library of Congress Cataloging-in-Publication Data

Names: Bates, Laura, active 2014, author.
Title: The burning / Laura Bates.
Description: Naperville, Illinois : Sourcebooks Fire, [2020] | Audience:
    Ages 14-18. | Audience: Grades 10-12.
Identifiers: LCCN 2019045287 | (hardcover)
Subjects: CYAC: Bullying--Fiction. | Rumor--Fiction. | Social
    media--Fiction. | Mothers and daughters--Fiction. | Schools--Fiction. |
    Witchcraft--Fiction. | Scotland--Fiction.
Classification: LCC PZ7.1.B3772 Bur 2020 | DDC [Fic]--dc23
LC record available at https://lccn.loc.gov/2019045287

Printed and bound in the United States of America.
WOZ 10 9 8 7 6 5 4 3 2 1

For Evie

THE BURNING

Content Warning

This book deals with issues including sexual bullying, sexting, and revenge pornography.

WHEN I WAS ELEVEN, MY English teacher told me that fire is like a tiger. He was teaching us about similes, I suppose. He said a tiger is orange and fierce and leaps forward, and it can be beautiful but also deadly.

Mr. Watson was wrong. Fire is a thousand times more deadly than a tiger. It can't be stopped with a bullet or a fence. It destroys everything in its path.

A single tiny spark gobbles up oxygen and burns hotter and hotter, growing bigger and bigger. Everything it feeds on becomes part of it, like a monster that bloats and swells as it devours its prey.

But fire isn't evil. It isn't good. It just is.

I'm not saying I know better than Mr. Watson or anything, but in my opinion, it would have made a lot more sense if he had said that fire was like a rumor.

Because fire is sneaky. You might think you've extinguished it, but one creeping red tendril, one single wisp of smoke, is enough to let it leap back to life again. Especially if someone is watching, waiting to fan the flames.

ONE

HAIRBRUSH. TAMPONS. TOOTHBRUSH. TOOTHPASTE.

The front door opens with a shudder and an ominous creak. Dark-blue paint cracks and peels above a tarnished brass knocker.

Deodorant. Watch. Shoes.

"Come on," Mum pants, heaving two bulging suitcases over the threshold and into the dark hallway.

I'm a list-maker. Lists give me grip. You can hold on to a list. Doesn't matter what's on it. Today, it's everything I had to remember to pack at the last minute. Things I couldn't put in the car last night because I'd need them this morning.

The list has been helping me to breathe. Like a spell to ward off evil. I've been chanting it under my breath since I woke up, and I haven't been able to stop. Because, as long as I keep repeating the things I need to remember, somehow I can distract myself. Pretend I'm not really walking out of my bedroom for the last time. Not really stepping into a car loaded with everything we own. Not really driving past the park where I fell off my bike for the first time. Not watching the swimming pool where I trained three nights a week disappear in the rearview mirror.

Hairbrush.

Passing the fish and chips shop.

Tampons. The library. *Toothbrush.*

The pet shop where I bought my ill-fated iguana. RIP, Iggy Poppet.

Toothpaste.

But now we're here. And even the list isn't powerful enough to blot out the new house in front of me.

I hesitate. Somehow, stepping through the door will make it real. Make the move from Birmingham, England, to Scotland real. I look back to the car, parked a little way down the street, its doors standing open, more luggage and overstuffed bags threatening to spill out. Through the back window, I can see a tattered box labeled ANNA'S ROOM: DIARIES, PHOTOGRAPHS, DAD'S BOOKS.

Nothing left to go back to, anyway. I take a deep breath, adjust the bulky cat carrier under my arm, and step inside.

The hallway has a musty smell, its whitewashed walls and wooden ceiling beams lit by one naked bulb. The moving van, which whisked away most of our earthly belongings the night before we left, has arrived before us, and piles of labeled boxes teeter precariously on all sides. Mum's already bustling into the big, airy kitchen, which also serves as the living room. There's one of those

4

big cast-iron stoves radiating warmth and our new brick-red sofa, still covered in protective plastic.

A massive old fireplace dominates the room, empty but framed by a handsome wooden mantelpiece. I empty my pockets, shoving my car trip trash on top of it. Old Styrofoam cup. Crumpled snack bag. Half a candy bar. It looks a bit less imposing now.

Gently, I set down the cat carrier, and one very grumpy black cat unfurls out of it like a puff of smoke, letting out an indignant yowl to tell me exactly what he thinks of being cooped up in the car for so long.

"Sorry, Cosmo," I whisper. I bend down to ruffle his soft fur with my fingertips, craving the comfort of his familiar warmth, but he turns tail with an angry hiss and disappears through the kitchen window into the back garden. I sort of wish I could follow him.

I shrug off my jacket and half slump onto the crackling, plastic-covered sofa. "Don't even think about it!" Mum warns. "We've got hours of unpacking ahead of us, and the car's not even empty yet."

Suddenly the trees outside shake with a gust of wind, causing an eerie, shrieking moan that sounds like it came from the bones of the house itself.

I try to sound sarcastic instead of freaked out. "Are you sure this place is fit for human habitation?"

We only looked around the house once on a rushed, blustery weekend at the end of March, speeding around Scotland in a whirl, viewing five or six different properties a day, each less inspiring than the last. At the last minute, we squeezed in an extra stop in a tiny fishing village named St. Monans, where Mum instantly fell in love with the quaint, crooked streets and peaceful old harbor lined with pastel-colored cottages.

Our house looked right out over the water—a neat, cream, square front snuggled cozily among the blues and yellows and pinks. Four sturdy wooden windows gave it a welcoming, symmetrical expression, and a bright-red roof peeped down from above, a few of the tiles in disarray as if they'd been knocked loose by clumsy seagulls. I could tell Mum was smitten before we'd even stepped inside, but Linda, the real estate agent, clearly still thought she had to convince us.

"It's historical!" she said brightly, through a pasted-on, lipstick smile, as she struggled to force open the sticking front door.

Upstairs, we had to duck under sloping ceilings, and I practically twisted an ankle tripping over the uneven floorboards.

"Imperfections add such a sense of personality to a house, don't they?" Linda gushed, rushing into the next room without waiting for an answer while I rubbed my ankle angrily. I'd happily have traded a bit less "personality" for a bit more health and safety, thank you very much.

I shiver and look up the winding staircase, remembering how I traipsed upstairs after Mum that day, bored and fed up.

We whizzed through three bedrooms, one looking out over a jungly back garden and the other two tucked under the front eaves of the house, with views across the street and down toward the harbor, where a few brightly painted fishing boats bobbed on the tide. The bathroom offered a dripping tap and a green stain around the sink's drain. The ceiling beams were riddled with tiny insect holes, and even the large stones around the doorways were scattered with deep, uneven scratches. ("Witches' marks! Don't they add a lovely touch of character?")

The house was chilly, and several of the walls were flecked

with mildew. (*Still there*, I notice, casting a critical eye over the paintwork in the hall.)

We didn't have time to look in the attic, which Linda airily assured us was both "spacious" and "cozy." Call me cynical, but this made me suspect it might be neither. ("The last owners never touched it, and it was used for storage before they arrived, so it might need just a *teensy* bit of tidying, but rest assured there's plenty of room up there.")

We'd been in a huge rush to move in two weeks, though, and, as Mum had pointed out in the gas station on the drive home, beggars can't be choosers. "Got to get you settled in time for the start of the new school year," she said, with a smile that was just a little too wide. "It'll only be a half-hour drive into town for school, and I can drop you off on my way to work."

Two weeks later, here we are.

The front door bangs in the wind, and I hurry to help unload the car. As we heave the last few boxes into the hall, the sky begins to rumble and the first drops of rain splatter on the pavement. Mum slams the door shut and puts an arm around my shoulders. She smells of perfume and vanilla essence. I breathe in her smell as deeply as I can, clinging to its familiarity. "Soon, it'll feel like home, honey," she says with a reassuring squeeze.

I make an mm-hmm noise and wriggle away to escape up the creaking staircase, muttering something about unpacking my room.

Upstairs, I shove the box of diaries and photographs as far as possible under my new bed without looking at it. I sling my backpack on the bedspread, letting the contents slither out: *Hairbrush. Tampons. Toothbrush. Toothpaste. Deodorant.*

I try to breathe.

7

My laptop slides out on top of them, the green power light blinking at me. My stomach does a weird sort of wriggle. I turn my back on it and tug the heavy window open with a complaining squeal and a cloud of dust. Outside the wind rustles the too-long grass and ivy sweeps like a tidal wave over the crumbling garden wall. In the far corner of the garden, a squat shed crouches like a toad in the gathering dusk. Rain is drumming steadily down now, and the evening air smells wet and earthy. The hair on my arms lifts as a cold gust blows in. I pull a baggy black sweater out of the nearest bag and shrug it over my head, then pull my hair out of its ponytail so it falls around my shoulders, warming my neck.

Mum has already hung my new school uniform over the door of the closet. I frown at the bottle-green blazer and kilt and picture myself arriving at St. Margaret's Academy, a flat gray building I've only seen pictures of online, standing awkwardly on my own while gaggles of students push past me, chattering excitedly.

"Anna! Dinner!"

I sigh and head downstairs, leaving the window open.

In the kitchen, Mum has already unearthed a few lamps and a tablecloth, giving the room an air of familiarity. A pan of hot water and spaghetti is bubbling away on the stove. Spaghetti wasn't on my list of last-minute things, but Mum shoved it in the glove compartment, realizing we wouldn't have anything else to eat on the first night. The modern cutlery with brightly colored handles and the tall glasses look out of place in this creaky museum of a house, which Linda proudly assured us originally dates back almost four centuries. It's like the cottage has dressed up in our old house's clothes, but the pants are too short, revealing a weird patch of bare ankle.

"It doesn't look like much yet." Mum shrugs apologetically, and I feel my heart constrict. Mum has uprooted her entire life— job, friends, everything—and here she is apologizing to me. I don't know what to say, so I shrug too, in a way that I hope looks like "I don't mind, Mum, I love you," but I'm afraid actually looks like "whatever."

"We'll get there." She smiles. "It's a fresh start, and that's what matters."

TWO

SUNLIGHT GLOWS ON THE OTHER side of my eyelids. I lie looking at the rosy haze, disoriented. My hand shoots out automatically to grope for my phone on the bedside table. The phone isn't there. Neither is the bedside table. My knuckles graze the chalky whitewashed wall instead. I startle, eyes flying open, reeling at the unfamiliarity of the room. And I remember. *You don't have a phone anymore, Anna. Not after what happened.* I close my eyes again and collapse back into my pillow, letting the pink engulf me.

There's the strangest noise. It panics me. The sound of quiet. No low, permanent thrum of traffic. No sudden scream of sirens, stopping as abruptly as they started. No clattering of trash cans being unloaded into garbage trucks. No screaming of next-door's baby through paper-thin walls.

The shock of the change hits me all over again.

There's something heavy on my legs. Cosmo must have forgiven me at some point during the night, because he's curled up like a pool of liquid fur on top of the bedspread. I slip one foot out and stroke his silky head with my toes.

"Toto," I whisper, "we're not in Kansas anymore."

I let the sound of my own heartbeat thud in my ears. As I lie there, other sounds creep in, so much softer than the morning chorus I'm used to. A trill of birdsong, repeated a few moments later in a deeper key. The gentle whispering of the wind around the eaves. And something faint, rhythmic, as reassuring as the tick of a clock. Like someone catching their breath and then blowing out gently through their nose, over and over again. It awakens something in the back of my mind, but I can't pin it down. I lie there, listening.

Huh-aaah. Huh-aaah.

It's water. Slapping against the wooden-boarded harborside and slipping back with the tide. I breathe in time with the water. In. Out. In. Out. Fresh. Start. Fresh. Start. Fresh. Start.

I throw on an oversize plaid shirt and a pair of leggings and head downstairs, running my hand along the unfamiliar, smooth wood of the banister. Mum is already busy in the kitchen, pulling mugs out of cardboard boxes, digging in the bottom of a suitcase for spoons.

"I popped out to see if I could get any fresh milk, but shops don't seem to open here on a Sunday before eleven," she says apologetically.

Sunday. Only one day before school starts. We haven't exactly left a lot of time for settling in. The thought of school makes my heart pound, and I try to ignore it.

"Yes!" Mum triumphantly produces a box of cornflakes and a carton of dried milk from a box labeled PANTRY. "Knew it was in there somewhere!"

The table has been covered with a garish plastic tablecloth that must have been sitting in the bottom of a drawer at our old house since my sixth or seventh birthday party. On it is perched a rinsed-out baked-bean can full of yellow dandelions and blue forget-me-nots, some with roots still attached. A scattering of earth surrounds the base of the can and the paper label has been roughly ripped off, but I can still see the top of the word Heinz.

Mum watches nervously and follows my raised eyebrows as I take it all in.

"Just thought I'd cheer the place up a bit," she says.

"It's nice." The bowls haven't been unpacked yet, so I pour cornflakes into a mug and try not to make a face at the cardboard taste of the dried milk.

After breakfast, I wander into the village. It's a cold day, but braving the icy breeze outside is better than watching Mum pretend to unpack while she anxiously watches my every move. It's like she's already looking for the "new me," as if moving into the new house will flip some kind of switch and suddenly I'll be the new girl with the happy face and the squeaky-clean slate that she's come all the way here to find. My cheeks ache with forced smiles. Being in a different place doesn't mean it never happened. Why doesn't she understand that? It doesn't mean I'm not still hurting.

The sky is like metal and the surface of the harbor bristles with choppy little waves. I walk down West Shore, the long road next to the water, passing a series of little wooden boats nestling like birds under the shelter of the harbor wall. In the distance, a great concrete pier zigzags out into the water like a solid lightning bolt. I make a sharp left away from the shoreline and follow a narrow street that twists and turns into the heart of the village, through snug rows of ice-cream-colored houses with white net curtains fluttering at the windows. A little wooden noticeboard opposite the café proudly announces local news and events, with fliers for a bar trivia night, a community picnic, and a talk on gardening at the town hall.

I come across sudden, unexpected smells of coffee and freshly baking bread that are as alien to me as the morning birdsong. It's a far cry from the exhaust fumes and cigarette smoke of my old neighborhood.

In a small playground, three girls who are really too big for it are whizzing around on the merry-go-round. They take turns to run wildly round the edge, pushing it until it screeches in protest, then jumping on and shrieking, hands clasped in the center, heads thrown back, hair streaming in the wind as they twirl around and around.

And suddenly I'm watching three other little girls, in a bigger playground far away, like an old-timey, flickering home movie I didn't choose to play and can't look away from. One with straight blond hair whipping around her face. One with a long, shiny black braid bouncing on her back. One with light brown curls tangling wildly in the wind. I can't look away from her face. She's smiling so widely.

A car flashes past, interrupting my view of the playground and snapping me out of my reverie. I put my hand to my cheek and find to my surprise that it's wet.

"No use crying over spilled milkshake," I mutter to myself. That's what Dad would say. Then he'd laugh uproariously, slapping his thigh

13

like it was the most hilarious joke in the world. I'd roll my eyes, but his laugh was so infectious, I'd end up giggling in spite of myself.

It hits me like someone's stuck their hand right through my belly button, grabbed my stomach hard and twisted. I slump onto a bench, wondering vaguely if I'm going to be sick.

I never imagined what it'd be like to lose my dad. Of course I didn't. No normal teenager does. You don't think it could ever happen to you. It's something for sob stories and sad movies. And, even if you did, you would never imagine the actual details. The weird sensation that he's leaving a little bit each day, not just in one big, dramatic exit. The way he's so tired toward the end that the pain takes him somewhere else, and it's an effort for him even to remember that you're in the room with him. The way you never really get the chance to say goodbye because, by the time you do, it's not quite him anymore.

But, if I had thought about my dad dying, I'd have bet every dollar of the money I earned babysitting Mrs. Reed's nightmare baby next door that I wouldn't have been going through it alone.

If I'd ever pictured that moment, I wouldn't have imagined myself sitting, lost, on a peeling bench in a playground in a tiny fishing village in the middle of nowhere. I'd probably have seen myself on a different bench, in the garden of our old house, somewhere safe and familiar. There'd have been two hands holding mine and a head resting on each of my shoulders. Straight blond hair and a long black braid.

I guess things don't always turn out the way you think they will.

I round a corner into a narrow alleyway that runs between two rows of small backyards. There are low garden walls on both sides, some with little wooden doors or gates set into them, some with bushes and fruit trees growing on the other side to shield the houses from view. There's a small, yappy dog running in circles on one lawn, its owner standing in the back doorway with her hands cupped around a steaming mug, waiting for the dog to do his business. A couple of the gardens are overgrown with straggling weeds and moss-covered, moldy patio furniture, but most are cheerful and well cared for, in keeping with the bright, seaside feel of the rest of the village.

I walk past one particularly neat garden, with pretty flowers in perfect straight lines and a rusting basketball hoop screwed into the back wall of the house. There's a man sitting in a deck chair in a corner of the lawn, a can of beer by his side. I check my watch. It's 9:45. He looks like he might once have been very handsome, but someone has taken an eraser and blurred his edges. His stomach protrudes over the top of his waistband, and his cheeks sag slightly, as if the flesh is too heavy for his face to support.

As I watch, a boy of about fifteen or sixteen comes out of the back door and into the garden, not seeing the man sitting in the corner. He's tall, with sandy hair and a crooked nose beneath sea-green eyes. He strolls over to the little flower bed, bends down, and turns on a small sprinkler, which starts gently spraying droplets of water over the flowers.

"Done, Mum!" he calls over his shoulder, up toward the house, and, as he walks back to the door, he picks up the ball that's lying near the doormat and quickly dribbles it toward the hoop.

"He shoots…he scores," he mutters under his breath, looping the ball up through the air with one hand and watching it bounce off the wall of the house, missing the hoop by a good yard, and roll back down the lawn.

15

There's a snort from the deck chair, and the boy whirls round, looking panicked.

"You always did throw like a girl," spits the man, taking a long pull on his beer.

I suddenly feel embarrassed to be eavesdropping and want to walk away, but I'm partially screened from view by a gnarled apple tree, and I'm afraid that moving will draw more attention. I stand there, frozen.

"Dad." The boy's face falls. He takes a few uncertain steps toward the chair and his eyes twitch nervously back toward the house. "It's a bit early… Mum's…"

"Don't you tell me what to do, you little bitch." The man half heaves himself out of the chair, his fist swiping toward the boy as if to cuff him around the ears, and just missing as the boy steps smartly backward out of reach.

"Sorry, Dad." The boy keeps his eyes down, not meeting the man's gaze, and he settles back into his chair with a grunt, closing his eyes.

As the boy heads back into the house and moves toward the door, the tree no longer protects me from view. His eyes lock with mine, and I see surprise ripple across his face, before it quickly hardens into embarrassment and then anger.

I want to explain that I'm just exploring the village, that I'm new here, that I didn't mean to pry, but the situation is so awkward, and I'm so worried about waking his dad, that I panic and very quickly walk away instead.

My heartbeat slows as I make my way to the other end of the alleyway, the rest of the backyards in the row deserted, their owners probably enjoying sleeping in on the weekend.

The village is so tiny that I've thoroughly explored it within half an hour. Apart from the boy in the garden, the only other person even close to my age is a heavily freckled paperboy, who looks so shocked to see me that he practically falls off his bike, before flushing and whizzing off.

In Birmingham, where we lived in England, if I wanted to kill time, I'd buy the cheapest ticket for a kids' movie showing at the multiplex, then sneak into one of the other screens halfway through the movie and sit in the back row, knees pulled up to my chest, slowly sucking an entire packet of Skittles one by one so they'd last as long as possible. It was a technique I'd honed to a fine art in the last few weeks before we left. If you hopped from screen to screen, you could spend the whole day there in the dark, hiding, dipping in and out of other people's fairy-tale endings.

The closest thing to a Cineworld in St. Monans appears to be a monthly movie night at the community center: next up, *The Emoji Movie* on May 2. I look critically at the large cartoon poop on the poster. Somehow I don't think that'll offer quite the same opportunity for escape.

It's starting to spit rain by the time I leave the cobbled streets behind and find my way back to the cottage. I turn up my jacket collar, but the chill seems to creep in anyway.

By late afternoon, we're unpacking in companionable silence, carefully unwinding each individual plate from yards of bubble wrap. Mum takes out all the knickknacks first, carefully displaying

17

candles and vases and wicker hearts around the kitchen. She whistles cheerfully as she lights a few tea lights, their flickering flames bright against the gathering gloom outside. I don't think she even realizes she's whistling Dad's favorite song.

Even though there are still tons of boxes sitting untouched, Mum's unpacked the TV and the old DVD player and laid out a selection of movies. Family movie night always used to mean the same old classics: *Jurassic Park*, *Labyrinth*, *E.T.* Dad used to do stupid voices and talk through all the boring parts, and Mum and I would have to throw a blanket over him to keep him from ruining the romantic scenes with stupid, slurpy kissing noises. But none of the movies she's put out are ones we'd ever watched with Dad.

Still, it's comfortingly familiar to snuggle up next to her on the new red sofa, cross-legged under the quilt I've hauled down from upstairs, sharing a massive bowl of popcorn and sipping hot chocolate. Mum picks all the pink marshmallows out of her cup and puts them in mine and I exchange them for my white ones without a word.

———————

In the middle of the night, I wake up and lie with my eyes wide open, staring into the darkness, listening to the strange quiet. The wind must have picked up, because I can hear the dull wooden bumps of the little boats bobbing against one another in the harbor.

At home, there was always some light creeping round the edges of my curtains. The dull flickering of the sign above the liquor store on the corner. The amber glow of the lamppost outside my bedroom window finding its way in like a trusty night-light. Here, the dark presses in around me like velvet, making me feel suffocated. Against the black, I start seeing that gray school building again and feel the familiar nerves rising up the back of my throat. Tomorrow, I have to start all over again.

My bare feet feel their way along the unfamiliar, uneven wooden floor toward the bathroom. As I come back, a glass of water in my hand, I see a crack of light along the side of Mum's bedroom door. I push it open a few inches, enough to see her curved back as she sits on the bare mattress of her bed, face buried in one of Dad's work shirts. Her shoulders are shaking.

I want to run in and press my face into it too, tell her I miss him as well, and that moving into this house feels like a betrayal, as if we're pretending he never existed at all. But she's worked every second since we got here to make everything okay. Happy. Normal. And, if I go in, it'll mean admitting that it's not. So I push the door closed with my fingertips and pad back to my own bedroom in the dark.

THREE

THE WEATHER ISN'T EXACTLY ENCOURAGING when I wake
the next morning. Through the gap in the curtains, I can see a slate-
gray sky with thick, low clouds. Mum obviously hasn't managed to
get the central heating working yet, because my cheeks, nose, and
the one foot poking out of the bedspread are freezing cold.

I start to drag myself reluctantly out of bed, but the cold
squeezes me like a fist, and moving slowly isn't an option. I gasp out
loud and scurry into the bathroom. I jump in the shower and shriek
at the top of my lungs as drops of freezing water dance down my
back like tiny blades of ice.

"*Mum!*" I scream. "The hot water's still not working!"

"Hang on!" comes the muffled reply from downstairs. "Linda
said it might take ten minutes for the water heater to kick in."

It's probably a good thing that the choice words I'd like to offer Linda are lost in the rushing sound of the shower.

Pencil case. Notebook. Diary. Mascara. Compact. Hair tie. Sports bag.

Half an hour later, I stomp downstairs with a towel around my head, one arm in a blazer sleeve, shoving my pencil case into my schoolbag. I've wasted fifteen minutes searching for a hair dryer while the shower warmed up, leaving a trail of half-opened boxes spilling their guts out behind me, with no luck.

"Great, I'm going to be the new girl who arrives late, walks in after everyone else, *and* has wet hair," I complain, grabbing a cereal bar from a box on the kitchen table and heading for the car.

"Well, at least you'll make an impression." Mum grins, ignoring my eye roll as she starts the engine. "I couldn't find any clean socks this morning, but you don't hear *me* complaining about facing my first day at work with smelly feet."

"Ugh, Mum, gross. It's not like your first day will be anywhere near as embarrassing as mine," I say, brushing a few stray crumbs of breakfast bar off my seat belt as I buckle it. "The National Health Service is basically the same everywhere. And administrators in Scotland probably do exactly the same boring paperwork as they do in England. You'll fit right in."

"Gee, thanks," Mum replies drily. She puts the car into gear and screeches backward out of the driveway.

"You won't be the new girl for long—there's always something else coming along for people to gossip about." She catches my eye in the rearview mirror and trails off awkwardly. I notice there are dark yellowish circles under her eyes.

I swallow and look out the window. In heavy silence, I watch the ramshackle cottages fly by, some standing out from the white-washed ranks in bright blues and pinks, their red and gray roofs nestled closely together as if they're gossiping over old secrets. Mum turns on the radio, and the familiar strains of "Don't Look Back in Anger" fill the car. "Have they not heard it's the twenty-first century?" I mutter, trying to ignore the fluttering of nerves in my stomach.

We leave the tiny village behind and whizz past bleak, flat fields punctuated with miserable huddles of farm animals. As we reach the outskirts of St. Andrews, the town where my new school is, with its beautiful old buildings, I can't help thinking how different it is from my usual journey to school, stuck in jam-packed traffic among crawling buses and towering high-rise apartments. No. Not usual. My old journey to school.

That thought is a mistake. Allowing myself to remember the journey to school is a gateway, letting other thoughts rush in before I can block them. School. The first day of a new year. My friends—I catch myself, painfully—*ex*-friends, will be jumping off the bus, waving rowdily, shouting hello.

Suzanne is probably flicking through holiday photos on her phone while Prav looks over her shoulder and evaluates her fashion choices. Shouting and laughing as usual, like every year. As if I were never there. At least, that's the best-case scenario. Worst case, they're gathered in groups, discussing me. Going over the gory details like vultures picking a skeleton bare, passing juicy tidbits along, even though, by now, surely everyone has already had their fill. Tearing more strips off me. Wondering where I am now…

No. Don't think about it.

Pencil case. Notebook. Year planner. Mascara. Compact. Hair tie. Sports bag.

I clench my fists until my nails dig into my palms. It doesn't matter. A fresh start.

Before I'm ready, we've pulled up in front of St. Margaret's Academy, and I find myself confronted with the real-life version of the boxy building I've googled, set back from the road across a large grassy lawn. I let myself feel ever so slightly comforted by the fact that it looks a bit friendlier in real life, with green-blazered teenagers buzzing around, greeting each other excitedly and streaming into the main building.

"I don't know what time I'll finish tonight, but the ninety-five bus stops just outside the front of school and it runs all the way to St. Monans," Mum says, handing me a bunch of house keys and giving me a rough kiss on the cheek before I can dodge it.

"Good luck, honey," she calls as I slide out of the car and hoist my bag onto my shoulder. I glance back and see her quickly replace her worried frown with an encouraging wave as she pulls away. *Busted*.

Moments later, I find myself swept indoors on the green tide as a bell rings and students rush for their classrooms. I look down at the crumpled schedule and map that arrived in the mail two weeks ago. It seems like a lifetime since I stared blankly at it. Now here I am. Ready to start fresh. As if you can just leave yourself behind and pretend to be a completely new person. Step out of your skin and shrug it off like a snake. Anna Clark: ordinary teenager. Totally normal. Nothing to see here.

I picture a long, crackly snakeskin trailing dustily behind me along the corridor, down the school steps, between the brown fields, through the twisting streets of St. Monans and all the way back to England. My hands twitch involuntarily toward the back of my jacket, as if I could brush it away.

———————   ———————

The first thing on my schedule is a welcome session with my guidance counselor, a man in his early thirties whose relatively fancy suit and tie are undermined by a tuft of hair sticking up at the back of his head and brown laces in black shoes.

"Welcome, Anna," he says warmly, balancing a massive pile of books and papers in one arm so he can stick out a sweaty hand to shake mine. "I'm Mr. Phelps. We're all so glad to have you here at St. Margaret's." He glances surreptitiously at his watch. "Now, I know you've recently been through a very difficult time." I hold my breath. I can hear the snakeskin crackling in my ears.

"With the death of your father," he adds awkwardly, and my stomach relaxes so suddenly, it feels floppy and warm. I make a noncommittal *mmm* noise and stare at my shoes. The crackling fades a little. Mum kept her promise. Nobody here needs to know. Not the teachers, not the students, not the mailman. Nobody.

Mr. Phelps offers to do a big introduction to the class, but I beg him not to, and I must be pretty convincing because he glances at his watch again with a relieved expression and quickly agrees. "We'll let you get to know your classmates individually, then, Anna. But please know that I'm always here if you should need anything at all or have any problems. My door is always open." And, with that, he's gone.

FOUR

ENTERING THE CHEMISTRY LAB IS like walking into an X-ray machine.

The teacher gives me a nod and a mercifully brief "Welcome, Anna." Thirty pairs of laser eyes sweep from my scuffed shoes to my still-damp hair. At the last minute, I hastily shoved it into a ponytail. Now I wish I hadn't. I want to let it fall over my face and hide behind it. Silently cursing the missing hair dryer, I walk stiffly to an empty seat near the back, while necks swivel to follow me. It's like the longest walk in the world. My feet feel weird, as if I'm clumping like an elephant. I think I've forgotten how to walk.

Pencil case. Notebook... I try to hold on to my list, but it's faltering in the face of such intense scrutiny.

Thankfully, it's a practical lesson, and the array of glass beakers,

Bunsen burners, and brightly colored powders lined up at the front quickly reclaims my classmates' attention. I'm grateful to slip onto a plastic stool and fade into the background as their heads turn back to the teacher and she starts talking us through the experiment.

I join the back of the line for lab coats, and when I finally get to the cupboard, it's almost empty. I reach out to take the last relatively clean one at the exact same moment as a redhead with a sleek, straight bob and trendy black-framed glasses. Her nose is scattered with freckles that look like they've been delicately painted on, and her eyes are outlined in perfect, black liquid liner, a tiny flick at the end of her lash line. She laughs and thrusts the white coat at me, taking the one with a large burn mark across the front instead. "Don't worry, I can pull it off," she jokes, and her voice is deep and gravelly and doesn't match her appearance at all. She gives a little twirl and is gone before I can remember to smile.

We're given the choice to work alone or in pairs, and I quickly bury my head in my notes, ignoring the buzz as most of the class pairs off. As I pick up my plastic safety goggles and turn to the sheet of instructions, the classroom door opens again. A boy with thick, black, slightly too-long hair curling around his ears sneaks into the room, trying to tiptoe toward the nearest workbench while the teacher is bent over somebody's tripod. His backpack is open, books and papers almost spilling out, and his slightly frayed blazer hangs from one shoulder.

She waits until he's almost made it to a stool at the back of the room before she turns. "You're seven minutes late, Robin Allnutt—not the best start to the semester."

He looks up, one leg over the stool.

"Not the worst start to the semester either, though, Mrs. Beadle," he says politely, "once you take into account earthquakes, volcanoes, and other natural disasters." He gives her a dimpled smile.

She can't quite help an exasperated half smile of her own. "Be that as it may, you'd better see me at the end of the lesson, please."

"Yes, Mrs. Beadle," he says calmly, allowing the contents of his backpack to tumble out across his desk. Something tells me this isn't the first time he's been asked to stay behind.

On the other side of the room, a thin wisp of smoke rises up from a table crowded with boys. A tall, skinny boy with stiffly gelled black hair is using the yellow flame of the Bunsen burner to singe the shirt cuffs of the boy next to him.

"That's enough, Mark Chambers!" Mrs. Beadle turns away from Robin, snapping on the switch for the overhead ventilators while the other boys laugh and hastily extinguish the Bunsen flame.

"And don't think I can't see you too, Toby Taylor," she raps out sharply, and a handsome boy with olive skin and a wooden beaded necklace hastily drops the lit splint he had been slowly inching toward Mark Chambers's hairline.

The class gets down to work, and I turn my attention to the conical flask in front of me, using a metal spatula to stir a spoonful of pink powder into the water. Gradually, the liquid begins to calm, fine flecks of rosy pink settling at the bottom in a bright layer, undissolved.

Without thinking, I've already filled out the little box on my worksheet before the powder stops moving: *Cobalt carbonate + H_2O: no reaction.*

At least there's one tiny benefit to switching schools in the middle of the year: I already did this experiment last semester.

I pick up the flask and swirl it round, watching the pink powder fly back up into the water and dance again. I stare into the storm and it slowly calms again in the palm of my hand. Things can settle down again. Even after a tornado. The thought reassures me.

At the bench in front of me, the redhead has already moved on to the next stage of the experiment and is preparing to pour powder into a flask of hydrochloric acid. As she tilts the test tube, I realize it's far too full—she's used at least three times the correct amount of acid.

"Wait!" I leap forward, but she's already tilted the tube, shaking the powder out in a slow waterfall, floating down toward the surface of the liquid. In slow motion, she turns her head and sees my panicked face, and I see her black-rimmed eyes snap back in horror toward the flask as she realizes her mistake.

The liquid erupts, pink giving way to a violent deep blue, its surface hissing and boiling, leaping up the sides of the flask. But the warning was just in time—she stumbles backward, a little of the powder remaining in the bottom of the test tube, and, although the blue solution spurts upward and a hissing turquoise foam slithers down the outside of the flask like a volcano, she has already let go, and it drips harmlessly onto the safety mat.

"Close call." She laughs as the teacher rushes over, but I can tell she's more shaken than she's letting on. "Thanks," she adds, and this time, I manage a quick smile. She looks down at her lab coat and the large burn mark. "Guess this was the right one for me after all." Her lab partner, a girl with high cheekbones and long, braided hair, is shaking her head, but her shoulders are shuddering with suppressed laughter.

"Seriously, Cat, are you *ever* going to learn to read the instructions?" she demands, in a scolding tone.

Cat turns back to her lab table. "Why would I need to when you're always three steps ahead of me?"

"Yeah, well, not this time. If you could at least try to wait until the second week of the semester before you blow up the entire science wing, that'd be great. I'd like to learn a bit first, if it's all the same to you."

"Like you haven't already been through the entire semester's syllabus on your own time, Lish." Cat elbows her in the ribs and the other girl looks away, half-embarrassed, half-proud, and doesn't deny it. I watch them from behind, taking in their easy closeness, and try to ignore the loneliness that rushes through me.

I spend the rest of the day sitting at the backs of classrooms, keeping my head down, speaking only when spoken to, and trying not to attract attention. If I manage to blend in well enough, maybe I'll just disappear. After the past couple of months, being invisible sounds very appealing indeed.

FIVE

FOR THE NEXT FEW DAYS, I manage to keep a miraculously low profile. I bury my head in my books, hang around in the school library during break time, and empty the vending machine of cereal bars instead of facing the cafeteria. Each day that passes feels like a little victory.

Every evening, Mum pumps me for details about lessons and friends, and I paint her the most cheerful picture I can. At home, I make it sound like I'm the life and soul of the classroom, name-dropping my fellow students as if I've got more friends than I know what to do with. At school, I work harder at blending in than I've ever worked at any academic subject in my life. And it's quite successful. When people walk past me in the corridor, their eyes sort of slide right over me. It's as if I don't exist. Nobody is paying me any attention at all.

Until Thursday morning.

The drama studio is a large, square room with black walls and a slightly springy, soft black floor. The tiered seats have been pushed against the wall to make space, and the class is lounging around the room, waiting for the teacher, some sitting backward on chairs, some cross-legged on the floor. The girls have taken over one corner of the room (I recognize Cat and Lish whispering animatedly about something, heads bent together), and the boys are mostly grouped in another.

A tall boy with blond hair is standing on a chair with his back to me, doing a very mean but very accurate impression of Mrs. Lewis, the school librarian. "*Library time is quiet time, Mr. Stewart!*" he screeches, as the others fall about laughing.

"Nice to see you warming up, Simon." Miss Evans, the drama teacher, walks in, gesturing for him to get down from the chair. She can't be older than her late twenties, wiry and petite, with oval glasses and a lilting accent.

The boy pirouettes on the chair, giving a deep mock bow, and, as he straightens up, his eyes meet mine. Green eyes, sandy hair, and a crooked nose.

A sudden image flashes into my head: a back garden, a basketball...those green eyes lowered in shame. We look at each other for a long moment that seems to stretch like elastic between us even though it can only be a few seconds.

He clambers awkwardly off the chair, still staring at me. Then he very deliberately turns his back and goes to sit with the other boys. I think about following him, trying to explain that I wasn't eavesdropping, not on purpose anyway, but I don't know how to say that without bringing up what I saw in front of all his rowdy friends. Somehow, I think that would just make everything far worse.

Miss Evans seems to have a lot more energy than I do at 8:45 in the morning. While the other teachers dress in suits and jackets, she's wearing gray yoga pants and a bright purple T-shirt with the slogan: YOU CAN'T SCARE ME: I TEACH DRAMA!

She divides us into groups of five and tells us to take turns to stand up straight and then fall slowly backward, letting our other four teammates catch us. "It's all about developing trust and learning to work together as a team," she explains excitedly, bouncing on the balls of her feet as she walks round the room, watching our progress. "Wait until the last possible moment, so that the person really experiences the fall before the relief of being caught."

Absolutely no way am I trusting these four strangers to stop me from breaking my neck. I make sure I'm in the catching party every time. We gather around a girl with incredibly shiny shoes and a white-blond pixie cut, whose name is Lola. She shrieks as if she's diving into freezing water each time she falls backward, even though we catch her every time. There are little oohs and ahs from around the room as people swoon toward the floor, then bounce gently up again as their teammates link arms like a trampoline.

Across the room, the boys are bouncing a large ginger-haired boy named Charlie in the air with such force, he spins onto his front, snorting with laughter.

"What lovely, uh, energy, boys…" Miss Evans begins, then her voice rises as Charlie whirls through the air, his head missing the wall by a couple of inches. "Yes, very good, I think we're warmed up enough," she squeaks, moving hurriedly back to the front of the classroom.

"Some of you may think," she continues as we settle cross-legged on the floor, "that acting is all about drama." She pauses dramatically, her eyes twinkling, as if she expects somebody to respond, but nobody does.

"The truth is, it starts with knowing your character. Really knowing them. Inside out. Getting completely under their skin and seeing the world through their eyes. People today spend longer looking at their own face on a phone than they do looking into someone else's eyes."

I see a few people starting to zone out. We're teenagers. If she's planning to give us a lecture on the dangers of becoming obsessed with phones, we've heard it all before. What nobody seems to have realized is that they're also constantly telling us tech is the future, 80 percent of today's jobs won't exist by the time we reach our thirties, and we've got to have digital skills to survive. They can't have it both ways.

I tune back in in time to hear her say, "…an exercise in truly getting to know a person, under the surface. The real them."

Uh-oh. This does not sound good.

Miss Evans is moving around the room now, pairing people up, and my mind starts frantically scrolling through excuses to suddenly leave the classroom, but before I can think of anything realistic, she's tapping me lightly on the shoulder and telling me to work with Louise, a mousy, round-cheeked girl. Up close, her brown eyes are small and close together, and she has heavy bangs that end a bit too high, as if the hairdresser wasn't paying attention and kept cutting farther than was strictly necessary. It gives her a constant air of being slightly surprised.

"Louise, you're the questioner. And Anna, is it?" She smiles at me kindly, and I nod, sensing where this is going, but unable to stop it. "Anna, you'll be answering about yourself. A nice way for us all to get to know you." She gives us an encouraging nod and moves onto the next pair, handing out stapled pieces of paper covered in questions.

"You have half an hour to find out all you can about your subject. Some of you might think you already know each other well, but often our true selves remain hidden in plain sight."

She has no idea.

"Use these questions as a starting point, but feel free to throw in your own as well. And, most importantly, *listen*. At the end of the lesson, you'll be expected to give a brief presentation about your partner, so you need to get to know them very well."

I close my eyes for a moment. When I open them, Louise is looking earnestly at me as if we're about to go through some deep bonding ritual. Before I can try to take control of the situation, she's already asking the first question.

"What is your full name?"

"Anna Gwendolyn R—" I stumble and choke the word back, turning my confusion into a loud cough as Louise frowns and looks up from the worksheet.

"Clark. Anna Gwendolyn Clark." I look down at my hands in

horror, unable to believe I've almost messed up already on the very first question.

Louise is looking at me skeptically. "Gwendolyn?" she asks. "Seriously?"

"It was my great-grandma's name," I mutter, trying to stop my voice from trembling.

"Okay." She scans the questions. "What is your greatest fear?"

I almost laugh. Then I realize. I have to lie. Really, really well. Because, if anyone finds out the truth, I don't think I'll last more than a week at St. Margaret's.

"Spiders," I blurt out quickly, trying to ignore the images that are tap-tap-tapping at the edges of my brain, trying to inch in. "Always been terrified of them," I add nonchalantly. Louise looks disappointed.

On my left, I can hear Cat giving immediate, snappy answers to every question as if she's hitting tennis balls back to her partner.

"Catherine, but everyone calls me Cat…three brothers…Frida Kahlo…a roller-skating accident when I was seven…"

"Be honest," Miss Evans booms. "Bare your souls. Worm your way right inside one another's heads…"

I have to clench my fists to stop my hands from flying to my forehead, as if I could block Louise from reading my thoughts. She returns to the list of questions with fresh zeal.

"Ooh, here's a good one. If you could have a superpower, what one thing would you like to be able to do perfectly?"

And, for a moment, I speak the absolute truth, because the answer jumps into my mouth and somehow flows through me before I can stop it…

"*Forget,*" I say, at the exact same moment as Cat. I turn and look into her green eyes, startled, and she looks as surprised as I do. Louise tuts and looks annoyed.

"Cryptic much?" she mutters, making a note on the sheet.

"Okay, look," she huffs, after a few more evasive answers. "I have to present you to the class in like"—she glances at her watch—"ten minutes. Nobody knows much about you yet, so help me out here. What was your old school like? Why did you move in the middle of the school year anyway? What are you into?" She reels off the questions so fast that my head is spinning, frantically trying to work out the safest way to answer, to choose the least dangerous topic.

"I—" I stammer, feeling like a cornered animal facing a very determined terrier. "Well, we moved for my mum's new job, so—"

Louise looks increasingly thunderous, but Miss Evans is clapping her hands to get everyone's attention. If she was hoping for deep and insightful revelations, I think Miss Evans might be disappointed. We hear about roughly five thousand of the boys' sports achievements, but none of them seem to have discussed their families, fears, or failings. Then it's Louise's turn. She clears her throat and turns to the rest of the class.

"Anna Clark is…" She pauses dramatically. "An *enigma.*" There's a long pause.

"A what?" someone shouts.

"A mystery," Louise snaps, annoyed. Then she puts her dramatic voice back on again. "No history, no previous address, a mysterious past."

She's half joking, making up for my lack of answers, but people are craning in their seats to look at me, and Louise nods excitedly, warming to her theme.

"Will any of us ever really find out?" She holds her hands up like a preacher appealing to the congregation. "*Who is Anna Clark?*"

People laugh and clap as Louise sits, and I laugh and shake my head, pretending it's all a big joke. But my insides are gently shriveling up as if they're made of tissue paper and someone has set fire to the edges.

SIX

BY FRIDAY AFTERNOON, I'VE DEFINITELY noticed more people giving me curious glances in the corridor, and it feels like, thanks to Louise, my plan to blend in has suffered a serious setback.

I just want to get to the end of the day, escape into the weekend, and hope that people will have moved on by the beginning of next week. Not that St. Monans offers much in the way of escape. But getting out of this school will be a massive relief. Trying to stay under the radar is a lot more exhausting than I thought it would be.

I sling my bag on the floor and slump down in my chair as the history teacher starts droning on about the program of work for the year.

The boys in the back row are kicking a balled-up piece of paper back and forth across the thinly carpeted floor, aiming it under one another's desks. Simon sits in the center, a red pen jauntily stuck behind his ear. I watch the ball skittering from black shoe to black shoe. Occasionally, one of them picks it up, flattens the paper out, and scribbles on it, then screws it up and throws it onto another boy's desk when the teacher's back is turned.

"The coursework assignment," the teacher is saying, "will count for thirty-five percent of your final grade and affect which track you are placed in for next year."

My head jerks up. I picture the boxes and trash bags still littering our new house. I can't afford to mess up this time. I crack open a brand-new notebook and tune in to what the teacher is saying.

"…an eight-thousand-word project detailing the life of a local person of historical interest, living or dead. And, before you all rush off to interview the Bishop of St. Andrews, I'd encourage you to look for a unique subject if you want to score highly on this assignment. Dig deeper. Search close to home. Don't be afraid to do a little research…"

I hear a sharp intake of breath behind me, and something flies over my shoulder and drops into my lap. Keeping my eyes to the front, I slowly reach down and close my fingers around the crumpled ball. "*Pssst.*"

Under the cover of the desk, I smooth the paper out on my knees.

"*Toss it back!*"

I glance at the paper, expecting to see a blank page or a stupid drawing. But down the left-hand side is a list of names, all in the same handwriting. Next to each name, in different pens and pencil, are scrawled numbers.

Rachel: 5, 6, 4
Alisha: 9, 3, 8
Sarah: 8, 7, 8
Thea: 3, 1, 4

I feel my scalp prickle. There are only girls' names.

It takes a moment to hit me. These are marks out of ten. And something tells me they're not scores for academic effort. My eyes skim down the list and widen as they hit the bottom.

Mystery girl: 7, 9, 0

The zero is scrawled in red and underlined.

I feel the blood pounding in my neck and my ears glowing. I've never been a girl who can spit back snappy comebacks when guys make comments, who knows how to turn it around so the laugh's on them instead. I usually panic and my insides seize up, and I think of something really brilliant to say about four days later.

But today something just snaps. I'm tired. Tired of running. Tired of hiding. Tired of having to blend in. Before I know what I'm doing, before even thinking, I've seized my pencil and crossed out the names with thick, angry lines that rip through the page.

Underneath, I scribble:

Jackasses: 0/10

That makes me feel the tiniest bit better. I crunch the paper back into an angry ball and hesitate, thinking about throwing it defiantly back to the boys. But then I pause. I let out a long breath. Fuming silently is one thing, but there's no way it's worth getting on the wrong side of Simon, especially after I've already blundered further into his life than he'd have liked. It's pretty clear who pulls the strings around here. And the very last thing I need is any more attention.

I drop it into my pencil case instead. Then I watch, as if I'm seeing it in slow motion, as the little ball of paper bounces off my eraser, falls off the side of my desk, and rolls away over the floor toward the back of the classroom. My stomach feels like it has dropped through the bottom of my chair.

There's silence. Then, just as I hear the creak of someone moving in their chair, the teacher speaks: "Simon."

The creaking stops abruptly. "Yes, Ms. Forsyth?"

I turn my head casually to the side and glance behind me. The ball is resting on the floor, halfway between my chair and Simon's. I start surreptitiously tilting backward, gradually leaning my chair back farther and farther.

"Did you get all that?"

"Uh…yes, ma'am."

I slowly stretch my arm down, pretending I'm trying to scratch my ankle.

"Excellent. Then you won't mind reminding the rest of the class of the timetable for completing the coursework."

"Uh…" he mumbles, looking to both sides for help, but finding only sniggering from his friends. He chews the end of his pen, stalling for time.

My fingertips are inches away. I strain my arm to its limits.

"Two weeks to complete your initial research and present your chosen historical person for approval." She sighs impatiently. "Then another five weeks to write up your findings in extended essay form and hand them in to me after midterms." As she speaks, Ms. Forsyth turns to walk to the whiteboard, and Simon drops his attentive expression, darts forward, and snatches the paper just before my fingertips can reach it.

The moment the bell rings, I hear a scuffle and the rustle of paper being unfolded. As I bend down to scoop my notebook and files back into my bag, I see a set of legs saunter past. A foot kicks the leg of the desk, just by my face.

"Don't stick your nose where it doesn't belong. Bitch."

I freeze as laughter rains down around me. By the time my head whips back up, their backs are disappearing through the classroom door. I sit down again and rest my head on my desk. I didn't think this week could get any worse. Boy, was I wrong.

SEVEN

"THINK YOU MIGHT SEE ANY of your new school friends this weekend?" Mum asks innocently on Saturday morning as she slathers a piece of toast with peanut butter. I look at her. She's making a bit too much effort to sound casual.

Somehow, I don't think "I can't think of anything worse" is what she's hoping to hear.

"Actually, I've got a massive history project to start, so I need to hit the library this weekend. If there even is one in St. Monans," I add as an afterthought.

I watch her, leaning against the sink with the orange morning light falling through her long, frizzy, dark hair. Dad always used to say that I was exactly 50 percent of him and 50 percent of Mum. His hair was blond and poker-straight, Mum's is a mass of wild dark brown corkscrews, and mine is light brown with half-hearted waves. Now that he's gone, it feels like half of me has disappeared too.

"What about you, Mum?" I ask suddenly.

"What about me?"

"What are you up to this weekend?"

She looks surprised. "Oh, this and that. I've got some bits of work to catch up on and some more unpacking to do."

I want to ask if *she's* made any new friends, but I don't. It makes me ache to think of her just puttering around the house on her own all day. I picture her back in our house in England, before everything fell apart. Bouncing out of the kitchen on a Saturday morning on her way to yoga, coming back three hours later because she'd bumped into a friend and had ended up losing track of time. Guilt slithers around my stomach. It's my fault she's left her friends behind. Now all she seems to care about is watching me make new ones. And, honestly, I'm not sure if I'm ready to do that yet. I'm not sure I ever will be.

But I don't tell Mum any of that. I give her a hug and a wave and leave her surrounded by cardboard boxes, a pair of scissors in one hand and a rag in the other.

St. Monans Library is a quaint, low building in multicolored local stone with a simple, gray slate roof. When I ask the elderly librarian whether there are any local records, he's so surprised, he does a double take, polishing his half-moon glasses and putting them back on again to peer at me more closely.

"You'll find everything we have in the local history section, dear, but for kirk records or census data you might want to visit the Fife Family History Society archives or ask the vicar."

"Kirk?" I ask.

"The Scottish Church, of course." He tuts gently as if I should have learned all the Scottish words in the dictionary before I moved here. With all of two weeks' notice.

"Oh, right. Sorry."

I thank him and head for the shelves, not sure exactly what I'm looking for. Tucked behind the colorful children's corner and the rows of alphabetized thrillers and romance novels, I find the dusty local history section looking as if nobody has browsed there in decades. Faded spines sag against one another, and a few old copies of church leaflets and local newsletters are stuffed in at the end of the shelf.

I thumb through some of the newsletters, hoping for a story about a local hero or a town legend. Instead, I learn about the renovation of the village post office, the annual harborside egg-and-spoon race, and the sad loss of Mrs. Pistlethwaite's tortoiseshell cat. (Some kind of freak accident involving a mousetrap and a toaster.)

St. Monans is probably too small for anyone of great significance ever to have lived here. I gaze around the library. An exhausted mom with a baby asleep in its carrier is half snoozing on a beanbag in the picture-book section. A couple of teenagers are browsing in the young adult aisle, each pretending to read the blurb on the back of a book, but sneaking sideways glances at each other instead. A man in his late sixties with a raincoat neatly folded on his lap is typing painstakingly on the public computer with one finger. Raindrops meander listlessly down the windowpanes. It's not exactly the big city.

Weekends never had to be filled up before. They just sort of *happened*. Someone would be having a sleepover or a movie night, or we'd bump into each other in town and end up hanging out in a coffee shop for the rest of the afternoon without even realizing it. Time in this village seems to move about ten times slower than it ever did before.

I sigh and run my finger across the cracking spines. Some of them have gold lettering that's rubbed away until you can't even read them anymore.

Fish and Family: Two Hundred Years of Tradition in East Neuk Coastal Villages.

The Lands and People of Fife, 1740–1880.

Studies in the History and Archaeology of the Salt and Coal Industries at St. Monans, Fife in the Eighteenth and Nineteenth Centuries.

I can practically feel my brain groaning with boredom.

Hellfire and Herring: A Childhood Remembered sounds a little more promising, but a brief flick through doesn't seem to yield any local citizens whose lives were significant enough to write an eight-thousand-word essay about.

Finally, I select a dusty, slim volume on the history of St. Monans. I consider signing up for a library card so I can borrow it and take it home, and then realize it might be easier to read it here. It's not like I've got anything else to do today, and home isn't exactly the most relaxing place at the moment. I find a threadbare armchair in the fiction section and settle down to read.

I leaf through a chapter about Newark Castle, whose ruins I saw sticking up like broken teeth in the distance as we first drove into the village. Another chapter focuses on the old St. Monans windmill and the history of salt panning in the area, but it doesn't mention any particularly interesting local people. I flick through the rest of the book with little hope of finding anything useful, pausing to examine a series of diagrams and photos of the old church through the ages.

Even in the slightly faded pictures, St. Monans Church is beautiful and striking. The caption beneath one of the photos explains that it is supposed to be the closest church to the sea, and it's not difficult to believe. Built from weathered gray and brown stones, the building stands proudly at the very edge of the land, just a few feet from a sharp drop to the sea below. It looks like a patient watchman keeping a close eye on the turning tide. Pretty arched windows with latticed panes line the sides. In one photograph, the church almost seems to glow orange in the sun, its spire pointing heavenward like a warning finger while angry dark clouds mass behind it. Just as I'm about to turn the page, my eye is caught by a footnote in tiny print at the very bottom.

St. Monans has seen little scandal but for the naval attack of 1544 and the trial of a local woman for witchcraft in the mid-seventeenth century.

Witchcraft? I blink and read it again. I flick through the rest of the chapter and turn to the index. Then I skim the remaining pages. There's no other mention of the story anywhere in the book.

I snap it shut and gnaw thoughtfully on my fingernail. My curiosity piqued, I return to the shelf and carefully study every other reference book again, checking to see if there's anything about witchcraft, or another book by the same author. Nothing. I make a mental note to check in the school library next week.

The man with the raincoat has left, and the public computer is vacant, a blinking cursor in a box waiting for the next user to register or sign in.

Just touching the keyboard makes my heart beat faster. I choose a username and password and hit return. The screen whirs to life, and I feel the whirring begin in my chest as well, like a colony of insects has awoken in there and they're restlessly fidgeting around. My breathing speeds up in spite of my efforts to stay calm.

The internet connection is slow, and it takes a few seconds for the Google home page to load. A little fizzle of nervous excitement runs through me as the familiar logo appears.

I type in "witchcraft St. Monans." Nothing. Feeling my excitement start to ebb away, I try a few more searches about St. Monans Church, but it seems to be a dead end.

The mouse pointer hovers over the address bar, blinking at me. Daring me. Slowly, I type in a single *I*. Immediately, the computer fills in the rest:—*nstagram.com*. My finger hovers. In a moment, I hit return and feel my mouth fill with saliva as bright white floods the screen. I can't sign in. I know full well my account has been deactivated. But that doesn't mean I can't look. My fingers move like lightning. I add a forward slash and a name to the address bar and suddenly, a collage of Suzanne's face fills the screen. In the first photo, she's grinning behind a massive chocolate cake ablaze with sparklers, candles on the top in the shape of *16*. Tears prickle at my eyes like hot needles. How many times did we talk about our sixteenth birthdays? We always joked we'd make the parties on *My Super Sweet 16* look like village-hall affairs. And now here she is, celebrating hers four hundred miles away.

I click on the second photo, and it immediately fills the screen to show Suzanne in a photo booth wearing silly fake glasses, long blond hair tucked behind her ears. Prav is leaning in on her left in a red cowboy hat, pretending to smoke a pipe. *Click. Click. Click.* Each new frame is like a little dagger piercing my chest deeper and deeper, but I can't stop. It's so easy to picture myself in each photo: where I'd have been standing, what I'd have looked like… pulling a party popper over Suzanne. Sticking up my fingers behind Prav's head. Pulling her trademark braid across my top lip like a mustache. Standing on tiptoes to give her an exaggerated kiss on the cheek. It's like my life has carried on without me, and I've just been airbrushed out of the pictures.

The photos get older, moving on from the party to summer break, some showing Suzanne in a bikini beside a pool in Mallorca where her family have been going every year since she was little. Each picture trails hundreds of likes and a long tail of approving comments:

Hot stuff

OMG GORGEOUS

Sexy Queen!

Suddenly an older picture pops up, and I'm confronted with my own face, grinning cheesily. I'm standing back to back with Suzanne next to a mirror, our hands raised to our chests and clasped in the shape of guns like a James Bond spoof, each of us with one leg sticking awkwardly up behind us. I remember the afternoon we took it in her bedroom, laughing at each other's poses until we could barely stand. I'm no longer tagged in the photograph, but it's me just the same.

SLUT

The word hits me like a slap.

I start to scroll down. The comments go on and on.

Loose lips

Easy A's

Suzanne and the slut!

My vision begins to blur as I scroll on, faster and faster, until the words run into each other.

Bitchhoeskankwhoreslut—

I close the window and pummel at the keyboard in my haste to log out, heaving in great gulps of air. The silver-haired librarian looks over at me and raises his eyebrows in an expression of mild concern, and I force myself to smile and nod at him. As soon as he bends his head back over his desk, I stagger to the nonfiction section and sink down cross-legged, letting the shelves shield me from view.

The words aren't the worst part. It's the names. Each comment next to a username of somebody I know. Somebody I went to school with for years. Somebody I would have called a friend. Somebody who stood next to me with a towel on their head in the elementary school nativity play or exchanged panicked looks as we sweated over the papers in our mock college prep tests. Somebody who knew about the time I broke my ankle playing badminton in third grade, or the time I got lost and had to have a humiliating announcement made about me over the loudspeaker on a school trip to the city zoo. Somebody who knows all those things about me and still thinks I deserve those words. When did the rest of me disappear?

EIGHT

MONDAY COMES TOO QUICKLY.

As I walk into the clattering din of the cafeteria for the first time at lunchtime, I wonder if school cafeterias were originally designed as a special form of torture. I can't keep avoiding it forever: I'm running out of change, and the vending machine has run out of cereal bars. But I have to fight the urge to turn and march straight back out again. I grip my plastic tray tightly, inching my way between heaving tables. I scan the crowd as if I might find a familiar face, but meet only blank stares. Clusters of friends deep in conversation fork meatloaf and peas into their mouths, not even noticing me hovering awkwardly nearby.

"Hey, mystery girl!"

I open my mouth to snap back, but it's Cat and Lish, waving

me over to a corner table. Practically fainting with relief, I hurry over and slide gratefully into a plastic chair.

Cat reaches into her pocket and pulls out a crumpled ball of paper. As she smoothes it out on the table, I see the edge of the word *JACKASSES* and realize what it is. I look up to see that she's grinning broadly. She puts her hand out and shakes mine vigorously.

"Saw this on the desk as we walked out of history. Any enemy of Simon's is a friend of ours."

"I didn't mean—" I start, and then think better of it and return the grin.

"I'm Cat, she's Alisha," says the redhead, pointing toward the other girl. I nod, while they look at me expectantly.

"Oh, sorry. Anna. Anna Clark."

"So everybody wants to know. The million-dollar question. What brings you here in the middle of the school year, Anna, Anna Clark?" asks Alisha in a fake game-show-host voice, holding out an imaginary microphone.

I laugh nervously. "Who could resist the weather?" I answer breezily, taking a huge bite of mashed potato. As Alisha opens her mouth to ask another question, I swallow quickly and jump in. "How long have you been at St. Margaret's? Do you live in the city?"

"We're lifers." Cat laughs. "Here since the beginning of time."

"On the first day of school, Cat was so nervous, she threw up on my shoes, and we've been friends ever since," says Alisha.

Cat groans. "So we're still telling that story? Fantastic." She turns back to me. "I came up from St. Monans Elementary. It's a tiny village—there's nothing there—but Lish is from St. Andrews."

"No way," I exclaim. "I just moved to St. Monans!"

"You're kidding!" says Cat, then, taking my hand solemnly in hers: "Commiserations. Your social life may never recover."

"It's not that bad." Alisha grins. "We take pity on her and visit occasionally."

"Not that Alisha goes out much anyway," Cat shoots back. "Because she has the dubiously dorky achievement of best grades in the universe to maintain."

"So why the move?" asks Cat curiously, dodging as Alisha pelts her with peas. "Newbies usually come in at the beginning of the school year, not the summer. Was it for your dad's work? My dad's a doctor," she adds, picking a pea off the front of her top and popping it in her mouth to a grimace from Alisha, "so we moved around a lot before he got a job up here."

I bite my lip.

A coffin, black and horribly shiny, being swallowed by the greedy ground. Cold wind whipping my hair around my face and into my eyes. Blurry. The smell of damp earth and rotting leaves. Wet grass stuck to the side of my shoe.

I taste blood in my mouth and bite down harder.

Mum's smile, forced and unrecognizable. It would have been better if she hadn't tried to pretend. A smile worse than tears.

I shake my head, as if tossing it hard enough might shake away the images. I try to make my voice flat and nonchalant and let the words rush together. "My-dad's-dead-he-had-cancer-my-mum's-a-hospital-administrator-she-got-a-new-job-up-here-after-it-happened."

There's a long pause, during which I blink rapidly and shovel peas into my mouth like my life depends on it. To my great relief,

Alisha shoots Cat a look (I smile weakly as I hear a loud clunk, and I'm pretty sure she's also just kicked her under the table) and abruptly changes the subject.

"Right. Let's give you the lowdown. The 411. The skinny." She flips her braids over her shoulder and reverts to the game-show voice. "The essential survival guide to St. Margaret's."

Cat giggles. "It's not exactly Alcatraz, Lish. I think she'll be okay."

Alisha holds up a silencing hand and continues. "Number one. The teachers are mostly decent, but that doesn't include Mr. Barnes. Do not, under any circumstances, piss off Mr. Barnes."

Cat nods sagely. "Total asshole."

I snort. For the first time since I stepped through the doors of St. Margaret's, I'm remembering what it's like to relax. Not to be constantly on my guard. Maybe even to enjoy myself.

"Number two. Never eat the beef stew. Thursday lunches— avoid them like the plague. Bring your own lunch or go hungry. Trust me on this one."

"We don't know what they put in it," Cat whispers, "but Stacey Brown tried it last semester, and I swear she's never fully recovered."

I grin and nod obediently. "Beef stew equals death. Got it."

Alisha eyes me critically. "I don't know if you're taking this seriously enough. In 2011, fifty-one people died in Germany after eating E. coli–contaminated bean sprouts. It could happen with the beef stew. I'm just saying."

Cat rolls her eyes. "Hey, Miss Wikipedia? There's no E. coli in the cafeteria. And, anyway, I find that story hard to believe. Fifty-one people who all intentionally ate bean sprouts? Sounds unlikely."

Alisha ignores her and plows on, holding up three long fingers.

"Number three. Watch out for Simon Stewart. Some of his friends can seem okay, but—"

Cat cuts her off. "They're not worth it."

"Not worth what?" I ask innocently, widening my eyes.

"You know. Not worth *it*."

Alisha waggles her eyebrows suggestively, and I snort. "I think that might be the least sexy thing I've ever seen." She pretends to be offended.

"Just trust me," Cat says, in a low voice.

"That's interesting advice, coming from someone who was getting *preeeetty* cozy with one of them last year," teased Alisha. "Toby Taylor, wasn't it?" She starts crooning in a singsong voice: "Cat and Taylor, up in a tree. F-U—"

"Yeah, well, that just makes me even better qualified to advise, doesn't it?" Cat cuts her off sharply. Alisha looks surprised.

"I thought you said things were getting serious? When we talked after Charlie's party, you said—"

"Well, they didn't."

There's an awkward silence. Alisha seems to be expecting more details, but Cat suddenly becomes very interested in inspecting her midnight-blue nail polish. As I open my mouth to ask more about Simon, the bell breaks the silence instead. Alisha jumps up like she's been shot, stuffing the last mouthful of her lunch into her mouth as she shrugs on her backpack.

"Lish doesn't exactly play it cool when it comes to being late for lessons," Cat teases, looking relieved at the opportunity to change the subject. "She wouldn't want her grades to dip to ninety-nine percent."

Alisha just grins as she rushes off to class.

"Want to get the bus home together?" Cat asks as she stands, yawning and stretching her arms. I feel a flutter of something in my stomach, and it's so unfamiliar it takes me a minute to realize what it is. Hope.

"Sounds good."

And as I head off to my next class, still using the crumpled map as a guide, I allow myself to wonder for the first time whether maybe—just maybe—this whole fresh start thing isn't going to be a total disaster after all.

NINE

THE MOMENT I WALK THROUGH the front door that night, I'm enveloped by a cloud of smoke. Cosmo streaks out of the door before I can close it, disappearing down the front path toward the harbor.

I'd been looking forward to telling Mum about getting the bus home with Cat (though maybe not the part where she distracted the driver so much by begging him to play a Beyoncé album over the sound system that he ran straight through a red light). But all other thoughts are instantly pushed out of my head by the smoke, replaced by terrifying visions of flames and fire engines.

"Mum?" I call, panicked.

She appears in the kitchen doorway, her face red and shiny, her hair escaping wildly from a messy bun on top of her head.

"Don't worry! Don't worry!" She pulls a tray of something blackened beyond recognition out of the stove, opens the kitchen window and starts flapping a dish towel around, trying to get rid of the smoke. My eyes start to sting. "It's not nearly as bad as it smells," she says. "It's just a little bit crispy around the edges."

Mum has never been the world's greatest cook. Okay, that's a total understatement. She's terrible. Really terrible. We had this long-standing family joke that Mum's "cookbook" was the old notebook in the top drawer that was stuffed full of all the local takeout menus. But it never mattered, because Dad loved cooking. He said it helped him to relax after work. He'd come home after a long day in the operating room, throw his tie over the back of a chair, roll up his sleeves, and start chopping like a pro, a bottle of beer on the counter and David Bowie blasting from the speaker.

Mum always teased him that he sliced the vegetables with the same surgical precision that he used on his patients, and we'd make fun of the way he lathered up his hands before cooking as if he were scrubbing in for an operation. And he would reply that she should be careful who she made fun of because if we were ever left to fend for ourselves without his cooking skills, we might not survive. It's funny the things you joke about.

After Dad died, Mum pretty much relied on microwave meals and pasta, which was understandable. And safe. This is an alarming new development.

"Thought it'd be nice to have a home-cooked meal for once," she says, busying herself with the pans bubbling on the stove as the smoke finally starts to clear.

"You know, Mum, you really didn't have to…" I gasp as she lifts the lid of one of the pans and acrid steam fills the kitchen.

"Perfect!" She starts serving everything onto two plates, and I realize with a sinking feeling that the charred black thing she's now carving is a leg of lamb, and that it's still suspiciously glistening with wet pinkness at its center in spite of its coating of ash.

When I've finally choked down enough of the very overcooked asparagus and played with enough of the lamb to avoid hurting Mum's feelings (while hopefully dodging salmonella), I excuse myself and return to the problem of my history project.

The house is much colder in the evenings than I'm used to, so I sit on my bed with my bedspread wrapped round me. Cosmo has finally ventured back into the house now that the smell of Mum's cooking is beginning to subside, and I snuggle him into my stomach like a hot-water bottle. I open a book on witchcraft that I've borrowed from the school library. I was hoping it might mention St. Monans, but the village is so tiny, it doesn't seem to make an appearance in any book I've found so far. I drop it on my pillow, frustrated. I don't know what it is that's drawn me to this story—maybe it's just a red herring and I should get on with looking for someone else to write about. But that little footnote just keeps niggling away at me. A gust of wind rattles the windows, and that strange moaning I still haven't gotten used to seems to throb through the bones of the house. Cosmo whines and buries his head in my lap, and goose bumps ripple up my arms.

The book lands open, the pages settling on a chapter titled "Superstition and Local Beliefs." A passage near the bottom of the page catches my eye.

When an accused witch had vacated her property, either by being banished, imprisoned, or killed, the next occupier would often scratch rudimentary markings, in the shape of stars, flowers, or other symbols, into the stones of the house. A common practice designed to ward off witches, it was particularly common in these cases, where the new owner of the house would be especially keen to avoid the witch's spirit returning to seek vengeance.

The back of my neck prickles, and I hear Linda's voice as if she's whispering directly into my ear: "Witches' marks! Don't they add a lovely touch of character?"

I climb out of bed and walk over to my bedroom door, running my fingers over the stonework above the frame.

There they are. Deep, regular grooves that look like they've been scraped in with a nail. When I first noticed them, they seemed haphazard—accidental even. But now as I look more closely, I can see there's a pattern to them. Several are unmistakable attempts at stars and moons, although whoever made them was clearly not very talented with their tools. In the corner is one I didn't notice before that's obviously supposed to be a flower, with five overlapping petals and a rough stem slashed into the stone below. Could Linda actually have hit on a grain of truth within all the bluster? Could these be *real* witches' marks?

I'm tingling all over. I feel like I've been transported back in time, and I lay my ear carefully against the thick, whitewashed wall as if the house might tell me its secrets. I move out onto the landing and start examining the other walls as well, searching for more signs, half expecting to see the answers to my questions carved into a beam. As I crane my neck to examine the ceiling, my eye falls on the trapdoor that leads to the attic.

Five minutes later, I've dragged the desk chair out of my bedroom, and I'm teetering precariously, using my fingernails to pry open the trapdoor. It swings stiffly downward on squeaking hinges, releasing a shower of dead flies and a rusty ladder that squeals and shudders to the floor. I blink and splutter, almost losing my balance. All I can see above me is a black square of darkness. I hesitate, part of me wanting to rush back downstairs to Mum and the warm kitchen, potential food poisoning and all. But if there's anywhere for a house to hide its secrets... I grab the ladder with both hands and start to climb.

I seem to be sitting on a rough wooden floor. There's a damp, heavy smell as if the air hasn't circulated in decades. I can't see far enough to make out how big the attic is, or what's in it. The light from the hallway below is only strong enough to illuminate the first few inches of wooden floor around the hole. I can barely see my hand in front of my face.

I sit there for a moment, breathing into the dark. It smells stale and musty. My ears prick up at a fast scuttling noise that sounds like it comes from a few feet away to my left. My skin tingles and I try not to think about the number of creepy things that might have made this old, undisturbed ceiling space their home.

Carefully, groping in front of me with my hands, I clamber to my feet and reach out, spinning on the spot. My hand brushes against what feels like a string hanging down from the ceiling and I give it a tentative tug. With a little click, a single light bulb springs into life, flooding the room with a weak yellow light.

It's a large room, running almost the full length of the house, but the sloping roof cuts into the sides, so I can only stand upright in the center of the room, and I have to stoop to take more than a few steps to either side. The attic is littered with piles of old junk, casting long shadows in strange shapes as the single bulb blinks over them. Judging from the thick layer of dust that lies over everything, none of it has been disturbed for years, decades maybe. Linda wasn't kidding when she said it might need a touch of cleaning up.

I tiptoe forward, leaving a trail of smudged footprints as if I'm walking through a blanket of snow.

Almost everything is dilapidated beyond repair. I examine an ancient wooden dresser, but its drawers are empty, and a delicate birdcage standing nearby is so old and rickety that it falls apart in my hands. A leather suitcase lying under the eaves turns out to be full of antique children's toys. A grubby teddy and a hand-sewn rag doll stare up at me with sad, unseeing eyes. I imagine them lying there for years and years, unvisited by the children who once loved and cared for them.

I run my fingertips over the broken keys of a child-size piano and it lets out a waterfall of ghostly notes. I trace a random pattern in the dust on top of a broken telephone, its retro circular dial missing several numbers. There's a box full of old bottles, their labels so faded and peeling that it's impossible to tell what they might once have contained. In a towering wooden wardrobe missing one of its doors, I find a corset covered in cobwebs, still laced as if its wearer might return in a hurry at any moment.

Suddenly something soft flits between my legs. I let out a scream, crashing backward into a pile of old cardboard boxes. But it's just Cosmo, his bright green eyes reflecting the light, his tail raised in alarm at my shriek, looking even more scared than I am. He's pressed himself against the back wall, hair standing up all over his body. I breathe again and reach out to stroke him. Then I frown and look behind him. Something isn't right about that wall.

It's the back of the attic, the wall that faces toward the garden. On the opposite side of the room, the roof slopes down to meet the floor in a sharp triangle shape. From outside, the roof is an even triangle, so the roof should also slope down to meet the floor at the back too. But it doesn't. The wall cuts off the triangle, meeting the roof around a foot above the floor.

I scoop Cosmo up in one arm and move gingerly toward the wall, picking my way over what looks like a pile of old rolled-up newspapers. Up close, I can't see anything different about the wall. It looks the same as all the others: sturdy, slightly rough-textured, and thoroughly whitewashed. I place my hand softly against the wall, testing its cool roughness beneath my palm. I run my hands from the top to the bottom, feeling along the edge where the wall meets the ceiling. Nothing. I try experimentally tapping at the wall. It gives a dull, solid thud.

Stooping, I move awkwardly along the wall toward the corner of the room. As I move farther along, Cosmo suddenly starts writhing and thrashing to get out of my arms.

"Shh, Cosmo, what's wrong with you?" I stroke his head, but the fur is standing up all along his back, and he starts to give a high-pitched whine, his ears flattened, his eyes widened to the whites and focused on the corner of the room.

"What is it?" I murmur softly. I've never seen him behave like this before, and frankly it's giving me the creeps.

I look again, straining my eyes in the dim light. And suddenly I see it. A tiny crack, so slender that it looks like a hair, right in the top corner where the wall meets the roof. I reach up and probe it with my fingers. Nothing happens. Gently, I ease my nails into the crack and feel a slight movement. I dig my nails in again, harder this time, and the crack widens—I can see a tiny sliver of darkness opening up. I wriggle the tips of my fingers once more and tug hard. There's a harsh, grating sound, and a whole section of the concrete wall swings toward me on a hidden hinge. With a yowl and a flash of whirling claws, Cosmo leaps out of my arms and streaks away.

"Ouch!" I suck at a deep claw mark gouged into my hand.

The space behind the door is narrow, barely big enough for me to crouch inside. What looked like the back wall of the attic is actually a false wall, concealing a small hidden cubbyhole between the attic and the back wall of the house. It's filthy, with long matted cobwebs trailing from the ceiling. The light from the single bulb barely penetrates in here, and I have to wait for my eyes to adjust to the gloom.

It's like being inside a very small, empty brick room. The walls are damp and slightly salty, as if the sea air has been caught in here for centuries, gradually crystallizing. I doubt the last occupants of the house knew about this hidden space—they barely seem to have even visited the attic. I might be the first person to have entered in over a hundred years. Maybe even longer. I feel the hair raise along my arms.

The sloping roof grazes my hair, and my arms scrape against the cold brick walls. In the half darkness, I run my hands over the damp bricks, and one of them moves slightly under my fingers.

Feeling in the half-light, I grasp its rough, crumbling edges and pull. It wobbles slightly. I work away at it, easing it slowly from side to side until I manage to wiggle it out, and it slides suddenly to the floor with a clatter.

In the little dirty space behind, something metallic glimmers softly. I reach my hand in and lift out a fine silver chain with a metal pendant, hammered flat and shaped like a five-pointed star. I let it dangle between my fingers, swinging gently back and forth, its sharp points spinning like a confused compass. I have the strangest feeling I've seen it before. There's something half familiar about the shape of it, the way it slithers over my fingers like silk.

"Anna!" Mum yells from downstairs. "Can you help me with this box?"

I shove the necklace hastily into my pocket and heave at the door, managing to pull it closed behind me. I want to keep this to myself: my own private discovery. I don't want to bring it out into the light and make it feel ordinary by discussing it with Mum. Dusting the dirt off my hands and brushing the cobwebs out of my hair, I hurry downstairs.

TEN

OVER THE NEXT TWO WEEKS, we fall into a pattern. Mum occasionally drives me to school, but most days I take the bus. (The first time, I was worried about bumping into Simon, but when we arrived at school, I caught sight of him being dropped off by his mum, a wisp of a woman in a dark blue Volvo whose hands fluttered at the car window as Simon strode off without a backward glance.)

When I arrive at the Inverie Street bus stop in the mornings, Cat is usually already there, sitting on the low white-painted wall that runs along the end of someone's yard, listening to music or eating a piece of toast. The bus starts out practically empty, not filling up until it gets closer to the town. So we sit in the back row, Cat usually frantically finishing off the homework she should have done the night before.

When we reach the outskirts of St. Andrews, Alisha climbs on and joins us, sitting backward in the seat directly in front of us, her head poking through the gap, tutting at Cat's mistakes until she inevitably hands her book over and lets Lish correct it. Lish makes a show of pretending to be annoyed and put upon, but I can tell she actually likes being asked for help.

———————

One particularly drab, rainy morning, Cat is huddled under a polka-dot umbrella against the wall when I arrive, her head bent over an oversize black portfolio notebook.

"Should've listened to Lish," she mutters as I sit beside her. "She told me I'd never get it done in time if I didn't start sooner." She's adding scribbled notes in the margins with a fountain pen, annotating pages of photographs that have been artfully arranged under a simple title: "St. Monans: Seasons."

"Wow, did you take these?" I take a closer look at the pictures. They show St. Monans landscapes at different times of year—the harbor drowned in red under a wine-soaked summer sunset, the church iced with a thick blanket of white snow, the pier looking strange and harsh like a jagged knife against a brooding backdrop of storm clouds.

There are a couple featuring Cat alongside three red-haired boys who tower over her, laughing good-naturedly at the camera.

"Your brothers?" She nods. "Are you close?"

"Most of the time." She laughs. "It's not always easy being the only girl in the family."

"These are really incredible," I breathe, craning my neck to see the opposite page.

"Do you really think so?" Cat asks, sounding unusually shy. "I've always loved photography, but I've only started taking it seriously the last couple of years. I took a course in Edinburgh last summer, but I haven't shown anyone my photographs from that yet."

"Seriously," I confirm. "They're really great. You should think about doing this for a living."

"I'd love to, but it's really competitive, and Mum and Dad say it's not a stable career, so they're pushing me to go to university and do a 'real' subject first." Cat sighs. "I don't know if it's all dads, or all doctors, but I think my dad will do almost anything to see me follow in his footsteps."

The bus interrupts us, arriving with a wheeze of exhaust. We climb on and head to the back.

"It's not all doctors or all dads," I surprise myself by saying in a low voice, as it moves slowly off again. "My dad was a heart surgeon, but he never pushed me toward medicine. I got the impression he'd rather I stayed far away from it actually—he was always complaining about being dragged away when he was on call on weekends and holidays."

Cat pauses, then she says: "Is it okay if I ask you about him?"

"Yeah, you can."

"Do you miss him?" she asks quietly.

"Every day. At first, it was like someone had literally ripped me open and I walked around flapping in the wind and feeling like there were little pieces falling out of me everywhere I went."

She nods thoughtfully as if she's thinking about what that

must feel like, and I'm so grateful that she isn't jumping in like other people did at the time to tell me how that's *exactly* how they felt when their hamster died or they lost their favorite pair of earrings.

"Does it get any easier?"

I think about this for a minute. "I guess it does, because a few months ago, there's no way I'd have been able to talk to you about him like this. Maybe the big, gaping, nothing-will-ever-be-the-same-again type of pain will always be there, but somehow you find a way to go on living in the smaller moments. If that makes any sense?"

She nods and doesn't tell me it'll all be fine.

The bus stops, and Alisha jumps on, taking her usual seat.

"I *told* you that you needed to start on that earlier," she says immediately, while Cat sticks the tip of her tongue out at her and resumes scribbling in her portfolio. I start to pore over Cat's pictures again, admiring the way she uses the real landscape of St. Monans to create a startling and beautiful backdrop.

"You should see the rest of her stuff," Lish says proudly, watching me. She digs out her phone and passes it to me, the screen displaying Cat's Instagram feed. Her landscapes are dotted among countless selfies and pictures of her and Alisha: posing with milkshakes outside a café; laughing in retro sunglasses with the sun bright behind them; jumping up and down in the front row at a concert; sporting fake tattoos; pouting and making silly faces in their school uniform.

"Hey, what's your Instagram?" Lish asks as I hand the phone back to her.

I can actually feel the palms of my hands starting to go clammy. My easy, relaxed mood vanishes in a moment.

"Uh, it's…AnnaClark247." I hold my breath as I watch her fingers dance over the screen, tapping it in. She swipes deftly through a few pictures of our new house and then…

"Wait, there's almost nothing here."

Cat leans over her shoulder, frowning. I can't breathe.

"It's like you didn't exist before you arrived in Scotland!" They laugh, and I try and force myself to join in.

I shrug. "I've never been that into social media," I lie, trying to sound as chill as it's possible to sound while your heart is trying to climb into your mouth. "And I don't have a phone at the moment so…"

Cat looks as if I've just told her I'm a member of the undead. "You. Don't. Have. A. Phone?!" Her eyes widen with each word until they are almost popping out of her head.

"But…" She's practically hyperventilating. It would be funny if I wasn't now sweating so much, I'm afraid of fainting from fluid loss.

"But how do you—" She waves her hands in the air as if she's casting around for words to express the entire universe. "How do you talk? How do you message? How do you get anywhere? How do you google? How…" She trails off, contemplating the full horror of a phone-free existence.

"It's not that big a deal," I say, trying to sound like it's the most boring topic in the world. "It's actually pretty liberating. You know, switching off, living in the moment."

"How do you keep in touch with your friends from home?" she asks, and I feel the familiar cold rock sliding into my stomach.

"I still have a laptop. I'm not a total recluse!" I answer lightly,

71

even though I only used my laptop once since we arrived, to post a few pictures of the house on a brand-new account. Just thinking about it is making the hair on my arms stand up.

"Have you worked out who to write about for the history project yet?" I ask Lish, hoping it's not too obvious that I'm trying to change the subject. "I'm still at a total dead end."

She looks glum. "I spent three days googling lists of celebrities from Fife, and do you know how many Black women were included on those lists?"

I shake my head, but I can guess the answer.

"None. Zero. Not one." Lish sighs. "So, I'm thinking of doing Mary Somerville." She waits, but Cat and I both look at her blankly. "Oh, come on!" She disappears for a second, leaning down to rummage in her bag, and pops back up with a Scottish ten-pound bill, which she waves under our noses, pointing at the black-and-white portrait of a young woman in a bonnet. "She was a scientist and astronomer." She looks at us expectantly. "Hers was the first signature on the 1868 petition demanding parliament give women the right to vote?" Cat shakes her head. "The first female member of the Royal Astronomical Society?"

"Oh! Yeah, of course, Mary Somerville," Cat exclaims. "Maybe I should keep that, just to remind me..." She pretends to reach for the money as Lish tucks it back into her wallet.

I laugh a bit too loudly, giddy with relief that the conversation has moved away from my empty Instagram feed.

"Whatever." Lish plops back into her seat. "Who are you doing yours on, Cat?"

"The Bishop of St. Andrews," Cat replies immediately.

72

"But—"

"The genius part," Cat says confidently, "is that after she told us *not* to interview him, nobody else will have thought of doing it."

Alisha closes her eyes and shakes her head silently.

"Does it *ever* stop raining here?" I ask as water runs down the windows so thickly, the outside world is blurred.

"Yep," Alisha confirms. "For approximately three days in mid-July."

"If you're lucky," Cat adds, snapping her portfolio closed with a sigh of relief as the bus slows down outside St. Margaret's.

We link arms and squish together under Cat's polka-dot umbrella as we run through the downpour toward school.

ELEVEN

"HEY."

I blink.

It's Thursday lunchtime, and Ms. Forsyth, the history teacher, has just spent the last period melodramatically reminding us that disaster will befall us if we don't submit our project proposals by the end of the week. I'm so busy fretting about my total lack of a subject that I've sleepwalked into the cafeteria with a tray of food in my hands, automatically veered away from the noisy table, where Simon Stewart and Mark Chambers are cheering while Toby Taylor downs a pint of milk, and stopped dead next to a nearly empty table.

"Hey," repeats the boy sitting alone at the table, an amused smile playing around his lips. One white earbud snakes down to his phone, and a copy of *Of Mice and Men* is open next to him on the table. He's making notes in the margin with a scratchy fountain pen. I can faintly hear the tinny beat of a rap song.

"Do you need directions?" he jokes.

I cast around the room, about to tell him that I'm actually eating with my friends, but there's no sign of Cat or Alisha. Suddenly it hits me. Thursday. I look down in horror at the plate of brown slop I've unthinkingly accepted. The dreaded beef stew.

"Uh…"

"You can sit here if you like," he says, separating each word out as if he thinks I might have been hit on the head.

"Thanks," I mumble, joining him at the table and starting to prod doubtfully at the lumps swimming on my plate. He puts his headphones away and folds down the corner of the page he's reading. "English homework," he explains, and I wonder if he's making sure I don't think he's reading the book by choice. Which is ironic because it's one of my favorites.

But he takes me by surprise. "I'd rather be reading this." He jabs his thumb at a well-thumbed copy of *Slaughterhouse-Five* peeking out of the bag on the table next to him.

"Have you read *Breakfast of Champions*?" I ask eagerly.

"No, but it's on my list. I'm Robin, by the way. I think we have chemistry together."

His eyes are darker than chocolate.

I flush. "We do?" I stammer, my head whirling. There's a prickling of something like chemistry in my stomach too, but we've only just—

"Yeah. Mrs. Beadle's class?"

I feel the flush accelerate to a bright scarlet and wonder if there is a massive IDIOT sign flashing on and off above my head.

"Oh, right. Yeah. You came in late," I say stupidly. I think I'm going to fall through the floor with embarrassment. In a frantic attempt to act natural, I grab a fork and take a huge bite, then choke in dismay when I realize I've just swallowed a massive mouthful of beef stew.

Robin's eyes are dancing. "So, how are you finding St. Margaret's?" There's laughter in his voice.

"It's okay." I somehow manage to stammer the words out, even though my throat seems to have closed up. I cast around for something, anything, to talk about, desperate to move the conversation on.

"I'm screwed with this history project," I squeak eventually. "I thought I might find something about a fascinating figure from my local area in here"—I hold up the copy of *St. Monans: Past to Present*, which I've been carrying around with me all day in the hope of a flash of inspiration—"but the only thing I found was the briefest reference to someone who might have been vaguely interesting, and her name isn't even mentioned."

Robin picks up the book, and I notice ink stains on his forefinger. He flicks it open to the flyleaf at the back.

"Why don't you ask the author about it? It says he's local—he might still live in the area. This was published in 1994, mind you."

He slides the book back to me. Sure enough, the brief blurb describes the author, Glenn Sinclair, as "an avid amateur historian and birdwatcher, born and bred in St. Monans." There's a black-and-white photograph of a man in his sixties with crinkled eyes and serious sideburns.

Robin picks up his phone. "According to 192.com, the only Glenn Sinclair in Fife lives at Nine Gourlay Crescent in St. Monans."

"Seriously? You can just find that out?" I raise an eyebrow. "That's a little creepy."

Robin shrugs. "Welcome to the twenty-first century." He pushes his tray back and stands abruptly, swinging his backpack over his shoulder. "See you around."

I watch him saunter away and can't help wondering if I offended him by implying he had serious stalker skills. I can't quite shake the feeling that I seem to have failed some kind of test I didn't even know I was taking, and I feel annoyed, then annoyed at myself for being annoyed. I snap the book shut on Glenn Sinclair's cheerful face and set off for double geography.

"Where were you?" Alisha asks as I slide into the classroom just as the bell rings. "We waited for you at the fish and chips shop."

I think about mentioning Robin, but it's not like there's really anything to tell. "Sorry, I totally blanked," I reply, flipping open my notebook and craning my neck to see what the teacher is writing on the whiteboard.

Dress: Casual. Packed lunch provided. Coach departs from main entrance at 6:30 a.m. sharp.

"What's this?" I ask, nodding toward the board.

"School trip," Alisha whispers. She sounds excited. "This is the year we finally get to go on the field trip to the Isle of May—it's like a wild bird sanctuary—on a tiny island just off the coast. You have to do an ecology survey and fieldwork on seabird populations—"

Cat cuts in, leaning over Alisha to hiss: "But it's mostly an excuse to mess around on a windy beach for a day."

"Sounds thrilling," I answer sarcastically, taking one of the parental permission slips being handed around. Alisha laughs and starts doodling tiny stars and moons all over hers.

"Hey, Lish," comes a hissed voice from behind us. I start to turn around, but Alisha grabs my elbow and stops me.

"Ow!" I grumble, rubbing the claw marks left by her nails. "What the—"

"Don't look at them," she whispers, looking determinedly straight ahead.

I give her a questioning glance, but do as I'm told. "What's going on?"

"They're just being dicks," Alisha hisses out of the corner of her mouth. "It's a long story."

I look up at the teacher, who has wiped the board now and is launching into a long monologue about the formation of oxbow lakes. "I've got time."

"A bunch of us got drunk at a party over the holidays," she starts, somehow managing to talk to me out of the corner of her mouth while still taking notes, in her tiny neat handwriting, on everything the teacher is saying.

"Charlie Eppingham's parents were away for the weekend, and he has this massive house." She swiftly double underlines a couple of words and starts a new bullet point.

"What happened?" I prompt.

"We arrived late and people were already pretty wasted. Cat disappeared off somewhere with Toby"—Cat has suddenly become deeply absorbed in her own notes and doesn't seem to be able to hear our conversation, but the tips of her ears are suspiciously red—"and then Mark"—she jerks her head very slightly toward the skinny boy with the stiffly gelled hair in the row behind us—"tried to get me to go upstairs with him, but I wasn't interested."

"Had anything happened?"

"Yeah, we'd been fooling around a bit, we'd kissed, but I didn't want to take it any further, and he got pretty pissed off."

I nod and give up all pretense of trying to write down the different phases of riverbank erosion. I'll just end up copying Alisha's neater, more detailed notes on the bus later anyway.

"Well, that's it basically. I didn't think he'd remember afterward because he was so drunk, but the guys have been teasing him about it since we got back to school and—" She pauses, her voice catching in her chest. "It must have got to him, because apparently yesterday he snapped and told them I was a skank, and he'd changed his mind about screwing me in case he caught something."

"*What?* Mark?" I'm genuinely surprised. A few days ago, I saw Louise drop a pile of books outside the library and Mark hung back from the usual group of guys to help her pick them up. "But he seems quite—"

"Nice?" She shrugs. "They're all okay when they're on their own. But when they get together… I dunno, it's like they have to *perform* or something."

"He called you a slut because you *didn't* want to sleep with him? Does he not realize that makes literally no sense?"

"*Lish.*"

We keep our heads down.

"Lish!"

Cat surreptitiously scratches the back of her head and raises her middle finger to Simon, who is sitting directly behind her. She puts a protective arm round Lish's shoulders.

"It's okay," Lish mutters, shrugging her off, even though her face suggests it's not. "I'd rather just ignore them."

But then the whispered chant begins.

"Lish, Lish, looks delish,

"What a shame she's such a bitch."

Alisha rolls her eyes. "Children," she whispers to me out of the corner of her mouth.

"Lish, Lish, looks delish,

"Shame her 'gina stinks of fish."

I look sideways at Alisha. Her face has gone very still.

"Lish, Lish, looks delish—" they start again. I look up. The teacher is frowning as she continues to write on the board. I swear she must be able to hear the whispering, even if she can't make out exactly what's being said.

A memory is pressing against my brain, scratching at me, trying to get in. I don't want to think about it. Don't want to remember what it felt like to hear those chants.

The boys keep on chanting softly, Charlie enthusiastically taking up the rhyme, looking sideways at Simon. I sneak a glance at Mark, sitting farther along the bench. He's not chanting, but he's not looking at anyone either. He's writing furiously, his head tilted slightly away. The voices get louder, but the teacher still doesn't turn.

The feeling of being helpless, surrounded, rises up around me like water. I can feel the unfairness of it all over again, building up inside me, pressing against my throat until I want to scream. I whirl to face the boys behind me. "Shut the fuck up," I snarl.

"Anna Clark!" Miss Fairfax snaps immediately. "Detention on Friday for swearing, not to mention interrupting my class."

"But the boys—" I begin.

"Enough. I'm sure the boys were being annoying, but you are the one who swore in my classroom."

I burn with the unfairness of it. I hear snickering behind me as Miss Fairfax turns back to the whiteboard. Alisha finds my hand under the table and gives it a tight squeeze.

Thanks, she writes in her notebook, among the moon and the stars.

TWELVE

THERE'S ONLY ONE DAY LEFT to pin down the subject of my history project, so it's now or never. It's after six o'clock and already dark before I've climbed off the bus, waved goodbye to Cat, and found my way to Gourlay Crescent. It's a quiet road lined with identical, boxy, pebble-dashed houses, more modern and nondescript than the fishermen's cottages closer to the harbor. But there's something different about number nine. Unlike its neighbors on either side, the little patch of front garden has been cultivated to within an inch of its life, with a few late daffodils still bursting into bloom, while bluebells cluster around the front door and tall nodding tulips in bright yellows and purples line the short garden path.

I pause on the pavement, suddenly feeling foolish. This could be a total wild-goose chase. What are the chances that Robin found the right address for this guy? And, even if he did, it's weird, verging on rude, to turn up unannounced on an author's doorstep, demanding more details about a book they may or may not have written more than two decades ago. I stall, one foot on the front path, the other on the pavement.

A pros and cons list starts sketching itself out in my mind. Cons: Potential major embarrassment—not exactly a new experience for me. Pros: I really need this. If I turn up at school tomorrow without a proposal for my assignment, I'll be in trouble with another teacher, and with one detention already this week, I really can't afford to rack up another.

I picture Mom's face, drooping in disappointment, imagine how she'd react to hearing how badly I've already managed to mess up in the very first month, and my mind makes itself up. Before I can chicken out, I rush up the path and knock firmly on the door, fighting the urge to run away.

For a long moment, there's no response, and I feel a guilty sense of relief wash over me. I did my best. Not my fault he's not in. It probably would've come to nothing anyway.

As I turn on my heel, a small outside lamp flickers on, bathing me in an unnatural bluish glow as the door opens.

Glenn Sinclair sits in a wheelchair, his crinkly eyes peering out from a face considerably more weathered but no less friendly than the one in the photograph. His sideburns remain, but they've been trimmed into a less bushy shape, and his hair is graying and shaved closer to his head.

I say a silent thank-you to Robin and his sleuthing skills.

"Hello," Glenn says pleasantly, a note of surprise in his voice. "Can I help you?"

Awkwardly, I spin back around to face him.

Suddenly I have no idea what to say. I hadn't really thought this far ahead.

"Er, I—Yes, I'm so sorry to bother you." I hold out the book as if I'm offering my ticket to a train conductor, proving my right to be here. "I'm a student working on a local history project, and I wondered if I might be able to ask you something about this history of St. Monans."

"Gosh." He takes it and turns it over in his hands, looking even more surprised, but rather pleased as well. "I didn't even realize this was still in print." Then, opening the front cover and seeing the library stamp, "Good old library, eh? Well, you'd better come in."

I hesitate for a moment, then step over the threshold, following him as he wheels down a ramp toward the kitchen. The walls of the hallway are hung with framed paintings and old maps, and there's a slightly musty smell that puts me in mind of museums and old bookshops. As we pass a door on the left, I catch a glimpse of a study lined on three sides with well-stocked bookshelves, a cheerful fire flickering in a small grate.

"Do you fancy a cup of tea?" Glenn calls over his shoulder as he disappears into the kitchen. I catch him up at the doorway.

"Yes, please, if it's not too much trouble."

The kitchen is small and cozy, with jars of rice and pasta lined up along the countertop and gleaming copper saucepans hanging from low hooks on the wall. Glenn maneuvers around it with ease, handling his wheelchair deftly in the cramped space as he fills an old-fashioned kettle and sets it on the stove to boil.

I perch awkwardly on a rickety chair at the kitchen table. One end of it is strewn with documents and photocopies, some of them written in what looks like Latin. The papers are peppered with Post-its and pencil notes are scrawled in the margins.

"My latest project," Glenn explains, seeing me looking. "I'm researching the history of Newark Castle and the different families that lived there over the years. It's fascinating actually."

He breaks off as the whine of the kettle builds to an insistent shriek and pauses to pour two large mugs of strong tea.

"Well, then," he says, handing one to me and joining me at the table. "What did you want to ask?"

"It's about one of your footnotes," I begin tentatively.

"Oh dear. If I've got any dates wrong, it's entirely my own error—"

"No, it's nothing like that," I interrupt quickly. "You mentioned a woman in St. Monans who was tried for witchcraft. In the seventeenth century, I think you said." I pause and look up at Glenn, who is blowing on his tea. He frowns and locates a pair of brass-rimmed reading glasses from the kitchen counter and pushes them onto his nose.

"I was just wondering if you knew any more about the story," I press, watching his face as he flicks through the book. "I've got to write a history project about a person of interest in my local area, and I just thought… I don't know, I thought maybe she'd be a good person to write about. I was just curious about the story, I guess."

Glenn has found the page and is running his finger along the footnote.

"Yes," he murmurs thoughtfully. "I remember something about this coming up in my research, but I never fully followed up on it at the time. I was under pressure to get the book finished, and I didn't have time to get to the bottom of the story, but I remember finding some documents that referenced it. Hang on a minute." He whizzes out of the kitchen, and I see him disappearing down the hallway and into the study. A few moments later, he returns with a scruffy box filled with loose sheets and scribbled notes. "Somewhere in here…" he murmurs, leafing through it, pausing to look more closely at a page here and there.

As I slowly drain my mug, he becomes more and more absorbed in his task, appearing to forget that I'm there at all. I gaze around at the neat kitchen, noticing several well-stocked bird feeders hanging just outside the window. After ten minutes or so, I start surreptitiously trying to sneak a glance at my watch. The nervous excitement I initially felt is beginning to fade into frustration. It doesn't look like I'm going to get anywhere here, and I need to get home for dinner before Mum starts to worry.

Suddenly Glenn raises a sheaf of papers triumphantly with an "Aha!" so loud, it makes me jump in my chair. "Got it!" he cries, brandishing the sheets in my direction. If he's trying to leave me on the edge of my seat, he's doing a good job. I writhe with impatience. "It seems there was an accusation of witchcraft here in St. Monans at some point in the seventeenth century…" He sounds like a man who knows how to tell a good story and doesn't mind drawing it out for effect. I bite my tongue and try to resist the urge to jump up and shake the details out of him.

"The story starts a little while before the accusation, if I remember correctly," he murmurs, running his finger down the paper. "It was a young woman." He nods as if it's starting to come back to him. "She was a noted beauty, but she came from a poor fisherman's family. They were hardworking, decent folk and they scraped a living from the sea, selling their catch on market day and just about getting by with enough to eat, keeping a roof over their heads and very little else. Like most families in St. Monans during that period."

I lean forward, hanging on his every word.

"Well, the source I came across during my research suggested that this young woman caught the eye of a local nobleman, the son of a powerful baron who owned much of the land around these parts. He was probably quite used to having his way with whichever local maids took his fancy, but for reasons of her own, the young woman spurned his advances and made it clear she wasn't interested in his attentions." He pauses to take a long drink of tea, and I twist my hair between my fingers impatiently.

"Well," Glenn continues, "he wasn't used to being told no and he didn't like it at all, particularly not coming from a woman and one of much lower social status than him at that. So he pursued her relentlessly and eventually she gave in." He clears his throat and looks at me as if he's considering whether to continue. "At least that's the tactful version of events that were recorded in the source I came across. Whether he was more—ah—*forceful* isn't clear, but I imagine it's more than likely." He doesn't need to spell it out. I nod grimly.

"It seems that she soon found herself in quite a predicament, if you know what I mean." He looks questioningly at me, but I'm not sure what he's getting at. "She fell pregnant," he explains slightly awkwardly, and it suddenly occurs to me for the first time how odd it is for me to be sitting at this weathered wooden kitchen table, drinking out of a stranger's mug and discussing the life of a woman who lived four hundred years ago with a strange man I only met for the first time half an hour before.

"Well," he presses on, "in those days, it was scandalous for a woman to bear a child out of wedlock—*really* scandalous, I mean—and quite possibly highly dangerous for them both. And so, when the child was born, the young woman found herself summoned before the kirk session and duly questioned by the elders of the town about her baby."

"The kirk session?"

"It was a sort of ruling council, made up of the most respectable and wealthy men of the village."

"Just the men?"

"Oh yes, there wouldn't have been any women involved." He pauses as if he's trying to remember where he was in the story. "Now she was a strong-willed lass and quickly named the noble as the child's father, arguing that the baby was as much his responsibility as hers, but the minister and the other church elders who heard the case were regular guests at the baron's dinner table. They knew that protecting the son could be advantageous to them, so they obligingly declared the child officially 'fatherless,' despite the fact that everyone in the village knew the truth."

I snort in indignation. "That's ridiculous!" I cry, unable to stop myself interrupting, even though I want to hear more.

"Oh, I quite agree," Glenn says mildly, blinking up at me from over his pages of notes as if he's surprised to see I'm still there. "But these were different times, you must remember, and injustice was more often the outcome than not in such cases."

"What happened next?" I ask, suddenly realizing I'm leaning forward in anticipation, my elbows pressing into the table and my chin in my cupped hands. Glenn frowns and riffles through the rest of the papers, then starts leafing through the ones left in the file.

"It's unclear," he answers eventually. "There's the briefest reference to her having later been tried for witchcraft, but the details are sketchy. The trail just went cold. That's why the incident never ended up becoming more than a footnote." He gestures toward the book, which is still lying open on the table.

"Do you think you might be able to find out any more?" I ask, holding my breath.

He looks at my eager face and pauses. "I don't see why not," he says slowly. "You've made me curious now as well! I'd hoped to chase down the rest of the story twenty years ago, but I ran out of time, and I confess I hadn't thought about it again until you arrived on my doorstep today."

With a mischievous glint in his eye, he adds: "I can't be doing all the work, though—that wouldn't be right, since it's your project. I'll make an appointment at the national records office and see what I can dig up, but you ought to visit one of the bigger libraries in St. Andrews and try to find out a bit more about witch-hunting in Fife." He holds out his hand. "Deal?"

Considering that the deadline for presenting the subject of my history project is tomorrow, I'd agree to pretty much anything at this point. I shake his hand firmly. "Deal!"

THIRTEEN

AS I GET READY FOR bed later that night, picking up jeans and a sweater from the floor of my room to put them in the laundry basket, something silvery slides out onto the floor.

I'd forgotten all about the necklace from the attic. I sit in bed and let it slip through my fingers like liquid, wondering how old it is and who wore it. Why was it left, hidden behind that stone, for so long? Why didn't its owner ever come back for it?

The chain is made of the most delicate silver links, no more than a millimeter or so wide. It has become dull and tarnished with age, but the star must have been made out of a different metal, because it still sparkles and glitters, flashing in the light as I examine it. In the very bottom corner of one of the star's points, a little zigzag has been scratched carefully into the metal.

I run my fingers over it again and again, feeling the slight roughness of the engraving under them, and pressing the points of the star into my palm until they leave bright red indentations.

Before I go to sleep, I lift the necklace in my hands, as light as spun sugar, and let it fall gently over my head, so that the pendant comes to rest below the little hollow at the base of my throat.

Everything aches. Your thighs burn from crouching next to the nets. Your hair stinks of fish, and your hands are coated in so many scales they are like fine silver gloves. Your knife slips easily under the wet, smooth skin and the flesh slips out like firm, cold jelly.

When the man approaches, you think he is going to complain about the smell. His face is fine and proud. His brow is high, and his eyes are cornflower blue. You laugh when he asks your name. What could he possibly want with it?

He laughs back, and his teeth are white and straight. He asks again and you flounder, uncertain. Da is out on the boat, and your brothers have left you at the harborside to clean the catch alone.

It doesn't seem like it could do any harm, to tell him. Maggie from the village, born with the salt in her skin and the waves dancing in her eyes, or so Maw always told it.

He reaches out and pulls a scale from your hair, and you don't know how to say that's quite enough because you've never met a man like him before. It wouldn't do to give him a quick box about the ears as you would with one of the lads from the boats. So you duck your head to the fish instead and scoop out its ruby innards to glisten on the cobbled ground.

Their bodies slither through your practiced palms like dough in some girls' hands. Mind the top fins—some are razor-sharp—they'll slash your fingers to pieces.

He's still there, though. He crouches. Puts out a gloved hand to cover yours. You shake it off. Your eyes are low like you've been taught, but he leans closer, and you feel his breath against your neck. And so you stand and face him, chest heaving, head up, and your eyes look straight into his.

He laughs then and moves away, yet his eyes still flash at you over his shoulder. You bend back to the fish, but you feel the net closing in on you instead.

I wake, hot and disoriented. My throat is dry and my pulse is racing. The dream felt so real. I rub my hands together, still half feeling the sticky scales and the sting of salt water in the cuts on my fingers. It's a cool night, but my hair is damp with sweat. The pendant is digging into my neck. I touch the delicate star. It feels warm.

I rub my eyes and try to convince myself that it was only a dream. But it was as vivid as day—I feel as if I sat on those cold cobblestones myself. It was like I was seeing it through my own eyes—that I'd somehow stepped into someone else's memory. Someone who cleaned fish on the cobbled harborside…someone like the girl in Glenn's story.

"That's ridiculous," I tell myself. "Don't be stupid, Anna. You're still half asleep. Glenn's story moved you, and you dreamed about it. That's all."

I turn over, wriggling until my hot cheek finds a cool spot on the pillow. Gradually, my pulse slows, and this time I fall into a dreamless sleep.

FOURTEEN

FRIDAY'S MEETING WITH MS. FORSYTH is a success. I was worried that not yet even knowing the name of the woman I want to write about might disqualify her as a potential subject for my project, but funnily enough it seems to have the opposite effect.

"Wonderful," Ms. Forsyth breathes, clasping her hands together. "A real research project. I think your proposal has great potential, Anna. Just make sure you get going on your investigation sooner rather than later—you've got a lot of work to do and the project is due immediately after midterms, remember."

She looks so enthusiastic, I have to try not to laugh. Clearly, Ms. Forsyth doesn't exactly get out much.

"Digging out old records and getting to the bottom of local

myths can be tricky and take longer than you might think, so leave yourself plenty of time."

I nod, wondering if Ms. Forsyth is going to keep going on about research methods and whether it'll make me late for gym, which frankly would be absolutely fine by me.

"Here." Ms. Forsyth digs around in her handbag and pulls a blue swipe card out of her wallet. "I shouldn't really do this, but just this once…" She actually glances over her shoulder before saying: "Take my university library card," and I have to stifle a snort and quickly turn it into a cough because I realize that fraudulently lending out her library card is probably the most deviant thing Ms. Forsyth has ever done.

"You'll be able to browse the whole collection, and it'll give you access to more volumes than are easily available at the public library. Now you'd better get going—you wouldn't want to be late for gym, would you?"

No such luck.

The changing room is buzzing as I squeak open my locker and pull out the baggy gray St. Margaret's polo shirt, cotton shorts, and tennis shoes. Talk about stylish. I start pulling them on without enthusiasm, my arms prickling with goose bumps in the cold.

"What's going on?" I ask Louise, who is sitting on the bench in front of the locker next to mine. She is bent over her phone, frantically typing into WhatsApp with both hands.

"People are saying Emily Winters slept with Simon Stewart," she breathes, without looking up.

I can see the glowing screen over her shoulder.

OMG deets?????????

94

Don't know yet but 😊 😊

😮 Does Lola know?

If she did, Emily would be dead already.

Bitch fight at lunch?

LOL only if the slut shows her face.

🤞

I pull on my shoes without bothering to untie the laces and wander into the gym, where half the class is already sprawled on the blue gym mats. A small crowd is gathered around Simon, who looks like he's won some kind of trophy, boys slapping him on the back and laughing as he lolls back with his hands behind his head. Toby is smirking next to him, already pumping out push-ups, even though we haven't been given any instructions yet.

"Have you heard about Simon and Emily?" Cat asks as I plump myself down next to her.

"Yeah," comes a strained voice. I look up. Alisha is halfway up the rope above my head, her feet tightly pressed together to support her weight, her biceps shaking as she pulls herself higher.

"Nobody's seen Emily all day," Cat adds, shaking her head.

"How do you *do* that?" I ask, half laughing, half impressed. "I can barely hang off the bottom without getting rope burn."

"She's always been freakishly good at gym," Cat answers, lying on her back with her legs in the air, twisting the nearest rope around and around her ankle. "You should see her run—she's like a tornado." I feel a slight pang, noticing how lightly they wear their years of friendship. Cat and Alisha have made my first month at St. Margaret's better than bearable, and I already feel close to them, but every now and then I'm reminded that they've known each other forever, and I wonder if I'll ever catch up.

An image of Prav, Suzanne, and I falling over in a writhing heap in gym class after trying to create a human pyramid pops unwanted into my brain. I feel myself missing them, and then my stomach lurches unpleasantly as I'm forced to remember why I shouldn't. Why I'm better off without them. It's like watching my body take a roller coaster ride it's already been on over and over again but refuses to get off. *Real friends don't desert each other*, I think to myself firmly, pushing the image out of my mind.

"I might adopt Tornado as my superhero name." Alisha grins, slithering down the rope and landing with a thud on the floor next to us.

"Thunder thighs!" yells one of the boys, and when I look over, they're all smirking, though I can't tell who actually shouted.

Cat flicks them the finger and shouts: "You're just jealous 'cause she'd run rings round you!" But after the boys look away, I see Alisha glance down at her legs and tug her shorts a bit lower.

"Circuits!" barks Mrs. Roth, the teacher, from the corner of the gym, her voice booming out as if she's using a loudspeaker.

"So, what's the deal with Emily and Simon?" I ask Cat as we sit opposite each other for sit-ups, feet touching in the middle and knees bent, each lying back and then heaving ourselves up with rapidly decreasing levels of effort.

Cat takes a deep breath and talks so quickly it's like she's on fast-forward. "Simon's been with Lola Ross since forever, but they broke up last week, because Simon said it was too much stress having a serious relationship," she explains, panting slightly.

"Emily and Lola used to be best friends, but they fell out after Charlie Eppingham's party, because Lola went off with Simon and abandoned Emily, even though Emily was really upset because James Hastings had literally just dumped her that afternoon and she didn't even want to go to the party in the first place."

She ceases even pretending to do the sit-ups and sits with her arms wrapped around her bent knees, wiping imaginary sweat off her forehead. "It's pretty savage for Emily to have slept with Simon behind Lola's back," she concludes.

"But they'd broken up?" I puff, still straining away, but only managing to raise my head a few inches off the floor each time. "And he's the one who said he didn't have time for a girlfriend, then turned around and immediately slept with someone else."

"That's just guys, though, isn't it?" Cat says dismissively, scrambling up to move onto the next circuit station as the gym teacher's shrill whistle cuts through our conversation. "Sometimes I really envy Lish." She groans as we start heaving a massive medicine ball back and forth, while Alisha pumps out a set of apparently effortless push-ups nearby. "Look at her! She's not even doing the girl ones, and she's hardly breaking a sweat."

As we change into our swimsuits in the second half of the lesson, the conversation about Lola and Emily rages on.

"What I don't get is what either of them sees in Simon in the first place," says one girl, wriggling the straps of her swimsuit up over her shoulders. There's an immediate chorus of disagreement.

"Oh, come on!"

"Are you kidding me?"

"Have you *seen* him lately?"

97

"Apparently," Louise whispers, and everyone turns to listen, "Lola was completely frigid and never let Simon touch her. So in a way, you can't blame him if he got some elsewhere."

There's a soft noise like air being let out of a balloon and everyone's heads turn toward the door. Lola is standing there, her short blond hair tousled and uneven, her eyes red, her swimming bag over her shoulder.

"Lola." Louise looks genuinely mortified. "I didn't mean—" But the door is already slamming behind Lola.

There's a long pause, and Louise looks like she doesn't know whether to run after Lola or not. "Well, I did hear it," she says to no one in particular.

Gradually, the chatter starts up again, and people finish changing. Cat is half dressed, stopping to open a packet of chips, her swimsuit hanging down to reveal her boobs, which seem to have developed earlier than everyone else's. She hands Lish a chip, apparently completely unconcerned that her nipples are on display for everyone to see.

I, on the other hand, am secretly terrified that one of my boobs is bigger than the other, and, although Google assures me this is very common and will probably even out eventually, I live in horror of somebody else noticing or commenting on it. I pull my swimsuit on quickly over my underwear, wriggling them off down one leg then the other and pulling them out through my crotch, then I take my arms out of my gym shirt sleeves and slip them into the swimsuit straps under my top before shrugging it off.

The strange silver necklace from the attic dangles around my neck, and I quickly tuck it under the swimsuit, feeling it lie still and cool against my skin. As I splash through the footbath, I look down at my own bare feet, and for a fleeting moment it's like I'm looking at someone else's, heels scuffed with dirt and toenails ragged, glittering wet in the water at the harbor's edge. Then the chlorine smell of the pool hits me, and the image is gone.

As we stream out of the changing room, most of the boys are already lined up along the tiled wall of the pool, some of them fidgeting with the drawstrings on their swimming trunks, others holding their towels in front of their chests and trying to look casual.

Somebody shouts, "Rack!" and there's a ripple of snickering, but I can't tell if it was aimed at me or not, or if it was a compliment or not, or if my swimsuit is too low cut or not low cut enough. I'm at least fairly confident they won't have noticed my lopsidedness at this distance, so I settle for crossing my arms over my chest and adopting a slightly huffy expression, which I figure will probably work for all scenarios.

I slip into the pool as quickly as I can and duck under the water, gasping as I break the surface.

"Freestyle lengths to warm up, please!" shouts our teacher, and I push off and start to move through the water with a steady crawl. The second I start to swim, I feel the tension leaving my body. This is something I know. This is my comfort zone. I feel the water rushing past me, its silky touch massaging my skin, my arms slipping in and out, in and out, and my breathing effortlessly matching the rhythm of my strokes. I haven't mentioned my swim-team past to anyone at St. Margaret's, and I hear someone give a low, impressed whistle as I zoom off, but I'm enjoying my return to the water so much, I barely register it. I hadn't realized how much I'd missed this. Not just the swimming itself, but the feeling of being powerful, of being in control. In here, I know exactly what to do and how to do it.

When everybody has done their warm-up lengths, the coach floats a set of foam goalposts into each end of the pool and hands out blue-and-white water-polo caps with funny plastic ear protectors that make everyone look like helicopter pilots. "*Très chic*," Cat jokes, grabbing one and throwing her head back, striking a pose.

Alisha and a boy named Ahmed are made team captains, and Alisha immediately picks Cat, who is splashing around in the shallow end, clearly absolutely terrible at swimming and, I suspect, probably even worse at water polo. I feel that slight pang of jealousy pull at my belly button again as Cat smiles gratefully at her friend and marches over, swapping her white cap for a blue one. I'm just hoping Alisha will pick me next when, to my surprise, Ahmed shouts, "Anna!" and I find myself pulling on a white cap, while he claps me on the back. "Nice warm-up," he whispers with a smile.

The game is fast and furious. Nobody's very good, but what we lack in skill and accuracy, we make up for in aggression and splashing. One casualty is sent to the school nurse after taking an elbow to the eye within the first five minutes. I'm in my element, sparring with Alisha, who has better aim on the ball, but isn't as fast as me.

"Referee!" I exclaim as Lish swims underwater and grabs my ankles, making me drop the ball. Lish surfaces, blows a raspberry at me, and sweeps the ball out wide to Cat, who promptly headbutts it, swallows a huge gulp of water, and retreats to the side of the pool, coughing and shaking water out of her ears.

As the other side groans, Ahmed scoops the ball up and passes it back to me. There's nothing but open water between me and the goal. Prodding the ball ahead of me, I start to swim, aware of a mass of splashing behind me as the other team closes in. I reach the five-meter line and pause, drawing the ball back in my arm, ready to shoot. Just as the ball leaves my fingertips, I'm completely submerged by Alisha and several other members of the blue team as they converge on me, dunking me under the water in a whirlpool of writhing limbs. My goggles slip off in the chaos, and I struggle toward the surface, finding bodies in the way and beginning to feel my lungs burn for air.

Then suddenly, as I kick toward the surface, a hand snakes between my legs and squeezes my butt, hard and deliberately. For a moment, I freeze in total shock. The water turns to ice, with me suspended in it, and the world stops. Then I break the surface and it's over. The whistle blows, the goal is conceded, the hand has disappeared, and swimmers are surfacing and kicking all around me, laughing and splashing as they head for the steps.

I feel numb. It happened so quickly, I'm already doubting my own memory. Could it have been a mistake? Could I have imagined it? As I clamber out of the pool and wrap myself in my towel, Simon pushes past me on his way into the boys' locker room, his eyes meeting mine for the briefest second. Is there a smirk on his face or am I imagining it?

I stare after him in disbelief.

I feel weirdly separate from the other girls as we splash through the footbath and back into the locker room. As if there's a plastic bubble around me. I'm there and not there. I'm still in the pool, feeling his fingers closing on my flesh. Still underwater, feeling my muscles seize in sudden shock. Still hearing the muffled shouts through the water in my ears. And, at the same time, I feel silly for caring. It's not like it's a big deal. It's not like it hasn't happened to me before.

Mechanically, I drop off my towel and move toward the showers. As I pass the mirror screwed to the wall next to the hand dryer, I turn slightly to the side. I wouldn't have noticed it if I hadn't already known it was there, but when I look closely, I can see definite red marks on my butt, where somebody's fingers have dug into my flesh.

"Jeez, checking yourself out much?" Alisha teases as she speeds past me and into the showers. "You have a lovely ass, Anna, but it's a bit much to be gazing at it in a public mirror!"

Automatically, I try to smile, following Alisha into the communal shower and quickly rubbing shampoo through my hair as the chatter goes on around us.

"Has anyone got a razor? My legs are *so* hairy."

"Look at your thighs, though—I'd rather have hair than cellulite. At least you can shave it off."

"Girl, please. You do not have cellulite."

"Yes, I do! What's this, then? Fucking orange peel is what it is."

"Nobody's looking at your orange peel with those tits, trust me. They're so perky, it's not real. Mine sag like socks stuffed with juggling balls."

There's snickering. "Oh, come on! Socks stuffed with juggling balls? Seriously? No way."

"You guys, you can all shut up. I have a *whisker*. And I swear to God it grows back thicker every time I pluck it."

It's a simple game. We've never been taught it, but we all

know the rules. You say something nice about someone else. They contradict you and deflect the compliment by revealing a fault about themselves and complimenting someone else instead. And the circle carries on, round and round. Accepting the compliment is strictly not allowed. I know how to play, I'm pretty great at it actually, but I can't join in because if I speak, I'm afraid I might cry, or laugh, or say out loud what just happened, and I don't think that's allowed either.

FIFTEEN

DETENTION AT ST. MARGARET'S TAKES place in the cafeteria. I walk in, feeling like a felon. I've never had detention before, and it is definitely not part of my plan for staying out of trouble. Thank God St. Margaret's has a policy of only informing parents if you get two detentions in a semester. I take a seat at a table near the back and start working on my math homework, not looking up as other students file in in dribs and drabs and scrape back their chairs. The radiators are pumping out heat. It's already dark outside, and I feel my eyelids drooping repeatedly, almost letting my head nod forward into the book before the teacher paces past and my neck snaps up again.

The third time this happens there's a very soft chuckle next to me—not loud enough to attract the teacher's attention, but a definite chuckle nonetheless. I look around and find myself staring straight into those almost black eyes. I jump.

Robin slides a scrap of paper along the table.

Need a coffee?

I grab it, scribble underneath and push it back.

I wish.

He pauses, writes and passes it to me again.

What are you in for?

Swearing.

How rude.

You?

That'd be telling.

Let me guess...crimes against music? If you can even call that garbage you were listening to the other day music.

Robin makes a face of mock shock and uses a finger to slowly mime a single tear running down his cheek.

Ouch. Tardiness if you must know. Late three
times in two weeks.

Oh.

We've reached the bottom of the paper. I turn it over and
continue on the other side.

Need an alarm clock?

Haha.

He pauses and writes another line below.

You've made a mistake btw. Number four's
wrong.

What are you, the algebra police?

Just trying to help.

Concentrating on my homework instead of
yours?

Finished mine already

We've reached the bottom of the page again. He slides a new
scrap over to me instead. I write:

Got any plans for the weekend?

Nope. You?

Hot date with St. Andrews University library.

Sounds wild.

I smile and hesitate, my pencil hovering over the page. My heart is beating quickly and, even though thoughts like *Don't be an idiot* and *Chasing after boys is the last thing you need right now* are swirling around in my head, I find myself scrawling:

Wanna help?

I push it back quickly before I can lose my nerve and hold my breath, looking down at my homework. There's a long pause. I hear his pen scratching. He's only written two words.

Can't. Sorry.

I snatch the paper so quickly, it tears a little and thrust it back at him.

No worries.

Then I turn back to my textbook, hoping that my ears haven't turned bright red, although they're hot with embarrassment. Why would he want to hang out with me? Even though he already said he has literally nothing else to do. Why would he? *He's probably clocked your weird, wonky boobs*, says a mean voice in my head. I viciously rub out my answer to question four and start again. Infuriatingly, I can't see where I've gone wrong, but I'm certainly not going to give him the satisfaction of asking for pointers.

The paper doesn't come back. The second the bell rings, chattering breaks out around the room. Robin looks as if he's about to say something, but I jump up and rush off without looking back.

Lucky escape anyway, I tell myself firmly. In my limited experience, boys bring nothing but trouble.

It's drizzling when Mum drops me off outside St. Andrews University library the next morning, and I can hear bells pealing somewhere in the city. I hold my denim jacket up over my head with both hands and peer at the imposing, sharply rectangular building. It's three stories high with thick concrete slabs jutting out between each level like a layer cake.

I use Ms. Forsyth's card and sidle surreptitiously inside, shaking rain out of my hair. Remembering Ms. Forsyth's hesitation, I feel nervous in spite of myself, half expecting someone to pounce on me and demand that I verify my identity. But I shouldn't have worried. The front desk is empty and the only member of staff I can see is busy reshelving a loaded cart full of books and barely glances up as I enter. I experience a triumphant rush of relief, then catch myself and feel foolish. Sneaking into a library—jeez, what a rebel! The place is almost empty—I guess Saturday morning isn't the busiest time for a university library.

The walls are lined with books, and rows of shelves jut out into the room every few feet, creating countless little alcoves where students can sit and browse. Down the center of the room there are long communal desks, with each individual space marked by its own chair, power outlet, and retro desk lamp. At the back of the room, there's a massive printer and photocopier, and a series of computers that students can use to search the digital library catalogue.

I seat myself in front of one and experimentally tap in "Scotland + witchcraft." I'm taken aback when a list of titles obligingly appears below the search bar. I'd half expected nothing to come up at all, but Scottish witches are clearly a hotter topic than I'd realized. There are about fifteen volumes to choose from. I jot down the section number and set off to find the right shelf, pausing to snicker at a sign on the bathroom door informing students that masturbation in the library is a violation of university regulations. ("Shakespeare wanked too!" someone has scrawled on the paper in orange highlighter.)

The books about the Scottish witch hunt are all clustered on the same shelf, sandwiched between a selection of European history volumes and around forty different books on the Salem witch trials. I pull out the ones that look most promising and settle down at a vacant desk. It has a fancy leather surface that feels luxurious under my fingers, and the black desk lamp seems to be craning its neck inquisitively to see what I'm working on. I feel a fanciful urge to turn it on, as if it will make my research seem more serious and professional if I conduct it under my own personal little spotlight. Then I feel like an idiot and click it off again.

As I open the first book, I imagine myself studying here for real: rushing through research the night before a class; poring over the first draft of a difficult essay; cramming before finals. I find that I quite like the idea. I haven't thought much about my academic prospects recently. Changing schools (not to mention countries) halfway through the year when you're in the middle of studying and writing application essays isn't exactly a great way to boost your university chances. But for the first time, I start to wonder if I might still be able to turn things around.

When I open the oldest-looking book, it gives off a satisfying whiff of damp earth and long-forgotten secrets. A smell of history and nighttime walks that make excitement and possibility fizzle in my stomach. But leafing through it is disappointing—it's written in such dull, old-fashioned prose, I can barely understand a word.

I move to the next one, and this time I hit gold. In clear, simple language, the author explains that while many people are familiar with the Salem witch trials, a similar hysteria swept through Europe as well.

Between the sixteenth and eighteenth centuries, a series of witch trials occurred throughout Scotland, seeing thousands tried, condemned and put to death. Estimates for the number of people killed range between 4,000 and 6,000, three times higher than in England during the same period, though Scotland had just one quarter of England's population.

Seventy-five percent of those tried and killed for the crime of witchcraft were women. Execution rates were highest (90 percent of those accused) in local courts, where the powerful men of a village could become judge and jury in a biased investigation closely tied to ideas of morality and influenced by local clergy. With no professional lawyers present, the pursuit of witchcraft in these cases was often taken over by local landowners.

While those found guilty of witchcraft in England were usually hanged, witch burning was common in Scotland, as well as mainland Europe.

I shiver, and rub my arms briskly to get rid of the goose bumps.

There are multiple competing theories about the underlying causes of the phenomenon. Most of the periods of prosecution coincided with times of intense economic distress. The political situation at the time was unstable, with the British Civil Wars taking place between 1639–51 and the ongoing threat of English attack and occupation. In 1644–5, a Scottish civil war was fought between Scottish Royalists and Covenanters, quickly followed by war with England. During the English Civil War, Scotland was invaded and occupied by the Parliamentarian New Model Army under Oliver Cromwell until the Restoration of 1660.

Meanwhile, women may have been seen by the Scottish Church as something of a moral threat. Many historians have suggested that the witch hunt in Scotland may have reflected attempts to control women, to suppress their sexual expression or power.

Many accusations included reference to gender and specific sexual fears—like the common claim that witches fornicated with the devil, or a case where a midwife was accused of transferring labor pains onto the husbands of pregnant women. In some cases, accused women were tortured by being forced to sit on red-hot stools, with the reasoning that this would prevent them from further satanic sexual activity.

The methods used to identify and "prove" witchcraft were often cruel and torturous. An accused witch might undergo "ducking," in which her thumbs were bound to her big toes before she was thrown into a river or pond, with her guilt proved if she floated (leading to her execution) and her innocence only asserted by drowning. Women could be deprived of sleep for days on end, a practice described as "waking the witch," leading eventually to hallucinations and nonsensical ramblings which would then be used as evidence of guilt. Professional "witch prickers" would travel the country, determining guilt by finding small patches ("devil's marks") on women's bodies where the stab of a sharp needle wouldn't draw blood or cause pain. Later examination of their tools revealed that the needle could be drawn up inside the instrument at the required moment, and many witch prickers were later exposed as frauds.

Various powers believed to be held by witches caused widespread fear and alarm. It was thought that some could transform themselves into familiar creatures at will, and that others had the ability to transfer some essence of themselves or their memories into personal objects like handkerchiefs or items of jewelry. Others were thought to have the power of flight.

By the time I leave the library several hours later, another book checked out under Ms. Forsyth's name and tucked in my bag, my brain is whirling.

I haven't found any more specific reference to St. Monans, nor the name of the young woman accused of witchcraft there, but I'm more determined than ever to discover what happened to her. As I wait for Mum to pick me up, I lean against the hard stone wall of the library and try to sort through my racing thoughts. Needles and flames and fish guts glinting in the sun chase one another giddily around my head.

SIXTEEN

I CHECK THE HOUSE OVER for the umpteenth time, trying to see it through Cat and Alisha's eyes. I've hidden two embarrassing childhood photos behind the bookcase, swept a pile of bags that are still waiting to be unpacked into the cupboard under the stairs, and moved my stuffed toys from the end of my bed to the top of my wardrobe.

We've been planning a sleepover ever since Miss Fairfax announced the coach for the geography field trip would leave at 6:30 on Monday morning. It'll be too early to get the bus, so Mum promised to drop us all off at school and heavily hinted that asking my new friends to stay over the night before was a great idea. I think she might be more excited about this sleepover than I am.

I've already preempted a classic Mum culinary disaster by

picking up some frozen pizzas from the one small shop that was open on a Sunday afternoon in St. Monans. As we grate some extra cheese over them, I look sideways at her, cheeks slightly flushed, eyes bright.

"Mum. Don't take this the wrong way, okay, but please, tonight, just..." I hesitate.

"Be cool?"

"Yes!" I exclaim quickly, then, as she gives a wry smile, I add, "Sorry. You know what I mean."

"Don't worry, I won't cramp your style. Actually, I've got a surprise for you."

I follow her outside. At the bottom of the garden, in the corner between the shed and the ivy-covered wall, Mum has created a little nook sheltered from the wind. She's arranged a few large logs around a bare patch of earth, flat stones forming a ring in the center. A pyramid of firewood is waiting in the middle, smaller sticks and twisted paper kindling peeping out around the edges.

"I thought a space of your own might come in handy...and perhaps some s'mores?" She holds up some packets of marshmallows, chocolate, and graham crackers, and I give her a huge hug.

"Thanks, Mum."

Still wrapping me in the hug, she strokes my hair and I feel about eight years old again.

"You deserve this, Anna," she murmurs into my hair. "It's about time things went right. I told you everything would change if we just got away."

I can feel a hard lump throbbing in the back of my throat, but at that moment the doorbell rings, so I swallow it down, wipe under my eyelids with the backs of my hands, and run to greet Cat and Alisha.

———————

"Only someone who's not originally from Scotland would even consider a campfire at this time of year," Cat says later, pulling a fleecy blanket tightly around herself as we sit by the dancing flames. "But I have to hand it to your mum—it's actually pretty cozy out here."

It's a mild evening. Even at this late hour, the air is chilly rather than freezing, and a heavy dark yellow moon hangs low above us. The only sounds are the swish of water in the harbor and the odd muted clink as Mum does the dishes in the kitchen.

The smoke from the campfire trails up toward the sky in thin tendrils, clinging to our hair and clothes so everything smells rich and woody. Cat produces a bottle of her mum's homemade blackberry wine, which makes me snort with laughter, and then I have to try and explain that in Birmingham we'd be drinking vodka if we felt fancy, or more likely cheap cider. The more we drink, the more hilarious it is, and I keep trying to explain again why it's so funny, but Alisha and Cat don't get it, which just makes it even funnier. To be fair, when I heard blackberry wine, I thought it'd be like mildly alcoholic Coca-Cola, but the speed with which I'm dissolving into laughter suggests that it's actually quite a bit stronger than I thought.

Alisha is humming softly to herself, leaning forward with a marshmallow on the end of a skewer, turning it in the fire and letting it brown slowly on each side. Cat keeps pushing her marshmallows too far in so they catch fire and turn black, slipping gloopily off the skewer.

"Girls are like marshmallows," Alisha says grandly, making a sweeping gesture with her arm to indicate this is an important point and we should be paying close attention. Cat's marshmallow promptly plops off her skewer and into the fire again. She tries to pierce another one, but it keeps rolling away until she eventually just picks it up, shrugs and shoves it into her mouth, untoasted.

"Okay, I'm listening. How are we like marshmallows? Because we're so sweet and fluffy inside?" I flutter my eyelashes exaggeratedly.

"Uh, no. Also, side note: Never, ever flutter your eyelashes at a guy, okay? Trust me, I'm doing you a favor." Alisha shakes her head.

"Yeah," Cat adds. "You look less like a flirt and more like a possessed doll in a slasher movie."

"Jeez, thanks, guys." I take another swig of wine and feel it spread tingling warmth from my center outward.

"Okay, seriously, this is important," Alisha says, trying to thump her fist on the log next to her and almost overbalancing. "I'm making a very insightful social observation here, I'll have you know."

"Okay, okay, we're listening." Cat leans forward, elbows on her knees, staring intently at Alisha through the flames.

"Okay. Here's the thing. Girls are like marshmallows…"

"You've already said that," Cat interrupts, but I shush her and hand her the bottle, and she takes a large swig and subsides.

"Because there's literally no way to win. Marshmallows. Girls." Alisha is looking confused.

"Uh, Lish, you're making very little sense right now."

"No, wait, I have a point, I swear." She takes a deep breath and tries to pull herself together. "Marshmallows. They're either too cold, and they don't go all nice and melty in the middle, and it's a disappointment when you try to squish them between the graham crackers...or you try to get them that perfectly golden brown all over and they inevitably catch fire and burn black and taste all gross and sooty."

"Or fall off the skewer," Cat adds solemnly.

"Exactly." Alisha nods vigorously, then trails off and stares into the fire, the red and orange flames reflected in her large dark brown eyes.

"Still not getting the connection, Lish."

She starts and looks up as if she's forgotten we're there.

"Like girls, right? You're too cold and frigid and not giving guys what they want...until you do, and then it's too much, and you get burned."

Underneath the warmth of the wine, an uncomfortable feeling is prickling inside me. Those memories I can't bear to face are tap-tap-tapping again. I grab the bottle from Cat and gulp down another mouthful, trying to drown them.

"I mean, Mark was so pissed off with me for not being ready to go the whole way at Charlie's party, right? But what if I had? Emily slept with Simon—"

"So people say," I interject because it feels important.

"Right, maybe she didn't even do it, but people say she did, and suddenly that's enough to crucify her! I mean, her life is literally not worth living right now. So what the hell? How do we win? Where is the perfect, not-too-slutty, not-too-frigid middle ground?"

I stare into the fire, seeing shapes in it that I'm not ready to confront, faces I'm not ready to remember. And one picture, one picture that shimmers and waves in front of me, yellow and orange, burning itself into my eyes all over again.

"There is no perfect middle ground," Cat whispers, and her trembling voice takes me by surprise, wrenching my eyes away from that wretched picture.

"Cat?" Lish asks, moving over to sit next to her.

Cat is looking into the fire, and her eyes are shining.

"I slept with Toby," she says quietly, "at Charlie's party."

"Oh my God, Cat, why didn't you—" Lish starts, but Cat waves her into silence and keeps talking, fast, as if now the words have started she can't stop them.

"We used a condom, but it must have slipped or something. I thought it didn't matter because it was literally the first day after my period, but I…" She trails off, and I see the shock cross Alisha's face as she realizes where this is going.

"You got pregnant?"

Cat doesn't raise her eyes from the flames. She just nods. There's a long pause.

"You had an abortion?"

Slowly, she nods again.

"Why didn't you tell me?" Alisha has her arms around her now, cradling Cat's head against her shoulder, rubbing her arm and letting her cry. I can see the hurt in Alisha's eyes, but she's hiding it, focusing on Cat.

"I couldn't. I couldn't tell anyone. I didn't want to risk my parents finding out. I just wanted it to be over. I didn't even tell

Toby, I just stopped answering his calls. Not that he ever bothered to try and find out why," she says slightly bitterly.

The orange light is dancing in her eyes and the glow of the flames bounces off her hair, making it look redder than ever.

"It's one decision. The right one. It's not that I feel guilty for making it—I don't. I feel sad. I wish it hadn't happened. But that wasn't why I didn't tell anyone." She pauses, like she's working out how to explain. "I didn't feel like anyone else would let it just be one decision, you know? I knew it'd be the only thing they thought about when they saw me, like it would *become* who I was. I knew they'd make me *that* girl. And I didn't want to be that girl."

"Oh, Cat. You were doing the right thing. You haven't done anything wrong." Words spill out of Lish, low and urgent and persuasive. "You used protection. You wouldn't know the condom had failed. And, when you found out, you took responsibility and you made a decision—a decision that's totally yours to make."

I watch them, folded into each other like origami, the way girls fit together when they've hugged so many times, they know exactly how their bodies fuse. And I feel a hollow place inside me where my jigsaw pieces are missing.

"I know." Cat sniffs. "I know it was the right thing to do. But then, why do I still feel like a burnt marshmallow?"

And just like that, I'm sitting on the same log, squashed right in alongside them, and Cat's hand is in mine, and we stay there like that for a long time.

There's a tiny, warm, blackberry-tinged voice inside me saying that this is real. This is friendship. I'm not glad that Cat's hurting, of course I'm not, but I can't help feeling happy that she's confided in me. Not just Alisha. Both of us. Maybe things really aren't going to fall apart this time.

But somewhere underneath, there's a nastier voice that I pretend not to be able to hear. A voice that hisses: "*Friends? They don't even know your real name.*"

SEVENTEEN

A ROWDY CHORUS IS ALREADY shaking the coach when I climb on behind Cat and Alisha at 6:30 the next morning. Simon and his friends have taken over the back few rows, and they're half singing, half roaring at some private joke.

Miss Fairfax is standing by the steps with a clipboard, ticking us all off as we board.

"Wearing casual clothes is not an excuse to completely flout regulation skirt lengths, Catherine," she frowns, eyeing Cat's indigo denim miniskirt with disapproval. "It distracts people from their work." Her glance toward the back of the coach indicates exactly who she thinks is at risk of distraction. Cat nods meekly, but rolls her eyes when Miss Fairfax isn't looking.

"Like it's my responsibility to control their eyes," she whispers as she clambers up the steps, massaging her temples.

I've never paid much attention to Toby Taylor before; he always just sort of blended in with Simon's crew. But I eye him closely this morning, sitting in the far back corner, twisting his beaded surfer necklace round his finger.

"Nice legs, *Caterina*," someone calls mockingly as we start making our way down the aisle, and Cat immediately gives him the finger.

Just for a moment, I swear I see Toby's eyes dart over to her, and something jump in his face like he's about to get up, but the moment passes and he just slumps lower in his seat and looks out of the window.

"Jeez," another boy calls, "it was a compliment."

"Compliments are like jokes," Cat says drily. "If you have to explain what they are, they haven't worked." There's a chorus of laughter, and she flips her hair behind her ears and keeps walking. I make a mental note to ask her how she does that, staying so calm and collected, coming up with the perfect response, especially with Toby sitting there at the back.

Alisha moans and puts her hands over her ears. "Don't they know it's still the middle of the night?" She plops down in a double seat halfway along the coach and promptly curls up to sleep, her head against the window and her body sprawling across both seats. Cat and I slide into the pair of seats across the aisle, both buckling our seat belts.

"How do you *do* that?" I ask, deeply impressed.

"Do what?"

"You *always* know the right thing to say."

She laughs. "Trust me, I don't. I dunno, I just call it like I see it, I guess?"

I shake my head. "Wish I could see it the way you do. I'm always coming up with the perfect comeback about three days too late. And the way my head's aching this morning, it'd probably take more like a week."

As soon as the coach sputters into life, Cat pulls out a notepad and starts sketching with quick, feathery pencil strokes. I crane my neck to see what she's drawing, but she snatches the pad away. "Keep still, will you?"

"God, don't draw me!" I laugh and try to turn my face to the window, but she tuts and grabs my arm, pulling me back around to face her, her eyes flicking from my face to the page, her head on one side.

There's a silence, and I can feel last night's conversation hanging heavy in the air between us, but it's like there's an unspoken agreement that we won't talk about it again.

Without warning, Robin's head pops up from between the headrests behind us.

"Are you going to eat both of those?" he asks, gesturing at the unopened cereal bars sticking out of my pocket. I stiffen. I haven't seen him since he rejected my semi-sort-of-not-really-date suggestion and I feel the embarrassment I'd managed to push out of my mind over the weekend surge back in full force.

"Be my guest."

I hand one to him and he grins, settling back into his seat with a copy of *The Taming of the Shrew* and putting his earphones back in.

"He seems to be a total bookworm," I observe, trying not to sound overly interested. The only good thing about Robin making it clear he isn't interested in spending time with me is that at least I haven't told Cat and Alisha how I feel about him. Not that I even know myself exactly how I feel about him. But thank God I don't have to deal with the embarrassment of them finding out it's not going anywhere.

"Well, he has to be, doesn't he?" Cat says matter-of-factly, frowning at her sketchpad and rubbing something out.

"Huh?"

"A bookworm. He doesn't have much choice." She swivels the pad triumphantly toward me. "Ta-da!"

My face jumps off the page, all pointed chin and heavy eyebrows. My eyes are bright blue and feathery curls cascade round my cheeks.

"Wow. That's…wow!"

"Thanks," she says, ripping it out and handing it over. "Keep it if you want."

I tuck it carefully inside my notebook.

"Hey, what did you mean when you said Robin has to be a bookworm?"

"Oh. I forget you're new." I smile, taking it as a compliment. She glances back at Robin and lowers her voice slightly. "He looks after his mum at home—she's got advanced multiple sclerosis, and I think she has a caretaker during the day, but he does everything for her the rest of the time, which doesn't leave him much time for homework."

I stare at Robin in shock. He's buried deep in his book and doesn't even look up.

"He's always arriving late, cramming his homework in during break, and catching up on papers over lunch."

I feel a rush of sympathy, then a sudden lightness. "So he looks after her on weekends too?" I ask casually.

"Yeah," Cat replies. She's flipped to a new page in her notepad and is scribbling furiously. "Like I said, almost twenty-four-seven."

"Are we sure this thing is seaworthy?" Alisha asks some time later, looking doubtfully at the *May Princess*, a sturdy little pleasure boat moored patiently alongside the pier in the small town of Anstruther.

"Don't be so silly, Lish." Cat pats the side of the boat as if it's a thoroughbred horse. "Of course she's seaworthy. And you can actually see the island from here—even if we sank, you'd probably be able to swim ashore." Under her breath, she adds: "A brilliant swimmer with a morbid fear of the sea. I've never heard anything so ridiculous."

"I heard that!" says Alisha, testing the end of the gangplank gingerly with one toe and still looking far from convinced.

Cat sighs impatiently. "It's probably one of the safest ways to travel, Lish!"

"If a boat sinks, you are three hundred times more likely to survive than people who are in a plane crash," Alisha immediately replies absentmindedly, holding up her hand to shade her eyes from the sun as she watches Simon sitting on a post at the very end of the pier, holding court with classmates gathered round him.

"Well, there you go!"

"That doesn't make me feel any better about going on this boat," Alisha says grumpily. "It just makes me more freaked out about flying."

She looks up and realizes we're both staring at her openmouthed as if she's a total weirdo.

"How do you—"

"I like to google when I'm nervous, okay?"

She's still fretting as we pull away from the pier and set off into the choppy waters of the Firth of Forth. The boat is split into two levels. There's a lower deck where you can walk around the edge and watch the water, or shelter in a low viewing room with rows of plastic chairs. On top of the viewing room is the captain's little cabin, with all the navigation equipment and an uncovered viewing platform where braver passengers can face the wind and get an even better view.

Alisha makes a beeline for one of the benches that runs around the edge of the lower deck, gripping the rail at the side of the boat like her life depends on it. As we start to pick up speed, bumping over a couple of waves, she moans softly and closes her eyes, leaning her head on her forearms. I'm tempted by the upper deck, where students are chattering in excitement, their hair whipping in the wind. I can see Robin standing at the front, his black curls wildly tousled, narrowing his eyes against the salt spray. But out of loyalty, Cat and I sit on either side of Alisha, rubbing her back and murmuring encouraging comments about how sturdy the boat feels and how quickly we'll reach the island. We exchange an exasperated smile over Alisha's bent head as the foaming gray water rushes by.

For the first time in as long as I can remember, I feel a sense of deep calm and something else I can't quite put my finger on. Alisha groans and grips my forearm hard, and as I look down at it, her nails digging into me, I realize: it feels like belonging.

EIGHTEEN

THE ISLAND IS LITTLE MORE than a massive rock rising out of the sea, around a mile and a half long and covered in scrubby grass and plants. At one end, where we scramble ashore, the land slopes down gently to meet the water, and a basic concrete landing platform has been built. The rest of the coastline is made up of taller cliffs plunging down dramatically into the waves, sheltering the odd little cove or gravelly beach.

As we file off the boat ("Oh, sweet, sweet solid ground," Alisha sings), we are divided into groups, handed clipboards and packed lunches, directed to different areas of the island, and instructed to be back at three o'clock sharp for the return voyage. I find myself separated from Cat and Alisha, but my breath catches in my chest when I see Robin sauntering in my direction and realize he's in my group, along with mousy Louise and a quiet, slightly overweight boy named Martin.

Together, we traipse across the island toward our allotted location: a small, rocky cove shaped so perfectly like a semicircle that it looks as if some ancient sea monster has taken a large bite out of the landmass. To get to it, we have to scramble down a steep path that zigzags across the cliff face like a dramatic scar. Robin and I lead the way, sending little stones skittering ahead of us as we scuff our shoes on the sandy path. It's a warm day, and I pull off my sweatshirt and tie it round my waist, enjoying the sea breeze on my bare arms.

I've nearly reached the bottom of the path when I lose my footing and slither a foot or so before managing to grab on to the sturdy trunk of a shrub growing out of the side of the cliff. "Careful!" Robin shouts, leaping back to grab my elbow, almost knocking me over again.

"Thanks." I laugh, jumping down the last bit of path to land on the shingly beach. I can still feel the warmth of his hand on my arm. As Robin lands beside me, I squint back up to where Louise and Martin are making their way slowly down, clutching each other occasionally for support.

"Should we go back and help them?" I ask.

"Nah, they'll be fine," Robin replies, casting around among the pebbles as though he's lost something.

"What are you looking for?"

He doesn't answer, but keeps looking, picking up stones, turning them over in his hand, and then rejecting them one by one.

"Aha!" he cries at last, his fist closing round a flat, flinty stone around five inches in diameter. "Come with me!" And, without warning, he takes my hand and pulls me down to the water's edge. I can't help shouting as the waves splash against my bare legs and soak my yellow Converse shoes, but Robin just laughs, pulling me in farther.

He looks out to sea like a golfer judging the distance from the tee and pulls his arm back, then sends the stone flying over the water, hopping and skimming over the waves until it falters, loses speed, and disappears with a loud plop.

"Nice."

"Want me to show you how?"

I laugh and bend down to select a flattish stone from beneath my feet. Closing one eye and squinting the other, I skim the stone out across the waves, and it bounces energetically until it's outstripped Robin's effort by several feet.

"Wow."

"My dad taught me," I blurt out, then wonder why I needed to make an excuse. He just nods and hands me another stone. I take it, weighing its heavy warmth, and skim it over the water. Robin sends another stone skipping after it, so they look like they're chasing each other.

Behind us, Martin and Louise have collapsed triumphantly onto the pebbly beach and opened their lunch packs. "There's no signal here," Louise moans, tapping helplessly at her iPhone screen.

"Shall we get started, then?" Martin is frowning at his clipboard and already munching on a slightly stale-looking cheese roll. "It looks like we have to record every puffin, razorbill, guillemot, or kittiwake we see."

"What on earth is a kittiwake?" Louise asks, sounding distinctly underwhelmed.

"They're seabirds," Martin says, flicking to the next page. "There are pictures to help us identify them. Look, that's a razorbill there, up on that ledge." We all crane our necks. The sun is bright and I can't even see the ledge, let alone a seabird that I'm almost certain I wouldn't be able to positively identify as a razorbill.

I open my packed lunch, ignore the roll, and pick unenthusiastically at the sea-salted chips. "Why do they always put in those squashy brown bananas? They make everything else smell so gross."

"Why are the chips always sea salt or cheese and onion?" mutters Martin. "They're like, the worst flavors."

Louise seems to come to the decision that if she can't communicate with the outside world, she might as well throw herself into the task at hand. She starts making notes on her chart, and she and Martin begin cataloguing the bird population with gusto.

"Oh look, our first guillemot!" Louise cries with genuine enthusiasm.

Robin gives me a mischievous glance and whispers, "A guille-what?" and I try to hide my smile so Louise won't think I'm laughing at her.

Then Robin yawns, rolls up his jacket like a pillow, and falls asleep. I mull over Cat's words on the bus. I guess he doesn't always get much sleep at home.

At first, I stay close by, at least pretending to be a team player by half-heartedly directing Martin's attention to a few black specks in the sky. ("Um, that's another seagull, Anna.") But after my third failed attempt to identify a seabird, I sense that they'd actually be

better off without my "help" and start wandering along the shoreline instead, picking up little broken pieces of shell and trying to fit
them back together.

I edge closer and closer to the water, finally taking off my
shoes and socks and letting the feathery edges of the waves ripple
over my toes as I pick my way over the pebbles. I pounce on the
shiniest ones, with their marbled colors and glinting surfaces, then
discard them as they turn to dull brown in the palm of my hand.

An outcrop of rocks looms ahead, and I skirt around it, wading
ankle-deep, then walk back up the beach on the other side, so the
rocks hide the others from view. I stop and hoist myself up onto the
edge of a large boulder, lying back and letting my hair spill down
the side, mingling with dried seaweed. My fingers fiddle with the
rough shell of a barnacle. I close my eyes, listening to the distant
cries of the seabirds, tasting the salty tang of the air and enjoying
the warmth of the sun on my eyelids.

The seabirds grow louder until I'm floating away on a chorus
of cries. It sounds like a mournful choir as if they're grieving, crying
out in one voice, like they're calling my name. *Anna. Anna. Anna.*

I open my eyes. It feels like just moments since I closed them, but
I'm stiff and disoriented, the sea is rushing around the base of my
rock, and the sun has dipped much lower in the sky. I shiver and sit
up, massaging my hip where it's been digging into the rock.

"Anna. Anna!" The yell makes me jump. I slither down from
my rock and around the rocky outcrop, looking back along the

beach to where I left the others. Someone is hurrying in my direction, his pants rolled up to his knees, holding his bag on his head to keep it out of the water. I think it's Robin. The tide is coming in and the beach is shrinking fast. I shade my eyes and look up at the cliff. Louise and Martin are already two-thirds of the way up, hurrying along the pathway and looking back over their shoulders.

I look around for my shoes and socks, but there's no sign of them. The rising tide must have washed them away. The waves lap insistently against the base of the cliff, making an angry slapping noise. In a rush, I realize the danger of the situation. If we don't reach the pathway before the tide rises too high, we could be trapped here. Robin is still stumbling toward me through the surf, and as he draws closer, I can see that his usual faintly amused expression has been replaced with one of genuine panic.

"Anna!" he shouts again, and I start to splash toward him, ignoring the sharp coldness of the water, which has risen up round my shins. Within moments, he's reached me.

"Where did you go? I was looking everywhere for you. I've been calling and calling for the last five minutes," he pants as we start wading back toward the path, the water sucking greedily at our calves.

"I was just lying on the other side of the rocks," I try to explain, sweeping the hair out of my face with a salty hand. I struggle to keep my footing as the sucking waves roll the stones underfoot like shifting marbles. "I'm glad you called. I'd drifted off."

"What else was I going to do? Leave you lying there like a tragic mermaid to be swept away by the rising tide? I'd have starting calling sooner, but I didn't realize how quickly it would come in."

The closer we get to the path, the slower our progress. The water slaps at the base of the cliffs and soon we're struggling thigh-deep against the current's insistent tug. We're only about twenty feet away from the path now, but the waves seem to jump suddenly higher, and I find myself half walking, half swimming through freezing, waist-deep water. I start to shiver uncontrollably, my teeth chattering.

I'm genuinely panicking now. I picture myself being dashed against the rocks by the waves, drifting away, battling against the current for as long as I can before the energy drains from my limbs and I can't fight it any longer...

I pull myself together and stride forward, but the stony ground is looser than I'd bargained for, with the water pulling and sucking at it, and I fall hard and suddenly, my head crashing under the surface. I feel my whole body convulse in shock as the cold encloses me. I struggle to find my footing as salty water floods into my nose, burning the back of my throat.

Suddenly an iron grip fastens around my wrist, and I'm wrenched painfully upright, my torso hauled up out of the water.

"Steady," says Robin, trying to sound jovial, but looking worried himself, his eyes flicking toward the path. "Just a few more feet—don't worry."

The tide rushes back again, lowering the level of the water around our waists. "Come on!" Robin shouts, and we grab the opportunity, splashing toward the path. I start to clamber up and out of the water, Robin hot on my heels.

"Wow!" Robin grins up at me, punching a fist in the air. "That was wild!" But, as he laughs, the waves rush back in behind him, hitting him in the backs of his knees, taking him completely by surprise. I see his mouth jerk from a laugh to a yell as he starts to fall backward away from me, his body slipping sideways.

I jump forward without thinking, hooking my fingers into his belt and leaning backward into the cliff wall with my whole weight, anchoring him. His back arches away from me and then slowly he regains his balance, crashing toward me and knocking me over, slamming my shoulder into the rocky path.

Fear and adrenaline leak out of us as we get to our feet and stumble the rest of the way up, safely out of reach of the water. Together, we stagger onward up the path until we're out of danger, slowing to a half-crawl as we finally manage the last few feet and collapse onto the grass at the top of the cliff, our chests heaving.

For a long moment, we stare at each other, neither of us able to do more than gasp for breath, our faces smushed into the grass, our eyes locked. The moment seems to float in time, like everything around us is on pause. There's a funny ringing in my ears where the roaring of the sea has left behind an empty space, and the colors of the grass and the sky and the water seem to merge into one another as if we're in a soap bubble, like we've just stepped outside the world and everything is holding its breath.

And then Louise and Martin are there, talking loudly over each other, Martin pompously warning us how close we were to missing the boat, while Louise seems to be taking a selfie with my bedraggled body sprawled in the background.

As we board the boat again, I follow Cat and Alisha to a bench toward the back. Alisha is rubbing at my hands to try and warm them up, and Cat is attempting to dry my dripping hair with a slightly grubby towel she found under one of the seats.

"How did yours go?" I ask them, and Alisha rolls her eyes. "Literally four straight hours of Simon making terrible jokes about how he doesn't need a worksheet to tell him how to spot birds."

"Ugh."

The wash from the boat churns frothily out beneath us and stretches lazily back toward the island. I watch the island grow smaller and smaller, bathed in the warm amber light of the evening sun. The waves that leaped at my waist just half an hour before look like nothing more than gentle ripples from this distance. Farther along the coast to our right, about three miles southwest of Anstruther, I can just make out the brooding outline of St. Monans church steeple, blurry in the sunset, pointing straight up toward the clouds. I rest my head on Cat's shoulder, and she casually lets her arm fall across my back. My whole body aches as if it's been pounded with hammers. The scrape on my arm stings, and my head is starting to throb. My throat is raw from seawater. But in spite of it all, with Cat's arm around me, I feel that warmth of belonging again.

As we draw into Anstruther, the boat slows to a chug, navigating its careful approach into the harbor. Robin is curled up in a corner, gazing out at the water, and I'm just debating going over to say goodbye when we swing alongside the pier and I notice the battered old Fiat in the parking lot. Suddenly I remember that Mum had promised to pick me up here. I'm not sure I'm ready for her to meet my whole class, especially considering how keen she is for me to be friends with absolutely everybody. I quickly hug Cat and Lish and run down the pier while the others are still clambering off the boat.

A few others also traipse off to join waiting parents, but most of the students are slowly loitering along toward the coach, heads bent over their cell phones as they get a signal again for the first time since the island.

The coastal breeze picks up as I reach the car, and I let its fresh, salty coolness soothe my aching head. I look back at the crowd to wave to Cat and Alisha. The sun is dipping low behind them and it turns the whole group into smudged silhouettes as they straggle down the pier, outlined against a red sky. I lift my hand and somebody lifts theirs in return. Another figure seems to be calling out to me, probably shouting goodbye, but it's too far away to hear clearly. I grin and shout back: "See you tomorrow!" feeling my words whipped away on the wind and knowing they probably can't hear me either.

The person seems to shout again, and I shrug, lifting my hands to my ears exaggeratedly to try and mime that I can't hear them. I see one figure—is it Simon?—peer down at what must be his phone and then gesture to several of the others, passing it around until a group of them are crowded tightly around him. For a moment, I think I see Cat looking in my direction, standing oddly stiffly, but the setting sun shines into my eyes and I think I must have imagined it.

I open the car door and put one leg into the footwell before turning curiously one last time toward the pier. The figure I thought looked like Simon seems to be shouting something in the direction of the parking lot, his hands cupped round his mouth like a megaphone.

His words twist away on the wind, but in the moment before the car door slams I think I catch just one, dancing teasingly in my ear before the breeze snatches it away.

It sounds like, "*Sssluuut.*"

NINETEEN

I SHIFT IN MY SEAT, wincing as the seat belt brushes against my scraped arm, and lean my forehead against the cool window. "Just breathe," I tell myself, over and over again.

"Just breathe." I try to calm down, focusing on counting five beats in and five beats out, watching my breath condense on the window and disappear. I try to reason with myself.

It's going to be okay. There's no reason to think that Simon was shouting about me. The sun was in my eyes—he might not even have been facing in my direction. Even if he was, I could easily have misheard him. I'm being paranoid. There's no way this could have followed me to Scotland. No way.

I fiddle nervously with my wet hair, twisting it around and around my finger until water drips out. The most important thing is not to let Mum realize anything's wrong. Maybe nothing really is wrong. Probably nothing is wrong. I'm sure nothing is wrong. But she's looking at me strangely, stealing quick, worried glances away from the road. Can she tell? Did she hear something as well?

"Anna, what the hell happened?" she bursts out eventually.

"What do you mean?"

"Your arm!" She gestures at me with one hand, the other still gripping the steering wheel. "It's bleeding."

I look down in surprise. My thin shirt is clinging damply to my shoulder, a small red stain soaking through.

"It's nothing, Mum, just an accident. I fell on the beach when we were climbing back up from doing the survey."

"It sounds dangerous," she sniffs.

"It wasn't, Mum, not really."

We screech to a halt, and I look up, confused, knowing we couldn't have got home so quickly—we haven't even left Anstruther yet. To my surprise, Mum has pulled up opposite a little electronics shop called East Neuk Technology. I watch, baffled, as she leaps out of the car, slamming the door behind her, and dashes across the street, prompting an angry honk of the horn from a passing driver as he swerves to avoid hitting her. Mum disappears into the shop, and I can just see her through the window, deep in conversation with the owner under a blinking neon sign that proclaims: LAMINATION: 3P PER SHEET. Moments later, she is out again, marching back across the street and clambering into the driver's seat, thrusting a small box into my lap as she turns the engine on.

I look down at it, nonplussed. It's a refurbished iPhone 5s.

I look at Mum.

"Practically brand-new, he said," Mum tells me, her eyes on the road. "And there's a new SIM card in there too."

"But—"

"I know we decided it was best for you to switch off for a while, but I need to know you can always reach me if you need me." Mum is blinking a lot and the tip of her nose has gone pink.

"Oh, Mum, I'm fine, honestly," I croak, feeling guilty that she's so worried. I lay my hand briefly over hers on the gear stick. "I love you."

I open the box and weigh the silver phone in the palm of my hand. There's a small scratch in the top right-hand corner, but apart from that, it looks just like my old one. The blank screen reflects my image back at me. My hair is tangled wildly around my face, and there's a long scratch across my cheek. I feel queasy.

"Thanks, Mum."

The evening seems to last forever. Mum has made a weird fish pie with lumps of mango in it ("Delicious," I lie), and I pretend to eat, pushing it round the plate with my fork. Finally, I slip away to my room, saying I'm exhausted from the field trip and need to get to bed early.

"Of course, love." Mum hugs me for a full thirty seconds longer than usual. "Sleep well."

Sleep is the last thing on my mind. As I pad up the stairs, the *Casualty* theme music starts to drift up from the kitchen, and a few seconds later I can faintly hear Mum chatting on the phone.

"Unbelievable, they didn't even seem to have so much as a first-aid kit between them…I know…well, exactly… Just *imagine* how much worse it might have been…"

Up in my bedroom, I plug in the new phone and switch it on. It glows in the dark. If I had Cat or Alisha's numbers, I could call them, just to double-check. They'd probably tell me about whatever stupid joke Simon had told to get everyone's attention, and we'd laugh about it together. But I've never asked for their numbers, because I never had a phone to put them into. So I have no choice but to wait until tomorrow. Wait and see.

I look at my bedside clock. It's only 9:03 p.m. I don't feel tired, in spite of the fact that my body is throbbing and my muscles are aching. My mind is wide awake and whirring much faster than I want it to. I need a distraction.

Scrabbling in my bag, I find the book I checked out of the university library and flick through it until I find a chapter titled "Treatment and Punishment of Women and Witches." I start to read, not taking the words in at first, trying to trick my brain into thinking about something else. But before long I'm genuinely absorbed in the text.

Women who were thought to have broken vital societal rules of behavior or to have sinned against God and the Church were punished in a wide variety of ways. Some punishments were designed to curb particular habits or behaviors, and others to shame and humiliate. In the most serious cases, a woman found guilty of witchcraft would be condemned to death.

I think about the woman from St. Monans, the one whose story I've been trying to uncover. I picture her the way I dreamed about her, vibrant and proud and full of life. Suddenly I feel afraid of what I might find if I keep trying to discover what happened to her.

Those found guilty of misdemeanors by the kirk session might be confined to the "cutty-stool," a wooden stool placed at a raised height above the rest of the congregation during the Sunday service so that they could be publicly shamed and scolded for their wrongdoings. The minister would sermonize about their faults while the rest of the congregation watched, a deeply humiliating experience.

Another common method of punishment was a "scold's bridle," a heavy and painful contraption designed to prevent the wearer from talking and to inflict great pain on her if she did. The scold's bridle was a heavy metal frame attached to the head, sometimes with a metal cage covering the face. When fixed onto the wearer, sharp spikes would be forced into her mouth, pressing against her tongue or cheeks. If she kept still and silent, the bridle wouldn't inflict too much pain, but talking would cause the spikes to pierce the mouth and tongue, so forcing the wearer into silence.

It was a humiliating punishment, often used for public shaming, and, in some cases, a method of torture. There were many offenses that could cause a woman to end up in a scold's bridle, including blasphemy, bad language, or being accused of witchcraft. The bridle was sometimes used to prevent the accused witch from being able to chant a spell against her accusers or speak a charm that might allow her to escape or transform. But women could also be forced into the bridle simply for being seen as nagging or shrewish, noisy or quarrelsome, in a time when it was strongly believed women should be seen and not heard. One historical account even suggests that some men had iron hooks fixed next to their fireplaces at home, so that when their wives became too scolding, they could send for the town bridle and chain her to the hook, wearing it, until she behaved.

I let the book slip from my fingers, thinking about what it must have been like to know that you couldn't speak openly even in your own home.

And then I start thinking about all the things I can't say. Things I can't tell anyone. Things I wish I could erase. My throat starts aching, and I swallow over and over again. I promised myself I wouldn't cry. New country. New school. New start. But is it? What did Simon shout? What were they all looking at on their phones?

Maybe there are some things you can't outrun.

TWENTY

WHEN I GET TO THE bus stop the next morning, Cat isn't there. I sit alone on the empty white wall, scuffing my heels against the pavement and checking my watch every twenty seconds until the bus comes. She isn't on it. She's never been late.

I spend the entire journey to school making up a list of plausible excuses in my head and repeating it over and over. *She's ill. She overslept. She got a lift. She's ill. She overslept. She got a lift.*

But when we reach the outskirts of St. Andrews, Alisha doesn't get on either.

As I walk through the main entrance of St. Margaret's, an eerie quiet seems to follow me. Swirling whispers die as I approach and spring back to life again in my wake. Eyeballs are everywhere. Their gaze crawls all over me like a thousand scuttling spiders. I try to resist the urge to scratch myself.

Am I imagining it? Is that cluster of older girls looking me up and down, or are they focusing on the noticeboard behind me?

"It's not all about you, Anna," I whisper under my breath, desperately trying to reassure myself. "Jeez, you only just got here—most people don't even know who you are yet. Get a grip."

A group of boys I don't know are laughing as I turn a corner. When they see me, they seem to laugh louder, or am I just being paranoid? One of them looks me up and down and smacks his lips. Or is he just chewing gum?

As I step into the art wing for first period, I feel the anxiety loosen its grip on my chest just a little. I breathe in the reassuring scent of oil paints and turpentine as I tie on a splattered apron and scrape my hair into a high ponytail. Neither Alisha nor Cat is in the same art class as me, so I settle down at a workbench on my own. Within fifteen minutes, I've decided that I've definitely been imagining the whole thing. I was exhausted last night. Stupid of me to let my mind run away with itself.

I study the canvas I've been working on for the last two weeks. It's a portrait of a young woman in oils, standing on a beach with a floaty dress whipping around her knees in the wind, her face half turned away, her hand up with fingers splayed out as if she's trying to stop someone from taking a photograph of her. It isn't clear whether she's laughing or crying, and I think I'm going to leave it up to the viewer to decide. The colors aren't exactly what you'd call naturalistic. The sea is a swirl of bright pinks and greens, the beach fluorescent yellow. The turquoise dress flutters under a ripe purple sky. Only the girl's face is colorless, her ambiguous expression captured in soft charcoal black.

Art isn't really my strong point, and I've worked really hard on this painting. It's the first thing I've made that I'm actually proud of, and I'm thinking of giving it to Mum for her birthday. I picture it hanging in the cottage, a shock of color against the whitewashed wall.

I pick up where I left off last week, using the finest of paintbrushes to dust the sky with delicate flecks of gold. One of the stars starts to spread out of control, threatening to swallow up the others like a black hole. Humming softly under my breath, I fetch an empty jam jar from under the sink in the corner and go to the supply cupboard for turpentine.

I'm only gone for two minutes. But, when I get back, the canvas isn't there.

I look around in surprise. Was I so lost in thought that I went to the wrong workbench? I cast about the room, expecting to see the bright painting at another workstation, but it's nowhere in sight. My classmates all seem completely absorbed, bent over their own work, some painting, others dabbing away at pieces of pottery or sketching in large portfolio notebooks. I put down the turpentine and do a full circuit of the room, checking every bench and even stooping to look under the tables.

Could I have absentmindedly carried the painting into the supply cupboard with me? I go and check, even though I already know the answer.

Slowly, the reality of the situation begins to dawn on me. But it feels ridiculous. Why would anybody move my painting? My heart sinking, I approach Mr. Barnes.

"Sir?"

He's bending over the kiln, putting a final dab of glaze on some slightly misshapen pots that are waiting to be fired.

"Sloppy," I hear him mutter crossly under his breath before he turns to face me, his bushy eyebrows drawn into a frown. "Yes, what is it?" he snaps.

I feel stupid even saying it. "Uh, my painting's gone, sir." I think I hear the softest echo of laughter, but when I look over my shoulder, everybody seems to be lost in their own projects. I turn back to Mr. Barnes. "It was here at the beginning of the lesson, but I went to get some supplies and it's…gone."

"Gone?" asks Mr. Barnes. "Don't be so ridiculous. Where did you leave it?"

I gesture miserably toward my empty workbench, knowing how silly I look.

"Oh dear, students." Mr. Barnes raises his voice, making sure the whole class can hear. "We appear to have a miraculous event in our midst today." People start nudging each other. Barnes's meltdowns are famous. And incredibly entertaining to watch. Unless you happen to be the one he's pulverizing.

"One of our canvases," Barnes continues, pretending to be astonished, "has grown legs and trotted off all by its merry self." There's a snort behind me.

"You might well laugh, Mr. Ogden. It is indeed a most dramatic and entertaining event." Other people are snickering too. "Just think," Barnes says, getting into it now, "how lucky we are that this first-ever example of an inanimate object discovering a mind of its own should have happened here, in classroom fourteen B at St. Margaret's Academy."

And just like that, the joke is over. His eyebrows snap even closer together and his voice drops to a silky, threatening purr.

"Anna Clark." I look at him miserably. "If you think it is acceptable to invent some preposterous story about a vanishing painting to excuse the fact that you haven't brought in your work, then you have another think coming. You know perfectly well that I insist on punctuality and professionalism. There are no exceptions."

"But, sir, I didn't—"

"Don't interrupt me when I'm speaking." Now the snickers are starting to ripple around the classroom. Mr. Barnes's head snaps up. "This isn't a joke, Miss Hughes. And perhaps anybody who thinks it is can join Miss Clark in her failing grade of a D minus for this assignment." The room falls deadly quiet.

"Sir, please—"

"Enough, Miss Clark! I will not tell you again. No excuses. Today was your final opportunity to work on these pieces before they're handed in. If you have no work to present, you will fail this module. That's the end of it."

I subside into furious silence.

———————

———————

I fume my way through the rest of the morning's lessons, not sure whether to be more angry at Mr. Barnes for not believing me or at whoever stole the painting in the first place. Even if they thought it was funny originally, they could at least have owned up when it became clear how much their prank was going to cost me.

In fact, I'm so angry, I forget to worry about who's looking at me or to listen out for whispers.

Rounding a corner, I find my path blocked by a group of boys I don't know. But, as I try to walk past, one of them deliberately steps in front of me, blocking my way. I move to walk around him and he sidesteps, trapping me between him and a row of lockers.

"Hey, Anna," he sings in a mocking voice, "fancy a threesome?" Some of the others laugh rowdily. I try to barge past him, banging my injured shoulder painfully against the lockers, but he moves sideways again, backing me against a locker door, his hands firmly planted on either side of me, towering over me.

"C'mon," he croons, "don't be like that. I know you want it... I've seen the photos." He moves closer, his breath hot on my face. "Isn't this what you like, Anna Clark?" And then his voice drops to a whisper. "Or should I say Anna Reeves?"

A jolt of shock runs through my body like electricity. I drop to a crouch, dive sideways and escape, running down the corridor. I hear laughter and shouts behind me, but I don't turn around.

How does he know that name?

As I near the main entrance, I see Simon appear at the opposite end of the corridor, surrounded by his usual gang. He sees me, and his eyes light up. I walk faster; see him speeding up to reach me. I break into a jog, just as he raises his hand to point in my direction, then finally I stumble through the main door as the bell rings for the next period.

I don't walk far. I can't. I have to see it. I have to know. I stumble down a few streets, far enough away from school to avoid the risk of being spotted, until I reach a small, tree-lined square with a fenced garden in the middle. The gates are open, but there's nobody inside, and I slump down against the trunk of an oak tree and pull out my phone.

I google "Anna Reeves photos," and find what I'm looking for almost immediately. Someone has set up a Facebook profile and it's not exactly easy to miss. I can't log in, but I don't need an account to view it—the profile is public. Of course it is. As public as possible. How did I ever think I could outrun this?

The main profile picture is an old one of me, cropped from a photo on someone else's account. I'm at a party (I recognize the glittery halter-neck top I'd saved up for two months to buy) and the side of someone else's smiling face is still just visible next to mine at the edge of the photo. Under the bio section it says: Founder of Sluts United.

And then, the first post, there it is. The picture I've been running away from, the feeling I literally left the country to escape, the shame that's been poking and prodding and trying to get back inside my mind ever since we got here.

The photograph I've tried over and over to forget, the one I've deleted all copies and evidence of. And yet here it is again, turned against me like a weapon, in vivid color, as bold and bright as the day I first took it.

Nipples standing erect. Stomach exposed. I feel sick and close my eyes. My blood is rushing loud in my ears. Everything else is quiet. I can feel it, sitting there, in front of me, just waiting.

I swallow and look at it again. I click and zoom and pore over it, as if looking for long enough might erase the pixels and dissolve it, dissolve me.

I'd pinched my nipples. It seems so stupid now. In the first picture I took, they were flat and round and I wanted to look more like the girls online, girls I'd seen in videos on cell phones and girls I knew he'd seen so many more of than me. Girls he'd expect me to look like. So I pinched them until they stood up hard against my skin and now I wish, I wish I hadn't.

And then I realize with a start that it's not the nipples that bother me the most. It's the things I hate, laid out on a cold, bright screen for anyone to see. The crease where my armpit meets my upper arm and the flesh bulges just a little. The cellulite that puckers like citrus fruit on my upper thighs. The half-moon beneath each breast as it pushes the skin down. The way one side droops more than the other. The imperfections I carry around with me every day. The parts I cover with painstakingly selected sleeve lengths and carefully positioned waistbands and artfully draped sarongs. All these years of choosing the me I show the rest of the world hurled back in my face. My body on the page like a body on a slab. Powerless. Vulnerable. Intimate. Inanimate.

I look until my own skin very slowly starts to blur and tremble and collapse in on itself through the prism of my tears.

More than fifty people are listed as friends—Simon Stewart...Charlie Eppingham...Louise Campbell—I can see their grinning faces in the list. Theirs and so many others—all from school. Whoever created the profile must have searched for St. Margaret's, and it looks like they've added practically everyone in our year. Some are people I've tentatively started making friends with; some I've barely even met. I choke back a sob. Well, they all know me now.

Oh God, Robin. Suddenly he leaps into my head and a fresh bolt of adrenaline surges painfully through me. The idea that he might have seen this stuff makes me want to be sick. I feel his eyes, locked onto mine, the grass pressing into my cheek. And now he thinks I'm a massive slut like everyone else. Oh God, he's seen... everything.

Panicking, I jab at the picture with my finger, desperate to delete it, to make it disappear. But, without a Facebook account of my own, there's no way of accessing it and I only succeed in accidentally zooming in, my own flesh glaring up at me, filling the screen.

My fingers fly over the screen. I create a new profile, entering the bare minimum of information, using my old email address and not bothering to fill in any personal information or add a picture. As soon as I'm in, I return to the Anna Reeves page and click again on the photo, scrambling for the report button.

The first option is simple enough. I'm in this photo and I don't like it. Click. Then a new set of options fills the screen. I hesitate.

- ☐ It's a bad photo of me
- ☐ It's inappropriate
- ☐ It makes me sad
- ☐ It's embarrassing
- ☐ Other

I hover over the options. Where's "All of the above" when you need it? Finally, I jab at It's inappropriate.

"The best way to remove this photo is to ask Anna to take it down," the site chirps helpfully. "Message Anna to resolve this or continue to report this?"

"Yeah, right," I mutter. I've tried that before. I click "report photo." And that's it. The window disappears, but the photo is still there.

After everything I've been through, after all the lengths we went to to get away, I'm right back where I started. How could this have happened? I've been so careful. I haven't left a trace. How did he know where I am, the name of my new school? It doesn't make any sense.

How did he find me?

It's a strange combination, anger and shame. It feels like acid burning in your veins. I open a new message window on my phone and type in a number I know by heart. Then I write:

Please. Just leave me alone.

And I hit send.

TWENTY-ONE

BY THE TIME MUM GETS home from work, it's just late enough to casually tell her I had a free period at the end of the day and got away early. I feel guilty about lying, especially when Mum's face lights up.

"Fantastic! Want to bake some cookies with me? Let's experiment—cherry and dark chocolate?"

"Um…"

"No, you're right, too basic—what about lemon and basil? Raspberry and ricotta?"

"Mum…"

"Strawberry and sardine? Just kidding." I force a laugh.

I have to get out of the kitchen. I'm terrified Mum will be able to see it in my face, recognize the signs. I can't bear the thought of her finding out that it's happening again, not after she's left her entire life behind to try and give me a fresh start.

"I'd love to, but I have homework. I'm really buried actually—I thought I'd just take something up to my room," I say, digging around in the fridge and grabbing a couple of slices of leftover pizza. Her face falls. "I'll definitely be happy to sample the results tomorrow," I say quickly, and then, with a supreme effort at jollity, "but if you think I'm eating a fish-flavored cookie, you're going to be sadly disappointed."

Mum grins and waves a tin of tuna menacingly in my direction. "All right, love."

Behind her there's a whole pile of bags still waiting to be unpacked. Her eyes slide over to them as she reaches for the flour and sugar. And I want to tell her she can unpack instead; that she doesn't have to be baking cookies to make it feel like home, but I don't know how to say it without sounding mean. The ironic thing is Mum never used to bake cookies. Since we arrived in St. Monans, she's made four batches.

I manage to escape before Mum notices anything's wrong. But upstairs in my room, there's nothing to distract me from the storm inside my head.

This isn't happening.

This can't be happening.

I left all this behind.

I close my eyes, desperate for it all to go away…

You stumble hard and fall on the grass, the wind knocked out of you. Laughing, you scramble up again, looking back down the slight hill to the church. It glows warm in the late afternoon sun, the waves lazily rolling beyond. A girl's voice pierces the air, high with excitement. "I'm coming for you, Maggie, I'm coming!" She hurtles out from behind a gravestone, skirts bunched up around her waist in spite of the telling-off she'll get if anyone sees. Her fair hair fans out wildly behind her in the wind, her cheeks flushed as pink as a child's.

You're both getting too old for these games now, Da would say sternly if he caught you. Girls of seventeen should be thinking of housework and marriage, not charging about like wet-haired colts. But the sun shines warm on your hair and Da is off on the boat, too far away for his strictness to contain you, and your legs ache to run.

As she charges up the hill toward you, you shriek and scramble away, the grass soft and cool under your bare feet. But she's faster, always has been, and her freckled arms soon snag around your waist, pulling you both down, tumbling across the hillside in a muddle of skirts and panting and laughter.

I jolt awake, panicking, and realize that it's dark and I'm still in my school uniform, lying on top of the duvet. I must have dozed off. For a moment, the giddy euphoria of the dream stays with me, then the real world crowds back in and I feel myself plummet back to earth.

I reach for my phone. It's 3:45 a.m.

1 new message

It's from a number I don't recognize.

Roses are red
Violets are blue

157

Anna's a slut
We all know it's true.

I stare down at the screen. For a heartbeat, my finger hovers over the reply button, then I think better of it.

Message deleted

The phone buzzes again, fidgeting impatiently in my hand.

1 new message
Hi, Anna. You don't know me, I'm in your chemistry
    class, but we haven't spoken. I was just wondering if
    you'd send me some pictures?
Message deleted

2 new messages
I know what you are.
Message deleted

1 new message
Once a whore, always a whore.
Message deleted

4 new messages
Hey, Anna...

5 new messages

Slut—

Message deleted

1 new message

Anna, it's Charlie. I'll show you mine if you'll show me
yours?

Message deleted

Message deleted

Message deleted

1 new message

Hi, mystery girl. Who knew you had so many sexy
secrets? So glad we're finally getting to know the real
you. SS x

How did they get my number? How can this be happening to
me again? And then it hits me, and I hate myself for not realizing
before. The message I sent earlier, asking him to stop. It backfired
on me, just like everything else. Like he was ever going to leave
me alone. All I did was give him my number. Why can't I ever do
anything right?

I navigate to the fake Facebook profile with trembling fingers,
but I already know what I'm going to see. At the top of the page,
there's a new post.

"Here's my new number! Text me anytime. Oh, and boys? I
really mean *anytime*," and there, staring at me in black and white, is
my new phone number, the one I've barely even memorized myself.

I bury the phone under my pillow and squeeze my eyes closed, willing myself to fall back to sleep. But sleep won't come. The muffled buzzing continues as if I've trapped an angry insect under my pillow. I fumble for it without looking and grope for the power button, holding it down until the vibrations reluctantly subside.

I lie wide awake in the darkness. The house is loud in the silence. Beams creak and crack and a low whistle comes sporadically from the chimney. I think about the others who lay in this room before me, looking up into the blackness of this ceiling. Were any of them ever this terrified about what would happen when morning came?

TWENTY-TWO

MORNING STUBBORNLY ARRIVES. THE THOUGHT of pretending to be ill or making some other excuse not to go to school crosses my mind, but I can't risk alerting Mum that anything is wrong. I think about just deliberately missing the bus and ditching, spending the day in St. Monans, but then the school might call Mum to ask where I am, and anyway she's already offered to give me a lift. I will time to slow down, but everything seems to speed by faster and faster instead. Breakfast, the shower, the drive to school all rush past in a blur as if I'm watching my own life on fast-forward. Until the moment I step out of the car and everything around me freezes like somebody has pressed the pause button. I think I might dangle here forever, stuck in time, watching Mum's rear lights disappear into the distance and wishing, wishing that I didn't have to walk into the building.

I start taking slow steps forward. Then the hissing starts.

At first, I think I'm imagining it. The faintest *sssssssssssssssssssssss*, like air being let very slowly out of a tiny hole in a tire. As if there's a little snake behind me, or a very big one somewhere far away. But, as I walk, it becomes gradually louder. Very slowly, more snakes join in, until I'm walking through a mass of hissing vipers. But nobody else seems to have noticed. Everybody's eyes are looking straight ahead. Nobody's lips are moving.

SSSSSSSSSSSSSSSSSSSSSSSSSSSSSSSSSSSSSSSSSSSSSSSSSSSS SSSSSSSSSSSSSSS

The hiss rises until it becomes unbearable. It surrounds me, until I feel like I'm walking through hot steam. I think I might faint. I force myself to keep putting one foot in front of the other.

I round a corner and a teacher steps out of a classroom ahead. The hissing dies away, instantly, replaced by the normal clatter of the morning. I almost bring my hand to my ear in confusion, almost wonder if I've imagined it all. Then he turns and walks through the door into another corridor, and it's as if somebody turned the volume back up.

SSSSSSSSSSSSSSSSSSSSSSSSSSSSSSSSSSSSSSSSSSSSSSSSSSSS SSSSSSSSSSSSSSS

My whole body is burning. I feel like someone has ripped off my protective shell, my outer layer of skin, and left me raw and exposed.

I abandon the idea of going to my locker and decide to head straight for math, my first class today. But the *sssssssssssssssssssssss* is all around me, twining itself like a choking noose about my neck, trying to yank me backward, trip me up, spin me round. I press on, walking as if I'm in a dream, only vaguely aware of the shapes of the other students around me as I focus desperately on just reaching the classroom door. Finally, I feel the door handle, smooth and cool and reassuring, under my palm. I stumble to the back of the classroom and slump behind my desk, hands shaking as I mechanically take out my books and pencil case.

I sit alone, trying to build a wall of silence around me as if it could protect me. Cat's in the third period for math, and Lish is in the advanced class, so neither of them is here, and my heart sinks as I realize I won't see them until lunch because we're in different English classes as well.

I don't hear a word of the lesson. Woodenly, I copy down formulae and stare straight ahead as the teacher talks. When she turns to the whiteboard to write out a list of questions, a boy I don't know in the front row swivels in his seat and holds up two fingers in a V shape in front of his mouth, graphically licking his tongue between them. The class watches in delight, some egging him on, most turning to see my reaction. I try to look as if I have no idea what they're talking about, as if there must have been some mistake, as if it's all happening to somebody else.

I look down at my book and pretend to be deep in concentration as I scribble away. None of them need to know that I am just writing *SHIT SHIT SHIT SHIT SHIT SHIT SHIT SHIT SHIT SHIT SHIT SHIT SHIT* across a page blotted with tears.

It isn't even halfway through the lesson when the first paper airplane skids onto my desk.

OPEN ME.

I look up, but the teacher is crouching next to a desk in the front row, patiently explaining something, and everybody else's backs are bent obediently over their books. I unfold it with shaking fingers.

A key that can open many locks is called a master key, but a lock that can be opened by many keys is a shitty lock.

Just in case I didn't get it, half the paper is taken up with a crude drawing of a cock and balls, a little dotted line spurting out of the top of it. Underneath there's a stick figure on its knees, mouth open, a puddle of liquid spilling out of its mouth and down its front. *ANNA* is scrawled above its head.

The drawings get more and more obscene. By the end of the lesson, my desk is littered in unfolded airplanes. One just says *WHORE.*

I'm falling through fog. I want to get up, to walk out, but my legs aren't working. Even after the bell rings, it takes me what feels like forever to gather up the paper, stuff it in my bag and start to move toward the door. It's like moving through treacle.

Slowly, corridor by corridor, I'm getting closer to my locker. Painful, unwanted memories are surfacing. Red daubed letters. *SLUT* painted across a metal door in blood-colored paint. I keep my eyes on the floor for as long as possible, but finally here I am: I have to look up to punch in my combination. I hold my breath and steel myself for the worst.

Nothing.

A smooth dark gray locker door like all the others. No slogans. No menacing signs. No dirty names. I feel a rush of relief. My stomach gently unclenches. I pull open the door.

With a slithering *whoosh*, what must be at least five hundred shiny wrapped condoms cascade out of my locker like an avalanche. They plummet to my feet, slithering across the floor and skidding away down the corridor in all directions. Students start to laugh, some standing on tiptoes to get a better view. Before I can even decide what to do, I spot Ms. Forsyth at the end of the corridor, in conversation with another teacher and walking straight toward me. My blood turns to ice. I cannot let a teacher find out about this. If the school knows, Mum will find out and then... I can't even bear to finish the thought.

Desperately, I sink to my knees and start scooping great armfuls up and shoving them into my backpack. They slip through my fingers and slide under my feet. I grab as many as I can, thrust handfuls back into my locker, but there are still pools of them glittering up at me from the floor, and Ms. Forsyth is getting closer and closer. I'm not going to make it. As I reach out again in a panic, the teacher Ms. Forsyth was talking to turns off into a classroom, and Ms. Forsyth looks up, sees me, and smiles. Then, in horrible slow motion, her eyes drop to the condoms all over the floor, and her face flicks rapidly from momentary amusement to confusion to concern.

"Anna?" she asks questioningly. I cast around for something, anything to say.

"Biology project," comes a smooth voice from behind me. "We're doing reproduction and public health—we have to come up with a public sexual-health campaign. Free condoms have been shown to reduce the spread of STIs and the rates of unwanted teen pregnancies by nearly sixty-five percent." And suddenly somebody else is there, next to me, on the floor, helping me gather up the rogue condoms like it's the most natural thing in the world.

The bell rings and students start to drain out of the corridor.

"I see." Ms. Forsyth is blushing furiously. "Well, yes. Good. Carry on, then." As she disappears into the distance, I stagger back upright, my legs like jelly, shoving the last of the condoms back into my locker. The girl next to me is short, with deep dimples and even white teeth. Her hair is cut in a dark bob, her hands covered in pen doodles. We've never spoken, but I've watched her creeping into lessons at the last minute, trying to disappear in the cafeteria. Drawing on her hands so she can avoid everybody's eyes.

"How did you—"

"Shh," she whispers. "Hang on." She spins around. "What the hell are you looking at?" A pair of younger girls, who were giggling and ogling at me, speed off around the corner. The corridor is now deserted.

"I'm Emily. Emily Winters."

I slide back down onto the floor, my back against the lockers, my legs stretched out in front of me.

"I know," I croak. "Thank you."

She shrugs. "I know the feeling."

"I feel like my entire life is falling apart." It's the first time I've said the words out loud and actually speaking to another human being about it floods me with relief.

"It's like—"

"Uh, Anna?" Emily cuts me off, looking down at her hands, twisting her fingers together. "Please don't take this the wrong way, but I can't be seen with you."

"You can't...what?"

"I need to go. Now. I'm sorry, but I'm literally just getting my life the tiniest bit back on track, now that—" She breaks off, watching me work it out.

"Now that everyone's talking about me instead," I say slowly.

She looks uncomfortable and embarrassed. "I mean, I'm really sorry this is happening to you, honestly I am, but if people see us hanging out together..." She trails off again.

"Sluts United," I say in a small voice.

"Exactly. Sorry."

And she really does look sorry as she turns her back on me and walks away.

TWENTY-THREE

AFTER THAT, I DON'T THINK things can get any worse. Until they do.

By the time I reach the cafeteria, walking around school has become unbearable. The whispers, the looks, the way people glance at one another when I walk into a room, or let their eyes flick down to my breasts and quickly back up to my face again. Going to the cafeteria feels like entering the lion's den. But it's the only place I know I can find Cat and Alisha. I haven't had any lessons with them since everything happened, and I really, really need my friends right now. So I steel myself and walk in, holding my tray like a shield.

The steady buzz of conversation drops for a moment, as if the whole room takes a collective breath in. Then the noise breaks out again, louder and more intense, with little ripples of laughter racing away from me in all directions as if I'm a pebble that's been thrown into a pond.

I see Alisha sitting at a table on her own, frowning down at her yogurt, and I rush gratefully for the chair next to hers.

"Boy, am I glad to see you," I start, wondering how much she knows, how much she's seen.

She stands abruptly, her face like thunder. "Shut up."

I stop dead. "Lish?" I feel like I've just stepped into icy water.

Inside me a small, horrible voice is telling me I know exactly what's happening, but I'm not ready to accept it yet, I won't. I look pleadingly at Alisha, but she holds up a hand to silence me.

"I'm not good at the witty put-downs, not like Cat," she says breathlessly. "So I'm just going to be straight with you: This is *not* okay." She pauses awkwardly, like she's not sure what to do next. "And I'm leaving. Right now."

I feel like she's punched me in the stomach. And the nasty voice inside my head is crowing. *You see?* it trills gleefully. *You knew this would happen. They won't stand by you any more than your last friends did. Nobody wants to be associated with a slut.*

I'm trying to breathe, but my throat is squeezed painfully tight and it's difficult to get air in, let alone words out. "Alisha, wait, please, I can explain." I'm begging now, trying to hold back the tears.

She turns and gives me a withering look that stings all the more because it's so out of character. "Explain? How could you do that to Cat? How could you? There's no way you can explain. You're a bitch, that's all."

I stop in my tracks, reeling with confusion. *Cat? What have I done to Cat?*

169

And, before I can stop her, she's turned on her heel and marched out of the cafeteria. I make a dash for the exit, leaving my tray on the table, but Lish is a faster runner than me and she's nowhere to be seen.

"Hey."

I whirl round, expecting a fresh attack. Robin is leaning against his locker, watching me, his eyes warm with concern.

"Are you okay?"

"Am I okay?" The question strikes me as so funny, so ridiculous actually, that I start to laugh. And, once I've started, I can't seem to stop. Then I'm crying, and laughing at the same time, and Robin's looking kind of freaked out because I'm leaking tears and snot and starting to hyperventilate and all he did was ask if I was okay. With a supreme effort, I try to pull it together.

"No. Not really. That's the short answer anyway."

He half steps toward me, his hand outstretched as if to pat my arm, but then he seems to think better of it and awkwardly drops it to his side. "What's up?" he asks nervously, and I start to shake with laughter again, because, honestly, what a fucking stupid question. But it subsides quicker this time.

"Honestly? Like you don't already know? Where were you before first period this morning—on Mars? Because you'd have to have been on another planet to miss what was going on."

He pulls a crumpled detention slip from his back pocket and holds it up with his hands palms outward, like he's protesting his innocence. "Wasn't here. Late again."

Somewhere in a detached, numb part of my brain I remember he looks after his mum, that it makes him late all the time.

170

"So, you really have no idea what's been going on?" I eye him suspiciously. I want him not to know, I desperately do, but, unless he's been living under a rock, I don't see how he can have missed it. The pictures haven't stayed on Facebook—I've seen them flashing up on Snapchat and WhatsApp screens and who knows where else, passed under desks, shoved quickly into pockets as I've walked past.

"Well, no, I did hear something," he says slowly, watching me like I'm a wild animal, and he's worried I might attack (or, worse, start crying again). "I just… I dunno what to say. I'm really sorry."

"What do you say to the school slut after everyone's seen her tits?" It sounds like the beginning of a really bad joke.

"Uh—"

He's starting to look like he wishes he'd never started this conversation, and I can't blame him. I know he's trying to help, but Robin being nice to me somehow just seems to make things even worse.

After the boat trip, I thought maybe it could be the beginning of something. Things felt so effortless, so full of possibility. But now—now he'll see me the way everyone else does. Damaged goods.

"Why was Alisha so…?" He trails off, gesturing toward the corridor, down which he must have seen Alisha disappear. "I thought she was your friend?"

"Yeah, so did I," I murmur quietly, trying to take it in.

This wasn't how it happened before. With Prav and Suzanne. They abandoned me in the end, but it wasn't sudden and dramatic; it was slow and painful. They said they were there for me, that they'd stand up for me, no matter what. But they got more and

171

more busy, the worse things got. I'd look around, when the whispers started, and they were nowhere to be seen. And then, one day, I walked into the library and overheard them joining in, laughing at someone calling me a merry-go-round because so many guys must have had a ride. Things just fell apart between us after that. It was easier to laugh along than to have to stand up for me all the time, I get that. I just wish they hadn't given up so easily.

"Alisha said I'd done something to Cat. But I don't know what she meant."

"Oh." Robin looks embarrassed, like he's trying to decide whether to tell me something or not. "Well, it's probably that thing you posted on Facebook, isn't it?"

I look at him blankly. What does that photograph have to do with Cat?

He frowns and looks like he wishes he hadn't said anything. "I haven't seen it, or anything, it's just… People are talking." He avoids my eyes. "You know, the post about her? That's probably why she hasn't been to school in the last two days. I'd guess she's pretty upset you told everyone…"

I cut him off. "It's not *my* profile," I snap. "Someone else is behind it."

"Yeah, no, I mean, of course," he mumbles.

"You don't sound very convinced."

"Well, no, it's just, I don't know, I guess I just heard—"

"No, you don't know, do you?" I'm breathing hard now, consumed by the unfairness of it all. Why the hell do people think this has anything to do with Cat? Why is everyone so quick to believe that I'm such a slut? "You don't know anything. And you definitely don't know me at all." My voice breaks, and I walk away, trying to ignore the look of hurt in Robin's eyes as he watches me go.

I sink onto the toilet lid in the girls' bathroom, door locked, feet tucked up on the edge of the seat so no one can tell I'm in here. I turn on my phone, ignoring the twenty-three new messages, and find the profile again. I'm logged in this time, using my new private account, and suddenly I can see there are more posts, ones I hadn't seen yet. How are they posting all this so fast?

There are status updates posted on the timeline, each one filled with explicit descriptions of what I apparently like doing to myself and other people. Just reading them makes bitter bile rise up in the back of my throat. Then everything gets a million times worse.

I scroll down and stop breathing. Anna Reeves has written a post about Cat. About Cat having an abortion. With Cat tagged. In horrible, clear, black-and-white words for everyone to see.

I feel dizzy. I can't take in what I'm reading. It can't be there. It's not possible. Nobody else knew. How did he find out?

I picture Cat reading it, her horror and her pain, and I want to punch something. I want to go back in time. I want the internet not to exist. I want not to exist. Suddenly I remember Alisha's reaction in the cafeteria. She thinks I betrayed Cat's deepest secret. Of course she hates me.

Without warning, the bile leaps in my throat, and I scramble off the toilet and lift the lid, retching, heaving bitter acid into the bowl, my stomach clenching and unclenching as if it could thrust this panic and pain right out of me.

TWENTY-FOUR

I DON'T EVEN KNOW FOR sure where I'm going until I find myself walking out the front entrance of the school, my feet moving by themselves. Before I know it, I'm boarding the rickety coastal bus, thrusting a handful of change at the driver, who takes it without interest. Usually, I take the faster route on my way to and from school, but this local stopping service meandering through the coastal villages is the only one running at this time of day, and anyway I need the time to think.

Sitting halfway back in an empty double seat, avoiding the curious gaze of a middle-aged woman surrounded by shopping bags, I wait for the doors to hiss closed. There's only one place I can think of going to escape all this, only one thing that might distract me.

Two days, two days, two days, two days. A steady chant repeats over and over in my head. Two days in a row I've skipped out on school. How much longer do I think I can get away with it? Nobody has said anything about yesterday, so maybe I got lucky, but there'll be trouble sooner or later. I'm meant to have a French mock oral test today, and we're supposed to be starting new textile projects in art. Somebody is going to notice.

I'm half expecting somebody to stop me, or halt the bus. But nobody comes, and finally, with a wheezing noise as the engine whirrs into life, we move slowly into the traffic.

The bus judders along toward St. Monans, the brown country-side rolling quietly on either side as though it's just any other day.

The picture dances in front of my eyes. The one burned into the backs of my eyelids. The one that's haunted me for nearly a year now. My eyes half closed, my hair falling across the pillow. My shoulder still showing faint red marks where my bra had been. Lying back on the bed, my breasts poised on my chest. Nipples standing up pink like raspberries. My stomach slightly more tanned than the pale white of my chest, a faded contrast line showing where I'd worn a bikini on vacation the year before. The last trip we'd taken as a family, imprinted onto my skin.

I can never, ever take that picture out of their heads.

I lean my forehead against the slightly greasy glass, watching the landscape change from windswept fields to scrubby bushes as the bus ambles toward the cliff road.

Suddenly we turn a corner, and the sea spreads out in front of me, glittering in the sunshine. Far beneath us, white-crested waves rage and foam, rushing backward and forward and going nowhere. I watch them pounce and swirl, pounce and swirl.

The waves are hypnotic. The sun is beating through the smeared window, warming my hair and cheek. I can feel the charm on my silver necklace gently vibrating away to the rhythm of the bus, tickling my chest under my school shirt. My eyelids start to flutter.

The sun filters through your eyelashes, and the cliff path is striped with light and shade. You hear footsteps behind you. You heave your basket higher on your back and quicken your pace, but he easily catches up. You keep your eyes ahead. His footsteps sound like danger, and your pulse quickens.

You slow to allow him to pass, but his hand clasps your wrist and he presses you upward, half lifting you against the wall of the church. The summer sun has warmed the stones, and the heat radiates into your back. His lips find yours, and their softness startles you. He smells of tobacco and clean fabrics. His hand grazes your thigh, and nobody has ever touched you like that, not under your brothers' watchful eyes, and it's confusing and exciting and dangerous and you pulse with the shock of it.

Maggie. He remembers your name, and it sounds different, beautiful even, in his mouth. The sun beats hot on your brow. Your feet find the ground, and you look him in the eye. He laughs that easy laugh again and you speak to him, haltingly at first, then more animatedly, as the sea dances behind him. You're glad of the openness of the path and the risk of other passersby to force decorum. You're glad of the wind to whip away your words and the sea spray to calm the heat in your cheeks and the brightness of the day to mask your confusion as you shade your eyes.

The bus lurches to a halt, and my forehead bumps painfully against the window. I look straight out at St. Monans harbor, groping to remember where I am. In a rush, I grab my bag and stumble off the bus, hearing the doors close behind me with a clunk before it trundles on.

I'm left dazed on the side of the road, trying to get my bearings again. It feels like I just traveled in time. I've never experienced dreams like these. Something is nagging in the back of my mind. Something important, something I've read somewhere...

Suddenly it comes to me. The library book.

It was thought that some could transform themselves into familiar creatures at will, and that others had the ability to transfer some essence of themselves or their memories into personal objects like handkerchiefs or items of jewelry.

I grope frantically at my neck and pull out the pendant. It dangles innocently from my fingers. I look at it hard for a moment and then shake my head. *Don't be ridiculous, Anna. You're dreaming about her because you keep thinking about her. You're seeing tricks of your own imagination, not somebody else's memories.* I tuck it firmly back under my shirt.

The day is warm, and the harbor looks like a scene from a picture postcard with its brightly painted dinghies and little wooden boats gleaming cheerfully in the sun. A seagull calls out with its rasping cry and the smell of fish and chips wafts temptingly on the breeze.

1 new message

It's from a number I don't recognize. I suppose I shouldn't be surprised; I know my number has been published online for all to see, but it still comes as a jolting shock.

Wanna fuck?

I keep walking.

Pretty window boxes outside the harborside cottages nod at me, pansies and geraniums bobbing cheerily in the breeze.

1 new message
Hey, bitch. I said wanna fuck?

I turn into the village. The bell tinkles gently as an elderly man shuffles out of the tiny shop. He raises his newspaper to me in greeting, then tucks it back under his arm.

1 new message
Are you horny?

I walk past the little playground. The shiny silver slide waits in the sunshine. Swings move gently in the light breeze.

1 new message
Are you shaved?

Down one sleepy street, there's soapy water trickling from a driveway where somebody is washing their car.

Are you wet?

The sun is warm on the top of my head, and the salt air gently plays with my hair.

Do you take it up the—

I scream out loud and throw the phone at the pavement with all the force of my bottled-up frustration. It bounces off the curb with a crash, startling a nearby seagull so it rises into the air in alarm. The glass shatters, an instant spiderweb of damage spreading across the screen.

The pinging stops.

The smell of fish and chips still drifts on the air. It feels like the kind of day when nothing out of the ordinary could happen. I pick the phone up and slip it gently back into my pocket. I walk on, past the pebble-dashed houses, the tulips nodding at me as if they know exactly why I'm there.

There's a long pause after I ring the bell, and, for a minute, my heart sinks. Perhaps he isn't home. But then I hear him fumbling with the locks, and the door swings open. Glenn looks surprised to see me, standing on the doorstep in my school uniform in the middle of the day. But perhaps he notices my reddened eyes or the leftover smudge where I've swiped at my running mascara, because he gives me a broad smile and invites me in.

TWENTY-FIVE

THE WARM, SAFE SMELL OF freshly baking bread floats out of the kitchen to meet me and stepping into it feels like walking into a soft, pillowy hug.

Glenn bustles around, putting the kettle on and using a tattered oven mitt to pull out a tray full of what look like crusty bread rolls.

He gives the briefest of glances at my taut face, then turns back to the teapot. "Is everything all right?" he asks casually, running his hand over his short, gray hair.

I feel the lump rising in my throat again and swallow hastily to push it back down. Some deep, unexpected part of me suddenly wants to spill it all out, to throw myself down on one of his rickety wooden chairs and pour out everything that's happened. How scared and worried and humiliated I am. My terror that Mum will find out and be devastated that all her sacrifice in moving away has been for nothing. The sick feeling in my stomach every time the photograph swims before my eyes. My rage that this is all happening to me again. The bewilderment at why he wants to hurt me so badly. The terror that I will never, ever be able to leave this behind.

Staring down at my feet, I whisper: "Oh yeah, everything's fine, thanks." I clear my throat. "We had a half day because of teacher training, so I wanted to come by and see if you'd managed to get anywhere with the research. The project's due in a few weeks, so I'm sort of running out of time."

Running out of time. The phrase rings in my ears.

"Well." Glenn carefully pours the tea and spins round to get a bottle of milk out of the fridge. He rests it on the arm of his wheelchair and pushes himself over toward me, a plate in his other hand loaded with the fresh, hot rolls. "Yes, I did actually. Would you like a roll? I just made them this morning."

My stomach growls loudly, and I suddenly feel hungry for the first time today. Something about Glenn's warm, welcoming kitchen, the chewy golden rolls and the cup of strong tea he plonks down in front of me make me feel like I'm in a bubble, sheltered at least a little from what's going on outside. Nobody except Mum has any idea I've been to see Glenn. Nobody can find me here, throwing myself into the story of the young woman who is haunting my dreams.

While I hungrily slather my roll with butter and raspberry jam, Glenn pops into the study and comes back with a scruffy notebook, its cover stained with coffee rings. He pulls his reading glasses out of his breast pocket and carefully puts them on.

"I went back to some of my original source material and finally managed to put my finger on the book where I'd first read about the witchcraft accusations," he explains, licking his finger and leafing through the pages. "Last time we met, I remembered the story about the nobleman and how he left the young fisherwoman pregnant, but I've been trying to uncover more about what happened to her next."

I nod eagerly.

"Well, I traced the source material through its index and managed to find the earlier text the author was referring to. Yes, here it is." He pauses as if he's rather enjoying keeping me in suspense. It strikes me that Glenn probably isn't used to much of an audience. There's no evidence of a partner or children, no shoes in the hallway, no family photographs taped to the fridge.

"Margaret Morgan," he says triumphantly, interrupting my thoughts. "That was her name. Known locally as Maggie." Something leaps inside me. Glenn is waffling on, but it's as if the sea is roaring in my ears and I can barely follow what he's saying.

Maggie.

The tips of my fingers tingle with shock. Maggie.

Maggie, like the girl in my dreams. It isn't possible. I must have read the name somewhere else—skimming through one of the books in the St. Andrews library perhaps—and taken it in without even realizing. It must have been tucked away somewhere in my subconscious and slipped out into my dreams. That has to be it.

I can feel the slight weight of the pendant pressing against my throat.

I feel light-headed, and for the first time today the horror of what's happening at school recedes just a little, lapping at the edges of my mind instead of crashing over my head in great, terrifying waves.

There's something unsettling about all this too. I'm not sure what's going on and, on a normal day, I might think harder about the dreams, the necklace, might even freak out and take it off. But with everything that's happening, I feel reckless, like it doesn't matter what happens to me anyway. And I need to keep tugging at this thread, to see where it leads, because it's the only thing in my life right now that can distract me from the rest of my world falling apart.

Briefly, I consider asking Glenn about the necklace, but I'm afraid he'll think I'm a complete lunatic. What am I going to say exactly? "I've been having these strange dreams and a tiny part of me is wondering if they might actually be visions because I've come across an old necklace, and by the way I think it might have belonged to a witch, and she might have transferred her memories into it, which makes me wonder if I might be living in her house since it's covered in witches' marks and is over four hundred years old?" Yeah, that sounds totally sane. Not.

"The details in the source are sketchy," Glenn is saying, "but it seems that the nobleman who'd fathered Maggie's child was lost in an accident at sea, not long after she had been punished for bearing a child out of wedlock." Immediately, a face swims into my mind, a face with sharp lines and a high brow, set with piercing, cornflower-blue eyes.

"Now, of course, this happened around 1650, a time when Scotland was obsessed with the idea of witches and sin, and just annoying your neighbor or visiting a sick child was enough to risk arousing suspicion. So it's not very surprising that the villagers quickly accused Margaret Morgan of witchcraft. It would have seemed too big a coincidence to them, knowing that she had been humiliated at his expense, for the father of her child to die in dramatic circumstances so soon afterward."

I'm leaning forward on my chair, my roll forgotten, hanging on Glenn's words. But he stops and takes off his glasses.

"I wasn't able to find out much more than that, I'm afraid. The outcome of the accusation, and the trial, if there was one, wasn't mentioned."

I sit back in my chair, limp with disappointment, and Glenn seems to sense my frustration.

"Well now, you mustn't give up, not now that you're on the right track. Having a name changes everything—you should be able to turn up something in the kirk session records with that, and finally get to the bottom of what happened."

"What sort of thing will I find in the kirk session records?" I ask, hope rising again.

Glenn puts his elbow on the arm of his wheelchair and rests his chin thoughtfully in his hand. "It depends. They can be a real treasure trove." He takes a sip of tea. "The kirk session meetings attended to the business of the church, but the group also took it upon themselves to police the morality of their parishioners. They had the power to investigate everything from drunkenness to disputes between neighbors, and they could hand out punishments as they saw fit."

"Wouldn't punishments have to come from a judge or a magistrate or something?" I mumble, through a mouthful of jam.

"Not for minor issues," Glenn replies. "Especially in the more remote areas, the communities would police themselves. Cases would only be referred to a higher authority when there was a particularly thorny problem, or if the kirk session felt unable to make a decision." He selects a roll and splits it down the middle with a sharp knife. "They also often heard cases of witchcraft. But it would be likely to have been more mob justice than a fair court hearing in that period, particularly in a village as small as St. Monans."

"Where can I find the records?" I ask eagerly. Somehow I need more than anything to chase this feeling, this sense of importance in something outside of myself and the tangled, chaotic mess that has become my life.

He chuckles. "I've never seen such a keen student before!" He considers for a moment. "You might try at St. Monans old kirk in the first instance, I suppose."

"Thanks, Glenn, I'll do that. I guess I should get home," I say reluctantly, dreading what I'm going back to.

"Anna," Glenn says gently, and I look up, startled. I'd been staring at the door, lost in the worries that are already reaching out again, their tentacles threatening to choke me.

"I hope you have somebody you can talk to," says Glenn. "Just…" He pauses and looks down at his lap. "It usually helps, when things are difficult, to talk about it, that's all." He seems to worry that he might have said too much because he quickly bustles back into the kitchen and starts clattering around, clearing up our mugs. Or maybe he's noticed the tears welling up again and knows that I wouldn't want him to see them fall.

"Pop back any time you like," he calls down the hall as I open the front door. "Let me know how you get on with the kirk records."

"Thank you," I choke as I step outside into the dusk.

TWENTY-SIX

ALTHOUGH THE DARK IS DRAWING in, it's still earlier than usual when I step through the peeling front door and I hear a chair scrape quickly across the kitchen floor and Mum calling, "Anna, is that you?"

She's sitting at the table as I walk in, laughing at something on her cell phone.

"What's up, Mum?" I ask, surprised.

"Oh, it's just something Gloria sent." She smiles, tapping in a quick reply before putting the phone down.

"Gloria?"

"Yes, she's one of the women who works the same shift as me. The hospital has a yoga class on at lunchtimes at the moment, and we tried it out today, and"—she starts laughing again—"and the instructor clearly didn't know the first thing about yoga, so…" She gestures toward her phone, where I can see a GIF of Keanu Reeves doing a split in midair. "Oh dear." She subsides again, wiping her eyes. "I think you had to be there."

"Yeah, I guess so!" I shake my head, but I'm glad that Mum has finally started to live again. She's putting down roots. If this had happened just a few weeks ago, I'd have been absolutely thrilled. As it is, my stomach writhes, and I feel a fresh jolt of fear. I can't let Mum find out what's happening. I can't ruin everything, just when she's finally settling here.

Upstairs, my hands are already sweating before I even open my laptop. There's a new post. It's a link to a blog page. I click, knowing what will happen. They all appear. The pictures that came next. The ones he forced me to send or he said he'd release the first one. Of course, in the end, it didn't work like that. But I didn't know that at the time.

Weirdly, it doesn't hit me as hard as the first one did. Like someone has already pierced my chest and now they're just prodding around inside the wound, making it throb and smart. I already know the pictures by heart. Where my hands are. What it looks like I'm doing. Even though I wasn't—not that it matters now.

Each picture trails comments like jellyfish tentacles. I try not to click on them, but I can't shut out the words that leap out from the page, screaming for my attention.

5 new messages

Whore

Oh yes, baby, do it to me. Touch me there. Yes, yes, YES!

Slut

Call me, I already sent you my number

Hey, slut. Just wanted to let you know I've printed this
picture off and jizzed on your face. Twice.

I try to ignore them, clicking instead back to Facebook, on the one alert I'm looking for. It's short and it hurts.

Thank you for your report. The photo you reported
violated our community standards and has been
removed.

The window disappears, and there's a link to a cheery help page that reminds me I can block anybody who is producing content I don't agree with or find upsetting. Upsetting? What a word to choose. As if this is all just mildly annoying. As if just stopping myself from seeing it will even begin to help. It's everybody else I'm worried about.

I let out a breath, almost feeling a little relieved. And I try to close my computer, I really do, but I can't help searching the profile one more time. I know I have to look. I have to see. I need to know if it's still there. And of course it is. The photo I reported is gone, but the other photos and the post about Cat and my phone number are all still there, in black and white. And the comments are still multiplying and sprouting spin-off threads. One group is joking about whether I had to leave England because there were no guys there I hadn't slept with. Another is speculating about the looseness of my vagina. I look until I feel sick, punishing myself, drinking it all in like bleach, as if I might be able to drown in it if I just endure it long enough.

At last, I've gulped my fill; read every last comment on a comment on a thread on a post. Heard every last person's opinion of me. Seen boys bragging about screwing me even though I've never met them. Watched girls discuss how they'd kill themselves before getting into a situation like mine. Sacrificing me at the altar of their own social acceptability.

I click on another photo, trying a new tack. I ignore the options to flag this as a photograph of myself. Instead, I choose: I think it shouldn't be on Facebook. When the options appear, I feel dirty. I select: This is nudity or pornography. And I shut the laptop and let myself slide sideways onto the bed without even taking off my shoes.

You knew he'd come again, and this time you're ready, or you think you are. The evening light is fading over the harbor, and you're soaking tired hands at the edge of the water when his voice slides over you like honey. You parry his directness with some coy words of your own, and you think, yes, I can control this and maybe even enjoy it? And at first you do.

You talk as easily as you did before, about everything and nothing, and he asks about your life as if it's fascinating and mysterious. Which perhaps it is, to him. But it never has been to anybody else. You tell him about your brothers and how protective they are, but how sometimes they feel like guards not brothers, and you wish you could go out on the boat with them and let the salt spray sting your eyes and feel the ache in your arms as you pull in the nets instead of sitting by the shore like a tethered boat yourself, waiting to clean the catch and watching the tide come in.

You tell him how your temples ache from tedious nights spent leaning close to the lantern as you mend the nets, and the pinpricks on your fingers sear as he bends his head and kisses them. You notice his dark, straight eyebrows and the way he looks at you makes you feel like you matter.

You tell him about your oldest friend, Jane, and how you walk to market together every Saturday and that she warned you to run straight to her house if he ever came and spoke to you again, and he laughs and slips the finest silver chain around your neck. It feels like liquid warmth on your collarbones and you've never owned anything like this, but doesn't it mark you? Or does it mean he is sincere? And when you probe for answers, he laughs and says it's yours, Maggie Morgan, a gift for you and doesn't it have your initials on to prove it? And you feel its sharp points pricking at your fingertips, and you shiver with excitement because nobody outside Jane and your family has ever given you a gift before, and the joy of the secret wraps you like a blanket.

And maybe it doesn't matter, not really, that Da said unwed girls who speak to men in private should be given a good whipping, because nobody can see you with the tide receding as you huddle in under the harbor wall. It feels good, at first, to let your fingers brush his fingers as the light dips lower, and you drink the wine he offers and feel the warmth spread through your belly.

He looks you in the eyes and with a hand in your hair he tells you how beautiful you are, and you dare to let yourself imagine a different life. And this time when he kisses you, you let your lips kiss back, because why should you always be a passive object? Isn't life for living? Aren't they your lips anyway? But while you're thinking about the next summer's day and wondering if you'll walk with him in town next *time, perhaps, in front of everyone, while he carries your basket and you laugh again together, his hands grow more forceful and his breathing heavier.*

Suddenly he's more insistent. You feel the rocks pressing into your back and what felt soft before feels hard now and uncomfortable. You try to calm him with a hand, a word or two, but he doesn't seem so keen to listen to you, not anymore.

So you gather your skirts and start to rise, and when he pulls you back, you tell him Maw will be expecting you, laughingly at first. He pulls you back and you arch your back to rise, but he is everywhere and suddenly his lips are not so soft, his hands do not caress, and fear flutters under your rib cage like a butterfly.

He breathes into your neck, burying his face in you, grunting out words as if he can't control himself enough to speak full sentences. Telling you you're irresistible, that he can't help himself, that you should stop the innocent act, you must know what your body does to men.

You try to wheedle, like he wheedled you, with flattery and promises of next time, but he crushes the words on your lips and you start to panic, start to shout. But nobody hears as your cries float up to mingle with the cries of seabirds as they wheel in the darkening sky.

TWENTY-SEVEN

I WAKE IN A COLD sweat and fumble for the pendant underneath the school shirt I never removed last night, which sticks to my back and stomach now. I run my finger over the rough scratches again and again.

Not a zigzag. Letters. Initials. MM. Margaret Morgan.

My head is whirling. I can still feel Maggie's panic, her fear and pain. In the bathroom, I pull the shirt off over my tangled hair and try to ignore the start of recognition at the sight of my own naked torso in the mirror. The image jumps up again before my eyes and I work to push it down.

The pendant shines gently against my breast, and I let my eyes be drawn to it, the one thing that's different from the inescapable picture in my mind.

I twist it in my fingers. "What are you?" I whisper. "How did you get here?"

"Anna?"

I jump out of my skin. Mum is standing outside the bathroom door.

"You're going to be late!"

I stand under the showerhead, turn the water up as hot as it will go and let the droplets burn down my closed eyelids, but I can't seem to wash my dreams away. And I'm not sure if I want to. I let the necklace dangle from my fingers in the stream, water sluicing over the silvery chain. Is the necklace driving the dreams? Or have I just invented all this, my own mind wildly filling in the blanks, bringing Maggie's story to life in my sleep? My throat aches for her.

Part of me wants to take the necklace off, to get off this roller coaster that's taking me deeper and deeper into a story I'm scared to finish, but a bigger obsessive part of me wants to continue escaping into somebody else's life, and I feel a burning need to know more, to find out Maggie's story. And even though it's ridiculous, even though I tell myself my imagination is running wild and it's just my own mind working overtime when I sleep, there's still a tiny part of me that's afraid if I take the necklace off, I won't be able to see into her world anymore. So I let it fall gently back onto my chest as I step out of the shower and grab a towel.

———

Walking across the yard into school has become a marathon. As I try to cross the lot, I'm bogged down, trapped by groups of girls hissing and whispering and clusters of boys shouting, making gestures, reaching out to touch me. It's like they're all drawn to me, like I'm giving off some scent of scandal. Like something rotten attracting flies.

Something strange is happening on the other side of the yard. The crowd seems to be parting like water. Then I see her. Cat is walking toward the school purposefully, her jaw set, her eyes down.

With a jolt of guilt, I realize that I've been so lost in my own misery, I haven't given much thought to what Cat must be going through. The way people must be treating her. I wonder if her parents have found out.

As she walks through the crowds, people seem to be repelled from her like a magnet, clearing her a path, parting like iron filings. But there are whispers, just like the ones on my side of the yard.

We're like magnets with opposite charges. One attracting, one repelling. Both miserable.

And she thinks it's my fault. I can't bear the idea that she thinks I've done this to her. Before I know what I'm doing, I'm calling her name, struggling toward her through the crowd. At first, I think she doesn't hear me, but then I see her eyes harden, narrow, although she doesn't look up, and she starts moving faster, away from me.

I haven't even made it into the classroom before I hear my name. There's a fierce knot of gossip just outside the science wing, and I almost walk smack into it as I scurry toward my first class. In a panic, I dart backward around a corner, but I needn't have worried. They're so busy discussing me, they don't even see me. Heart pounding, I rest my cheek against the rough brick and listen.

"I heard she had to leave her last school because it got so bad and everyone had seen the pictures and everything."

"Bet the guy she sent them to still goes there, though."

"Yeah, but it's not so bad for him, is it? It's not his tits making the rounds."

"He's the one that put them out there."

"No, he's not. She shouldn't have sent them in the first place if she didn't want them getting out. Slut."

"He probably told her he wouldn't show anyone." Somebody sounds uncertain.

"It's her own fault for trusting him, then. Nobody made her do it." I peek around the corner. That's Louise, relishing the gossip. She sniffs. "You wouldn't catch me dead getting into a situation like that."

"Only 'cause you're too uptight to take your top off in the first place." There's a ripple of laughter, and Louise draws her head back like she's been slapped.

"It's pretty slutty whichever way you look at it," says someone else casually.

"God, her parents must be so mortified."

"I heard her dad's dead so—"

"Just as well he doesn't have to die of embarrassment at his daughter tramping around all over the internet, then."

I feel like my rib cage is shrinking, getting far too small to contain my stomach or my heart or my lungs. Everything is being squeezed smaller and smaller, and it's getting harder to breathe.

"Bet she's got Daddy issues on top of everything else."

I feel something inside me snap. Fury fills me like rocket fuel, propelling me forward, out of my hiding place, ready to... I don't know what…ready to explode, or hit them, or scream that it wasn't like that, that I didn't do it for attention, that I never wanted any of this.

Then the bell rings deafeningly, and the knot dissolves as everybody scampers into the science wing. They don't even notice me, standing there empty as a paper bag.

And, just as suddenly as it came, the anger subsides, leaving nothing but a heavy, heavy tiredness in its place.

———————   ———————

As the day drags endlessly on, it takes every ounce of courage and self-control I have to keep walking through lessons like a zombie, pretending I can't hear what people are saying, trying desperately to focus on my work as if it can somehow block out everything else, and failing miserably.

I have two classes with Cat, but every time I try to get near her, she disappears, arriving at the last minute and dashing out the second the bell rings. As she leaves one classroom, I overhear two girls talking in loud whispers about "killing her baby," and my heart contracts painfully as I see her lower her head and rush away.

"What the hell do you know about it?" I ask them angrily. But the only response is an arched eyebrow and a muttered, "No surprise that you're standing up for her; you've probably done it too."

What's happening to Cat is different, but it's the same.

I spend the whole of lunch in the bathroom, slouched in the farthest stall, pulling my knees up to my chest whenever anyone comes in so they can't see my feet under the door.

By the time I walk into the classroom for my last class of the afternoon, every drop of fury has completely subsided, and I feel like an empty shell. I wearily slump into my chair and try to focus on the film the teacher is projecting onto the wall at the front of the classroom.

A trembling antelope with spindly legs is chewing at some long grass, unaware of the crouching cheetahs surrounding it on all sides. Their muscles ripple as they crawl toward it on their bellies. Suddenly, a cat leaps through the air like it's spring-loaded, and the antelope jumps as if it's been shot and skitters away, darting back and forth, zigzagging through the grass as it tries desperately to escape. For a second, it looks like it's going to make it as it dashes madly toward a little copse of trees, then suddenly another cheetah bursts out of the trees and the poor antelope screeches in fright and sort of twists in midair and dashes backward, straight into the jaws of one of the other big cats. There's a horrible, wet crunching noise, and the picture switches abruptly to some rare insects in the Madagascan jungle.

David Attenborough's reassuring, sonorous voice drones on and on, and I let my head lean on my hands in the darkened room. That tired heaviness is back again, weighing down my limbs. I'm sitting next to the radiator and I feel the warmth creeping up on me, pulling me down even further. The buzz of the projector merges with the buzzing of the insects. I feel my eyes closing and welcome the escape.

Your ankles ache and you massage them painfully, trying to reduce the puffiness. The fire in your bedroom flickers cheerfully, but you feel cold.

It's been weeks since you last sat downstairs with your family in the main room after dinner. They can barely bring themselves to look at you.

You lower your head over the lumpy sackcloth in your hands and try again to tie it into the shape of a doll, but the light is dim and your fingers clumsy, and it slips to the floor. You groan as you bend to retrieve it, stopping to steady yourself with a hand against the wall before you lower yourself carefully back into the wooden chair. You look down at the swell of your belly, pressing out through your woolen dress. Pain catches in your throat. It's obvious to see now, though you hid it as best you could for the first few months. Now you hide inside instead, taking refuge in your own loneliness. The townsfolk jeer and whisper if you dare to set foot outside. Your world has shrunk to these four whitewashed walls.

You run the silver pendant through your fingers for the hundredth time, feeling the scratch of your initials in the metal as they graze your thumb. You took it to the harbor that day—the first time you felt the quickening in your belly—and held it for a long time, your arm outstretched over the waves. But as the silver slid through your fingers it felt too easy, too much like letting him get away with it, and you clenched your fingers in anger and pulled the chain back over your head like a talisman. It's a reminder of your fury. Now it gives you strength.

You groan and shift your clumsy body, trying to ease the throbbing pain in your back. You are nauseous constantly, and you swallow and swallow, trying unsuccessfully to calm your churning stomach.

You bend your head back to your task and jab again at the sackcloth face with a too-big needle, meant for mending nets. The eyes are all wrong, bursting out in rough brown yarn and the mouth is a lopsided slash where the smile should be. A cruel voice pipes up inside your head. "How will you ever raise a child alone in a world that hates you both?" If *only your neighbors knew their taunts pale into insignificance beside the harshness of the words you hurl at yourself.*

You are just seventeen. You know nothing. How will you be a mother if you cannot even make a simple doll? The needle slips through your fingers and lodges painfully in the center of your palm, sending a trickle of dark-red blood oozing onto the cloth. In a rush, you hurl the half-made doll into the fire, watching as the sparks fly up and the flames scorch it. Then you rest your face in your hands and sob.

TWENTY-EIGHT

THE CLATTER OF CHAIRS AND the jangling of the school bell jerk me back into the present. I stuff my pencil case and books into my bag, my mind racing. Maggie was so alone. I can still feel her anger and her helplessness, and in the weirdest way it makes me feel a little less alone myself.

At least until I walk out into the corridor and it begins again.

"Hey, Reeves, did you change your name because your parents disowned you?"

"Ooh, Reeves, nice nipples. Do the carpets match the curtains?"

I keep my head down and shoulder my way through the crowd toward the end of the corridor. I just need to make it out of here. I start listing U.S. presidents under my breath, trying to block out the noise.

Roosevelt, Truman, Eisenhower, Kennedy, Johnson, Nixon, Ford, Carter...

And then, just ahead of me, I see her.

"Cat!" I shout, not caring that people are turning their heads. "*Cat!*"

I see her back tense as she hesitates for a moment and then starts walking faster. No way she didn't hear me. I'm running now, barging people out of the way, stumbling painfully as somebody sticks a foot out to trip me, but managing to swerve past it at the last moment.

She's moving faster, half jogging as she heads for the bus stop and the rowdy crowd surrounding it, a sea of students crushing Coke cans and opening chip bags and cracking jokes.

"Cat," I wheeze, catching her up just as the bus pulls in. Her face is flushed, and she tears herself roughly away from me as I grab her shoulder and try to spin her to face me.

"Just listen to me, will you?"

But she's already climbing onto the bus, and I jostle on after her as the tide of students sweeps up the steps, and we move past the driver, one at a time. She wriggles ahead of me through the crowd and finds a seat at the back, while I'm trapped halfway down the aisle, standing up between the packed seats, forced to grab a hanging ceiling loop as the bus jolts into motion. I catch glimpses of her face, glaring out of the window as we move off, headphones jammed into her ears, never so much as glancing in my direction.

But she hasn't thought it through. All I have to do is be patient as we putter along through the five o'clock traffic, teenagers jumping off onto the pavement in threes and fours as we stop every few minutes on our way out of the city. It's only a quarter of an hour before the crowd has thinned enough for me to see her clearly, still stubbornly looking away. And within another few minutes, we reach the last stop before the bus sets out over the countryside toward St. Monans, and the majority of the students flow off the bus in one rush, shouting their goodbyes to one another and heading home. I see Cat's eye twitch as the girl sitting next to her gets up and moves to the exit.

As the bus sets off again, I sway down the aisle and plop myself firmly into the seat next to her. She's got to listen to me now. But there's only ten minutes or so to go before we reach the St. Monans stop, and I lose my chance again for good.

"C'mon, Cat. Give me a chance. Please."

Silence.

"Cat. I can see your phone screen sticking out of your pocket. You're not fooling anyone. The battery is dead."

She blinks, then yanks the earbuds angrily out of her ears and abandons the pretense.

"What do you want?" she hisses.

"The chance to explain. It wasn't me, Cat. I didn't set up that page. I didn't write anything on it. I'd never, ever betray your secret."

"Yeah? Then who did?"

"It's hard to explain. It's to do with my old school, a guy I used to know before I came here. He forced me to…"

"Look, no offense, Anna, but I really don't need to hear your pathetic sob story about how tragic it is that you made some terrible decisions, okay?"

"I'm not giving you a sob story!" I snap and, even though I feel awful about what's happened, I'm struggling not to be a little annoyed with her too. "This isn't even my fault. Look, it wasn't me,

202

okay? Why would I ever do that? Why would I deliberately post those pictures of myself?"

"Of course, it's all about you and your slutty pictures, isn't it? That's much more important than the fact that my entire life is ruined."

"No, it's not! And I *didn't*—that's what I'm trying to tell you!"

"So, what are you saying, that that's not you in the photos? That you've never seen them before? That someone somehow magically found out about the"—she looks around and lowers her voice—"the abortion? Because I never told anyone except you and Lish, and she hasn't told anyone."

"I know, it doesn't make any sense. I can see that. I get why you think it was me, but it wasn't, I *swear*. I don't know who it was, or how they found out, but they must have realized that we were close, and they're trying to hurt me by forcing us apart. Can't you see that?"

She turns back to me, and I realize my mistake too late as her eyes flash with anger.

"Oh yes, of course this is all about hurting *you*. All about ruining *your* life. Massacring me is just part of the bigger plan to destroy you, right? I'm just collateral damage. You really do just think you're the center of the universe, don't you?"

"That's not what I said! You're deliberately twisting my words!" I'm so frustrated, I could scream. Why can't I just explain? Why won't she listen? I can see the bus stop looming as we draw into St. Monans, and I know it's hopeless, but I try one last time.

"Cat, please, listen. Maybe Alisha—" She jumps to her feet. This time I've gone too far.

"Alisha is my best friend." She says it in a low snarl. "We were best friends before you arrived, and we'll be best friends when you've gone." And, with that, she rushes down the steps and disappears into the village.

TWENTY-NINE

THE LATE SPRING SUN IS warm and soothing on my shoulders as I walk through St. Monans on Saturday morning. I deliberately set off early, before Mum's awake, leaving an upbeat note on the table and carrying a pang of guilt at the bottom of my stomach.

Gone to do some research for history proj.
Love you!

I feel bad about avoiding Mum. But the idea of being around her long enough for her to pick up on what's going on is infinitely worse. I remember how she seemed to slowly crack the last time around, how the cracks became longer and wider until it was like she couldn't hold herself together anymore. Running away, coming to St. Monans, it was the only way Mum seemed to be able to survive it. She fled to this place as a haven. I know she thought it was for me, but it was for her too, maybe even more so. I know it was. So I can't poison it for her.

Anyway, I tell myself as I set off, I really do have to go and track down the kirk session records. There's only a couple of weeks left until the project is due, and I want to know, no, I *need* to know what happened to Maggie. More than ever, I feel a connection to her. I owe it to her to find out what happened. Somebody needs to know. Somebody needs to care what happened to her. She deserves to be more than a footnote.

I set off along the shore road, letting the breeze play in my hair and enjoying the early morning sun as it bounces off the harbor. In spite of the light breeze, the water is calmer than I have ever seen it, and each little boat stands proud above its own perfect reflection. I can already see the old church in the distance, its spire standing out at the end of the bay's curve, beyond the line of pastel-colored cottages.

I'm almost feeling calm until I suddenly remember Cat's last words, start playing the scene over in my mind, see the hatred in her face again as if she's standing in front of me. So I double my pace and focus on the water and start listing every fish I can think of, but it's not enough to distract me, so I force myself to list them in alphabetical order, which is a trick I've used in the past when even lists aren't strong enough to block everything else out of my mind.

Angelfish Barracuda
Conch (maybe not technically a fish, but at this point I'm
  willing to give myself a pass)

Dolphin (see above)

Echinoderm (which is a fancy way of saying starfish, according to my old biology teacher. Okay, a starfish isn't technically a fish either. All right, maybe I should revise the category to sea creatures for the sake of accuracy)

Flounder

Great white shark

And now I'm stumbling up the rough stone steps, the church rising majestically in front of me and the sea stretched out like a mirror where the wall drops away to my left. As somebody who is 90 percent sure God doesn't exist but 10 percent terrified I'm wrong and he'll send me to hell for not believing in him, churches have always kind of given me the willies. Tentatively, I make my way around to the solid wooden door, turn a heavy door handle, and push. It's locked. I walk all the way around the church, but there's no other way in.

Feeling deflated, I wander past the weathered headstones, thinking how odd it is that a churchyard can be one of the most terrifying places in the world on a dark night and one of the most peaceful on a sunny day. Some of the gravestones are so worn that their inscriptions have disappeared altogether. A hazard of being laid to rest in the closest church to the sea in Scotland, I guess. On the other hand, I can't help thinking it would be worth the early anonymity to be buried in such a beautiful setting. The sea laps gently at the wall, and the sky is blue, and I wonder if there's anywhere more peaceful in the world to lie and wait for the weather to erase your name from living memory.

I'm so lost in thought that I don't see the man kneeling to trim the grass at the edge of a grave until I almost trip over him. I hastily apologize as he gets to his feet, wiping dirt-stained hands on his overalls and shielding his eyes against the sun to look at me. His face has the leathery hallmark of years spent working in the sun and wind, and I suspect that he's at least a little younger than the eighty or so years he looks.

"Are you all right, lassie?" he asks in a local accent, and I wonder if he's tended the graves here for a long time.

"Sorry, I didn't mean to intrude," I begin, but he laughs.

"No need to apologize—the churchyard's open to anybody." He looks around at the tombstones. "And you're not likely to disturb any of them in a hurry."

"I was actually looking for the vicar, or someone else who might be able to give me access to the kirk session records. Do you know where I might find them?"

He looks at me in surprise. "Well now, you'll need to go to the new church for that. St. Monans was linked with Largoward Parish Church in the 1980s when the congregations declined so much they were combined into one. The churches separated again around ten years ago, but any old documents belonging to St. Monans stayed in Largoward, I believe."

"Oh right, thanks." I'm already turning to leave, but he's lighting a slim rolled-up cigarette now and seems reluctant to end the conversation. I guess he doesn't get much company out here.

"What does a pretty young thing like you want with the kirk session records?" he asks curiously, blowing a thin stream of gray smoke out of the corner of his mouth, where the light breeze whips it away. "I've only ever had amateur historians and the like asking about the church records before, and they're usually old enough to be your grandparents."

"It's for a school history project—researching the local area."

"At school locally, are you?"

"Not far; at St. Margaret's Academy, in St. Andrews."

"You don't say?" He beams with pleasure. "My granddaughter's at St. Margaret's! I think you and she would get on like a house on fire. Perhaps you've classes together?"

"Maybe," I reply vaguely, thinking about finding my way to Largoward Church and wondering whether that too might be closed on a Saturday.

"Well, just you nice girls stick together now," he tells me with a wag of his finger and a kindly nod. He leans conspiratorially toward me and lowers his voice to a dramatic whisper. "Not all girls have the right sense of"—he pauses, chewing his lip—"*decorum* these days, if you know what I mean."

I must look baffled, because he seems to take my expression as encouragement to elaborate further.

"If you heard the stories my Louise comes home with about one girl in her year…" His facial expression shows exactly what he thinks of *that* girl.

I feel vaguely sick, but I don't know how to walk away without seeming rude, and he's warming to his subject.

"I don't know what's happened to young girls today." He sees my pained expression and puts a sun-burnished hand on my arm, patting it gently. "Not all girls, of course, darlin'. I feel sad for them, I really do. Getting themselves into these situations… The way some of them dress, you wonder what they expect is going to happen. What are their parents thinking, letting them go out like that?"

He sucks his teeth and shakes his head sorrowfully, looking at me as if he knows *I*, being *the right kind of girl*, will understand.

There's a brief pause, and I want to say something about the pressure, the huge pressure to wear just the right thing that's short enough and sexy enough and low cut enough, but also not too short and not too sexy and not too low cut, and how we don't say this for boys, do we? We don't police their outfits at all, and it's almost like their behavior stands alone instead of their entire character being judged on the basis of a few inches of material, and if something happens to them, we don't blame them for what they were wearing. But I can't work out where to begin, and so I stand there, silent in the breeze.

"I'm not one for gossip, mind you," he says.

And I somehow stop myself from replying, "Oh, you're not? Yeah, your granddaughter isn't either." Instead, I smile sweetly and thank him for his help and walk away, leaving another little piece of my dignity behind.

THIRTY

I HAVE TO DOUBLE BACK to the cottage to fetch my bike, and it's late morning before I reach Largoward Church and knock on the door of the small, homely vicarage next door.

The Reverend Peter Osbourne is a very tall man with square glasses and a thin, hooked nose that has a pale brown mole dangling at its very tip, giving it the most unfortunate appearance of a constant drip of moisture threatening to fall from the nostril. He seems just as surprised at my request as the gardener was, but he leads me to the small church hall obligingly enough and uses an ancient-looking ring of keys to unlock a small archive room at the back.

It's pretty clear nobody has been here in a very long time. The room smells dank and stale, and sagging cardboard boxes are piled in disarray in every available space. There's a desk in the corner with piles of outdated parish magazines and copies of sermons on it, and a stack of old, stained hymnbooks teeters on a desk chair that could only have been purchased in the 1970s.

"I'm afraid it's not terribly well organized." He chuckles, apparently thinking that he's made a funny joke instead of just stating the obvious. "But do feel free to make yourself at home and just drop off the keys at the vicarage when you've finished."

And with that, I'm alone with nothing but a buzzing fluorescent strip light and fifty or so moldy boxes to keep me company.

It takes all of about half an hour for my idealistic excitement to become as damp as the cardboard boxes. Digging through a stash of ancient documents becomes a lot less romantic when 95 percent of them are rehearsal timetables for the parish nativity concert or invoices for the boxes of cookies to be handed out at the weekly coffee mornings.

By late afternoon, I have still found nothing useful. The last weak sunbeams slant into the windows of the empty hall and light up the dust that dances and circles in the air. I sit cross-legged in the doorway of the archive room, sipping a cup of weak tea in a polystyrene cup that I've scavenged from the hall's little kitchen. The ghosts of four-year-olds' birthday parties and village bingo play before my eyes. Parents bustling in and out of the kitchen with cakes and ice cream and pineapple and cheese chunks on cocktail sticks. Old men in V-neck sweaters sharing a quiet smile and a joke on companionably placed plastic chairs. A ramshackle stage and velvet curtains framing a raucous Christmas pageant.

I sigh and hoist myself to my feet, casting around for the ring of keys. This seems like a dead end. As I look for the keys, my eye falls on a dirty satin sheet in the corner, most likely once used as a tablecloth for a game stand or perhaps draped around the shoulders of a villain in a skit. When I pull at the edge, it swishes to the floor with a *whoosh* of slippery material and a cloud of dust. Coughing and blinking, I see a final pile of boxes beyond, held together with parcel tape that's faded and peeling at the edges, looking like they've remained undisturbed for even longer than everything else.

Not daring to be too hopeful, I pull at the tape, and it falls away in brittle pieces in my fingers, all its stickiness long lost. And there, nestling inside the box, is a pile of neatly labeled lever three-ring binders, each full of photocopied pages of handwritten notes.

Kirk session records, Largoward Church, 1875–1892 reads the label on the spine of the first file I dig out. I feel a ripple of excitement and dig deeper. Largoward, Largoward, Largoward… Finally, I find what I'm looking for. *Kirk session records, St. Monans Auld Kirk.* My heart leaps.

I don't know exactly what I'm hoping to find, but Glenn mentioned that what happened to Maggie had taken place around 1650.

After a fair bit of scrabbling around, I finally find a file marked *Kirk session records, St. Monans Auld Kirk, 1656–71.* I open it eagerly and scan the first page.

These pages are photocopies of the original records which were copied before being destroyed in the flood of St. Monans Auld Kirk crypt during the storms of November 1965.

I leaf through the pages and am excited to realize that even

213

though they're written in old-fashioned English and there are a few words I can't make out, I can generally understand the gist of each document, although it takes me a while to decipher the flowery, ornate handwriting.

I drag the ancient desk chair underneath the fluorescent lamp, its squeaky wheels protesting, and sit where I can lift the pages closer to the light.

I pore over records of stolen pigs and overdue rent, disputes between neighbors and runaway children. I become completely absorbed in one particularly gripping case involving a cow, a blacksmith, and a very nasty case of syphilis. But I can't see anything that seems particularly relevant to my research.

"Where are you, Maggie?" I mutter under my breath, draining the last dregs of my stewed tea.

I flip open another file at random, containing the records from 1642–49, and as I flick through the pages, her name seems to jump out at me and grab me like a hand.

11th October 1649. Margaret Morgan of this parish stands accused of conceiving and bearing a child outside of wedlock. Witnesses John Needham and James Smith, neighbors to the Morgans, themselves do testify to hearing the delivery of the bairn some two weeks past, with wailing and with child's cries.

Margaret Morgan was thrice summoned before the kirk session and did fail to produce any marriage certificate to legitimize the child. Consequently, she is unanimously found guilty by all members of the session.

Now also the session addresses the scandalous attempts Margaret Morgan has made to smear a local noble with the stench of her own wrongdoing through her outrageous claims about her child's paternity. His character being well known to the session members and his good conduct being beyond reproach, these lies are dismissed without further consideration and the act of false testimony further added to the list of her transgressions.

It is hereby decreed that the child is fatherless and as such after due deliberation it is decided that Margaret Morgan, thus proved to be a harlot and a scandalous limmer, shall suffer appropriate consequences. Namely: that she shall be clothed in a vestment of sackcloth and doomed to stand as a gazing stock in the vestibule of the church for three successive Sabbaths, during the ringing of the bell, constantly repeating aloud the following words—"False tongue that lied."

Having thus atoned for these falsehoods, she shall then be consigned to the cutty-stool and elevated above other seating for purposes of her humiliation before the whole congregation who might reflect upon her sins and consider well their own avoidance of wrongdoing.

As far as I can see, it's the only entry that mentions Maggie. I take out a pad of paper, breathing fast, and begin to scribble down the entry so I can use it for my project. My mind is racing as quickly as the pencil flying across the page. How could they? It's so *unfair*. Even though I already knew this had happened, even though Glenn had explained how Maggie bore all the blame for her illegitimate child, seeing it written down in black and white makes my skin itch with anger on her behalf. And the punishment! She was publicly humiliated. For nothing more than telling the truth. And bearing the child of the man who forced himself on her.

I have to know what happened next. The witchcraft accusation came later, according to Glenn, and this file only contains records up to 1649. But, if I don't get home soon, Mum will be wondering where I am.

Quickly, I start sorting through the other boxes, heaving out all the binders I can find and separating out the ones from St. Monans in a messy pile. Then I put them in order, starting with the records from 1589–95 and working my way through to 1828, the latest date.

Shit. There's one missing: 1650–55. Those are almost definitely the records I need. If she was accused of witchcraft for supposedly taking revenge on the father of her child, it was probably not long after the birth and Maggie's humiliating punishment, when it would all still have been fresh in local minds.

I scour the boxes again, looking in every nook and cranny to be completely sure I haven't missed anything. The file is definitely not there. I groan in disappointment. But I do find something of interest. It slips out of a plastic document sleeve at the back of one of the binders, an unassuming little black book. It's slim and bound in what looks like leather. When I gingerly lift the front cover, the pages underneath creak and stick together, damp clumping them into sections. The first page is blank, but the second makes me fizz with excitement. In old, faded handwriting, so ornate and squiggly that it takes me a good five minutes squinting under the lamp to decipher, it reads:

The Diary of Stephen Browne
Ministerial Apprentice
St. Monans Kirk, 1648–51

When I see the dates, I gulp with excitement and scrabble at the first page. It immediately comes away under my too-eager fingernails, the damp paper tearing noiselessly like wet toilet paper, the writing reduced to illegible ink stains. I freeze in horror and pull my hands away. Then, very, very gently, I work my little fingernail under the corner of the second page and slowly peel it open. The writing is still legible, but my heart sinks. It seems to be in Latin. Gingerly, I close the book, slide it back inside the plastic sleeve and carry it carefully between my pages of notes as I set off to return the keys.

I'm planning to beg Reverend Osbourne to let me borrow Stephen Browne's diary, but first I ask him about the missing kirk session records.

"Ah yes, between 1650 and 1655? Unfortunately, the session minutes for those dates were already missing before the original records were photocopied," he explains. "They were never in the files to begin with. You could try the Fife Family History Society— they won't be able to help with kirk records, but they may have some other documentation relating to your project."

"Oh." I'm so disappointed, I'm almost on the verge of tears. "It's just…I was hoping… I'm trying to trace what happened to

Margaret Morgan, a local woman who I believe might have been accused of witchcraft."

He shakes his head—clearly, he's never heard of the story.

"The earlier records I found today suggest that she was forced to wear a sackcloth shirt and publicly humiliated just for having a child out of wedlock."

"Well, yes," he sighs, and the mole on his nose almost seems to quiver with disapproval. "There were different ways of expressing it in those days, of course, but fundamentally it sounds like this would have been seen as a violation of God's law. This girl engaged in fornication outside wedlock and delivered a bastard child—an example had to be set to maintain order within the parish."

I can't believe what I'm hearing. "So," I say slowly, "what you're saying is that she was asking for it?"

What I really want to say is that it wasn't her fault, it wasn't what she wanted, he forced her, but it's not exactly like I can explain how I think I know that without sounding as if I'm really losing it.

"Well, I certainly wouldn't use that wording," he splutters, fumbling to take the keys back and suddenly seeming in a great hurry to be done with this conversation. "But the punishment she endured does certainly seem to have been consistent with her own choices and actions."

He looks down at me as if I might be considering following in Maggie's footsteps, and his expression sours even further.

"Actions have consequences, young lady. You'd do well to remember that."

But they didn't, not for the father of Maggie's baby.

I was planning to ask permission to take the diary, I really was. But, as I look up at his drippy, dour face and his sanctimonious expression, I find myself quietly slipping it into my bag, smiling politely, and walking away.

THIRTY-ONE

MUM IS SITTING AT THE kitchen table when I get home, and she has her no-nonsense face on. Immediately, I feel the stolen diary burning a hole in my bag, and I surreptitiously move my hands behind my back, clutching it tightly.

"Oh, Anna," she sighs, and I suddenly feel my chest start to tighten. "I know."

I feel like the air has been knocked out of me.

"Why didn't you feel you could tell me, love?"

I lower myself very slowly into a kitchen chair.

"I can understand if you thought I might be angry." She pauses, looking at me closely.

"I didn't know what you'd think, Mum." I'm immediately on

the edge of tears, hardly knowing where to begin. "I didn't want to upset you."

"Oh, darling, it was only secondhand."

I blink. She pulls the cracked and broken iPhone from her pocket and lays it gently on the table in front of me.

"I—" The air is rushing back into my lungs so fast, it makes me dizzy.

"I found it when I was cleaning upstairs. What happened?"

"I dropped it. I'm sorry, Mum, I meant to tell you."

"Don't worry, love—we can afford to get another one from the secondhand place. But I wish you'd felt like you could say something sooner. Breaking your phone is one thing, but hiding it from me?"

"Mum, I—"

I look down at my hands. I hate Mum thinking I've been hiding something from her, and it's even worse knowing that I'm still not telling her the whole truth.

"Come here." She pulls me into a massive hug, and I let her, even though fifteen is definitely on the old side for sitting on your mum's lap. And I breathe in her smell of body wash and vanilla and something else that's uniquely *her* and try to let myself feel safe, just for a moment, but it doesn't work. I know I'm only pretending.

Upstairs, the nightmare starts again. I know I should stop looking. I know. But I can't. I have to know. When I don't look, I spiral into sickening panic, imagine what new posts are appearing, obsessing over the idea of everybody else being able to see them except me. What if there are new pictures? What if they say something else about Cat? I have to look. The imagining is even worse.

A new post on the original fake profile gives the username for a new Snapchat account and a link to a WhatsApp group. There's also a link to a profile on an anonymous Q-and-A website where someone is answering sexual questions, pretending to be me. I feel panic bubbling up inside me like hot water. It's spreading. I log in to my real Facebook account. There's a message:

> Thank you for your report. The photo you reported violated our community standards and has been removed.

I feel a wave of relief. Frantically, I click on the Anna Reeves page. The photo is gone. But there's a new link to another web page. I click it. Full of new photos. One shows the topless picture, but a winking emoji with its tongue sticking out has been roughly photoshopped over each of my nipples. Somehow it makes the picture seem even more obscene.

What's worse is that the other pictures aren't even of me. One shows a girl from the side, kneeling on all fours on a bed, naked. Her elbow is coyly positioned to cover her nipple, but her face is missing. Mine has been photoshopped onto her body instead. The next picture is even worse. I'm sitting cross-legged on a bed, one hand suggestively hovering over my crotch, the other rubbing my own breasts. Except it's not me. But there's my own face, staring back at me. It looks so real.

I feel the horror of it spreading through my chest, squeezing my lungs, making it hard to breathe. Sitting there, looking at myself, but not myself. I feel sick.

I zoom in on the picture, poring over it, looking for some

detail, some clue that it's a fake. It's there, of course, when you look closely enough. The slightly odd angle of the neck, the way the skin color doesn't quite match, a sliver of extra flesh where there should be wallpaper. But, if I hadn't known, with complete certainty, that it wasn't me, I almost could have believed it myself. Who else will take the time to look so closely?

I want to scream. It's not me. *IT'S NOT ME!* This is getting completely out of hand. I had nothing to do with those photographs. And there they are, plastered across the internet with my name on them for everyone to see. Even as I watch, they are racking up new likes and clicks. As if in a dream, I can see the comments starting to trickle in underneath them. The numbers are slowly climbing.

For a minute, I'm so frantic that I consider running downstairs and blurting it all out to Mum. I even half rise off the bed. But then I imagine Mum's face as she looks through these websites, picture her sharp intake of breath as she sees the photos, imagine her reading the invented claims about my sex life, and I sit heavily back down again. I look back at the writhing pictures. I imagine trying to explain that they've been faked. The worst part is that after everything that's happened, I'm not even sure she'd believe me.

As the panic rises, I try hard to stay calm. Mum doesn't know yet. She hasn't seen it. I just have to work harder to hide it until it dies down on its own. And in the meantime, if I'm going to survive the wait, I need to force it out of my head.

I open a new window and type a quick email to Glenn, asking him if he'd be prepared to translate the diary from Latin for me. Earlier I'd been so excited about it. Now it takes every scrap of self-control to focus on Maggie and her problems instead of mine.

I push the laptop away, wriggle under the covers, and squeeze my eyes tightly shut, but sleep won't come. The new images dance in my head, and I can see the words flashing underneath them in a horrendous, never-ending parade. *Bitchhoeskankwhoreslut—*

I jump out of the bed and reach underneath it, pulling out the boxes that have been stashed there untouched since we arrived. I rummage around until I find a pale blue V-neck sweater with dark blue trim and I pull it over my head before retreating back to bed. It smells of Dad. Fresh-cut grass and aftershave. Not the sharp, pungent smell of aftershave newly applied, but the lingering smell memory that's left behind after it's been left to settle in a closed drawer for months. I close my eyes, and Dad is hugging me tight, telling me everything will be okay. And even though I don't believe it, even though I can't see how anything is going to be okay, ever again, it's just enough to drown out the noise and let me fall asleep.

You cannot bear to sit inside for one moment longer. You long to feel the wind on your face and to smell the salt tang of the sea air. The day is cold and the sky is heavy, but your heart lightens as you wrap your cloak around you and step outside.

As you move heavily through the market, you feel their eyes all over you. You keep your head down and one hand on your swollen belly as if you can protect the child within from the harsh sting of judgment. You try to pretend you cannot hear their whispers, but each word adds new weight to the lump you carry in your throat. A woman steps in front of you, blocking your path. She sneers with contempt and spits at your feet. You are trembling and it takes all your self-control to keep your eyes low and move away.

Across the muddy street you see Jane, and she gives a cry and rushes to embrace you, ignoring the tutting and sharp intakes of breath that ripple around you both. It's like there's a shield around you and she has broken through it, uncaring. She kisses your cheeks and asks you how you are and you are so unused to kind words that they slip under your carefully constructed shell like a knife and you dissolve into tears. She wipes away your tears and throws her arm across your shoulders so that her flax blond hair mingles with your own dark red.

You walk together along the cobbled harborside, watching as the other girls slit the fish down their bellies as you used to do and spill their guts back into the bloodied water. It's like looking through a window into another lifetime. They shuffle nervously as if they think being near you could infect them. You have become the warning, the story nice girls are told as a caution. It stings.

Jane has visited him as you asked. She caught him saddling his horse outside the stable and confronted him with your condition—begged him for support on your behalf. Her voice falters apologetically, and you know the worst before she speaks again. He denied all knowledge of your existence. He laughed when she suggested such a match. And he threatened her with a whipping if she came again.

The wind has risen and at least now you can blame its salt daggers for the hot tears that spill from your eyes. You feel fury rising and the baby writhes within you.

Before you know what you are doing, you have pulled away from Jane and set out, striding along the cliff path. You hear Jane calling after you, but her words are lost in the wind and you do not turn back. Darkness is falling fast and the wind brings rain in great freezing sheets. Soon, your hair is plastered to your face and neck in wet ribbons. You struggle on, though the mud cakes itself heavy in the folds of your skirts and your back protests at the weight of your sodden cloak. Lightning splits the night in two. Thunder ripples overhead like God's own voice and the sea rages like a wild thing at your side. It leaps at the cliffs and the spray lands like spittle on your cheek.

You walk as though in a trance, dragging cold-numbed feet. You feel the water in your very bones, spreading tendrils of cold reaching through your veins to chill your soul. The lights of the village fade behind you, and before long the kirk rises, hulking out of the darkness to your right. Three lanterns flicker warmly in the vestibule. Once you might have sought refuge within, but there's no help for you there now. There's candlelight inside, and the young assistant priest is setting out the texts for Sunday service along each pew. Stephen. They announced his name when he arrived. For a moment, he looks up and his eyes widen in shock and something else: guilt perhaps.

He was there in the kirk session that night, when they all swore ignorance of your child's paternity. He watched, silent, as they called you a whore. He stood by while they gloried in your embarrassment and chose your punishment. His face spoke his discomfort, but he did not interfere, and now he cannot meet your eye. He looks like he would speak to you now. He takes a faltering step forward, but you give him a scornful glance and turn back to the storm. What help can he offer you now?

You catch up a lantern by its copper ring and struggle on. The flame throws its glare across the path ahead. The cold has turned your knuckles white as bone.

In the distance ahead, lights twinkle. You fix your sights on the pinpricks. Like walking on two blocks of freezing lead, you can no longer feel your feet. The lights seem to swim before your eyes. Sometimes there are three, sometimes five. They shift and dance like faerie beams. Your breath comes fast and ragged, puffing away in great clouds into the night.

The lights swell slowly into windows, pulsing out against the foul night. Light shines from them like a beacon, beckoning you on.

A house takes shape around the windows. A sweeping staircase leading up to a grand front door, six windows spreading out on either side, the facade stretching to three floors.

A silhouette darkens the nearest window, crossing in front of the fire. You feel his eyes on you, following your progress.

You stumble at the first step, feet tangling in waterlogged skirts. You throw out your arms, skinning the heels of your hands on the stone and the lantern smashes into fragments. Velvet dark swallows you whole. You lift your palms to your lips and feel the wet roughness of the grazes, but they are numb with cold. The pain will come later.

Abandoning the lantern, you scramble up the remaining stairs and throw yourself at the door, pounding against the wood with bleeding palms. The thunder has retreated now and the rain drums a steady beat against the windows. There is no mistaking the din you make, even above the noise of the downpour.

You wait.

Water runs from your forehead into your open mouth.

You hurl yourself at the door, not caring anymore about the cold or the rain. Pain bursts down your forearms and flashes at your elbows as you pound on the unyielding wood. You scream his sins into the wind. You shriek that you carry his child, a child he forced upon you. You draw every last shred of strength and you command him to face you. You know he is inside.

The firelight flickers through the windows.

Nobody comes.

THIRTY-TWO

I JOLT AWAKE, FEELING AS if I've just fallen from a great height. I can still feel Maggie's rage, her frustration, surging through my veins. She feels so trapped. Felt so trapped. It seems so real.

My open laptop is still sitting on the floor. Its baleful gaze has watched me while I slept. There's no escaping it. I can see a new email at the top of the page.

G. Sinclair
Hi, Anna,

Yes, I'd be happy to take a look at the diary. My Ancient Greek is a little rusty, but my Latin is fairly reliable, so I should be able to give you a fair idea of its contents.

Usually, I'd advise that an artifact this old should be returned to the proper authorities immediately, but since it's already sat in a damp room for nearly a hundred years, I don't see much harm in our taking a quick peek before we return it safely.

I do hope all is well. My door is always open to you should you need anything.

Very best wishes,
Glenn

When the doorbell rings that afternoon, and Mum yells up the stairs that a friend is here to see me, I have no idea what to expect. Cautiously walking down the stairs, I see Alisha's tall, willowy frame leaning against the front door, making polite small talk with my mum. My stomach twists in knots. Relief and gratitude are fighting with resentment inside me. I want her back on my side. But I'm hurt that she abandoned me in the first place.

"I'm sorry," she says simply as soon as we've left the cottage and Mum is safely out of earshot.

I try to sound haughty, even though a big part of me just wants to throw my arms around her. "What made you change your mind?"

"It didn't add up," she says slowly. "I realized it couldn't have been you, once the stuff started getting nastier and everything snowballed. Why would you have done that to yourself?"

"Exactly!" The relief is like a dam bursting. "That's what I've been trying to explain! But what about Cat? Can't she see that?"

Alisha looks uncomfortable.

"How is Cat?" I ask, in a low voice.

"Not great, to be honest," she sighs. "She's having a really rough time. It's not been as bad for her at school as it is for you—Cat's always been so popular, and people know how sharp her tongue is—I think that's shielded her a bit. But her mum found out about the abortion after someone from school told their parents, and she's in a lot of trouble at home. Her parents claim they're mad that she didn't tell them, not mad that she did it, but I don't think she believes them."

She shifts uncomfortably. "And she's pissed off at me because she thinks I'm taking your side," she admits, kicking the cobbles. "I tried to talk it through with her, point out that it doesn't make any sense, but she can't get past the post about her. Thinks there's no way anyone except you could have leaked the secret."

I sigh heavily. "I've gone over and over it a million times. I wish I could work out what happened. But I can't."

"To be fair," she says loyally, "it doesn't make any sense. We were the only ones who knew. And I haven't told a soul."

"I know." As much as it hurts, I do understand why Lish reacted in the way she did. I can see why she assumed it had to have been me who leaked Cat's secret. "Nor have I. It doesn't add up. I'm really sorry I messed up your friendship," I add miserably, half wishing she'd never even come over.

She shakes her head. "It's not your fault. I saw the Snapchat and the Q-and-A stuff." She looks at me carefully, like I might break at the mention of it, and suddenly her arm is looped around my shoulders.

I shake my head silently, hoping she can't see the tears in my eyes.

As we wander into the village together, I let myself lean lightly against her. And, even though it doesn't fix everything, it's like a tiny part of the stress and fear and panic I've been holding inside myself leaks out into her touch.

We buy snacks from the fish and chips shop and wander down the jagged concrete pier in the Sunday sunshine, enjoying the warmth that late spring has finally brought, even to freezing Scotland.

The stinging smell of vinegar clears my nose and makes my mouth water, and the chips feel warm through the paper in my hands. We sit side by side, dangling our legs over the water, occasionally tapping the surface with the toes of our shoes and watching the ripples move across the glassy surface.

"So?" Alisha finally says. "Tell me."

It's hard to know where to begin.

"There was a boy," I start quietly.

"Of course there was."

I give a half-hearted laugh. "At my old school. I liked him. Like, *really* liked him." Alisha nods.

"For a little while, I thought he liked me too. We started messaging. He was funny; he made me feel good about myself. I thought we were getting really close."

I sigh and bite into a fat chip, feeling my teeth sink through the crispy shell and into the soft potato center.

"Was he your first boyfriend?" she asks, squeezing some ketchup out of a little packet onto the side of the paper.

I nod. "I was really happy. I thought things were going so well. He seemed to really care about me."

I look down, twisting the edge of my T-shirt between my fingers. Lish waits, letting the silence hang in the air between us.

It's so difficult to explain, to take her back into my world the way it was back then, to understand how my head was in a whirl and home was unbearable, and anything, anything at all that distracted me was like a life raft I wanted to grab with both hands and never let go.

"My dad had died just a few months before, and things were tough—really tough. Mum had gone into her own world, and she was trying so hard to keep things normal for me that she didn't realize pretending things were all okay was killing us both. Everything in the house reminded us both of him. Neither of us was really coping. But she was so cheerful. It was exhausting. And stupid. I could hear her crying in bed at night. She knew I could hear her. We were both just pretending. We still do, in a way."

Alisha nods, letting me take my time.

"He was like an escape route from it all. He distracted me, but he also made me feel as if somebody could still see me—like I was a real person, you know, instead of just the girl whose dad had died, who people whispered about behind their hands and threw sad looks at across the classroom."

I stop and stare blankly at the little scudding clouds reflected in the surface of the water.

"So what happened?"

"One night we were messaging, and he asked me to send him a picture. I was so naive. I sent him a snap of my cat." Alisha laughs and for a moment I manage a thin smile.

"He said no, he wanted a picture of *me*, but I still didn't understand. I sent him a selfie of me making a stupid face, then a nice one, with a filter and makeup and everything."

Alisha face-palms. "Okay, I'm actually embarrassed on behalf of your past self here."

"I know, I know. But I was only fourteen. And nobody had asked me for nudes before. I was, like, what's the problem with this one? He had to really spell it out."

"When Cat and I first got asked for nudes, we went to Superdrug and took photos of every nail polish and foundation we could find that was labeled 'nude' and sent them all back," she says. I laugh. "But we weren't seeing the guys, which made it a lot easier to disappoint them. So what did you do?"

"I dodged the question and sent back cute answers and stalled and flirted for a few days until he started acting really hurt, saying he couldn't believe I didn't value our relationship as much as he did, threatening to break up with me, saying he was so upset that I didn't trust him."

I fall silent again, and even now I can feel the echoes of my panic, remember how desperate I was not to lose the first guy who had shown any interest in me.

"It felt like the end of the world. Like being with him was everything."

"So you did it?"

"So I did it."

Alisha nods as if she already knows the story. "And then he acted like things were really special, right?"

"Yeah, like it was taking things to the next level, like we were so much closer because of it. And I wanted to be so close to him. So when he asked for more I kept sending them. What's the big deal, once you've done it once?"

It's hard to talk about what happened next. It feels like someone is slowly squeezing, pushing the air out of me. "But then he wanted more. He wanted me to start...doing stuff in the pictures, stuff I wasn't comfortable with. When I told him I didn't want to, he started getting angry."

"Asshole," mutters Lish under her breath.

"He said I was uptight, a frigid bitch, and he started threatening me. Saying he'd spread the photos around if I didn't do what he wanted." I heave a long sigh. "And he did."

"Oh, Anna."

"It happened so fast. Things just got worse and worse. The pictures went around like wildfire. The things people said—the stuff they called me..." My voice falters. "I was the school slut. I was the punchline of every joke. Going to school became a nightmare."

"What about your friends?" She says it gently, like she's touching the edges of a wound, waiting to see if I wince away, not wanting to cause me even more pain. "They didn't stand up for you?"

"They tried to...sort of...at first." I push the heels of my hands into my eye sockets, watching the colors explode behind my eyelids. "It's difficult to explain. When it was just starting, they stuck up for me, told people to fuck off when they called me a slut, but it just—it snowballed. It became so big."

I gaze out across the water, taking deep breaths of the salty air, trying to think about it clearly when all I really want to do is curl up in a ball and cry.

234

"It was like they couldn't stop it, in the end, so they chose to save themselves because I was toast anyway."

"Save themselves how?"

"They just sort of faded away," I reply, in a low voice. Even now, I feel ashamed to admit how easily my so-called friends abandoned me. "They weren't around so often, they were busy, they didn't reply to messages."

"They didn't want to be tainted by association?"

"Yeah." There's a long silence. "But in the end they started joining in. I walked in on them one day, saying things that I never"—I try to swallow down a lump that's fighting its way up my throat—"that I never thought—" Alisha leans over and gives me a massive hug, and it chokes the sob out of me, fresh tears running down my cheeks.

"I get it. You don't have to repeat it," she says quietly, and I squeeze her hand in silent gratitude.

For a little while, I just rest my head against her shoulder and wait for my chest to stop heaving. I've tried to avoid this for so long, kept it locked away in my mind, forcing my thoughts away when they drifted dangerously close to remembering, scared of reliving the pain. But suddenly it feels like I need to face it, like telling Lish might somehow help to bleed a little bit of the hurt away. So I take a deep, shuddering breath and I carry on.

"The worst part was that one of the teachers found out somehow—someone must have told. I got a massive lecture about degrading myself and taking inappropriate pictures, and we both got suspended for a week."

"What?" Lish sounds outraged. "They punished *you*? With

235

everything you were going through?" She looks so angry, it almost makes me laugh.

"The school said they would tackle the bullying, but so much of it was online… They didn't even know what was happening, let alone have the power to stop it."

"Did your mum find out?"

"Once I got suspended, she did. She was devastated. She seemed to think it was her fault, like she'd done something wrong— like she'd made some huge wrong turn somewhere that had made me so fucked up."

"What did she do?"

"I think she panicked. She shut down all my accounts, deactivated everything. But the messages kept coming, and in the end she took away my phone altogether. It was kind of a relief by that point, to be honest."

"So you were just totally cut off?"

"While I was suspended, yeah. But, when I got back to school, things were even worse. Chris—that was his name—he got kicked off the rugby team because he'd had to miss a week of practice, being suspended, and there was some big tournament coming up. His friends started hounding me, blaming me for it, accusing me of ruining his life. Everyone hated me, and I couldn't take it anymore. I started ditching and my grades were slipping, even though I'd always done really well at school. Mum was freaking out…" I trail off.

Alisha hands me the extra napkin from our chips, and I take it and blow my nose.

"That's how we ended up here. Mum decided drastic times

called for drastic measures, and out of the blue she started looking at schools and houses in Scotland. Her gran was Scottish, and she's always loved it up here, but we never used to come much, because my dad hated the rain. She said it'd be good for us both, help her to put Dad's death behind her and give me a chance for a fresh start."

"But you couldn't outrun it."

"I guess not. But I don't understand how they found me. Nobody knew where we were going. I even started using Mum's maiden name, Clark."

My voice breaks, and I look down at the soggy napkin. "I was supposed to make her proud. I don't understand how this happened."

So many things still don't make any sense. I've been so careful. How did they know what school I was at? And how did they know about Cat?

"It's going to be okay," Alisha soothes. "Things will blow over, they always do." She doesn't sound supremely confident. She produces a plastic bottle of cider from her bag, and even though it's warm and tastes like cat pee (or at least what I imagine cat pee tastes like, based on the smell of Cosmo's litter box), I'm so happy to have one friend I can still talk to that I swig it anyway.

The hot chips burn our fingertips and melt in our mouths, and for a while we sit in silence.

"Did you love him?" Alisha asks quietly.

I think about it. "I don't think so. Not now. But I thought I did, at the time. It felt so like the real thing. Or what I thought the real thing would feel like. Hands sweating, heart racing, couldn't think about anything else." I reach for another chip. "I was so excited when he'd message me—it sort of made everything come alive, you know?"

Alisha nods, licking the salt off a chip before dipping it in ketchup.

"What about you?"

"What about me?"

"Have you ever—you know—been in love?"

She looks out thoughtfully over the mirrored water, gazing at the blurred place where the blue of the sea meets the blue of the sky and I wonder if she's thinking about Mark.

"I think"—she pauses for a long time as if she's weighing up what to say—"I'm in love with Cat," she says eventually. I'm so startled, I don't know what to say.

She flashes me a quick grin and I laugh awkwardly.

"Do you mean *in love* in love? Or, like, friendship love?"

"What's the difference?" she asks seriously. I look doubtful.

"I love Cat. I want to see her every day." She starts ticking things off on her fingers. "She's the first person I want to tell when good and bad things happen to me. Everything I do with her is better than if I did it on my own. I think she's an amazing person, and she makes me try to be better. She's completely different from me—she doesn't care about exams and she's obsessed with art and photography—but at the same time we're so similar, I can almost tell you what she's going to say before she says it." She looks up at me. "Doesn't that sound exactly like being in love?"

She's got a point.

"When I die," Alisha says slowly, and I look sideways at her and watch the sun shining on her shoulders, "if I was going to be buried with someone, and have my bones end up lying mixed up with theirs for the rest of time, I'd want it to be her. Not some guy."

There's a long pause.

I'm trying to work out what I think about what she's just said and also trying hard not to think about Dad's bones. "I guess I just never thought much about that kind of love before. They don't exactly make many movies about it, do they?"

"I dunno." She laughs carelessly, like she's trying to shrug it all off. "But aren't all those other things just as important as having sex with someone? I'll love Cat longer than any guy I go out with. This"—she gestures vaguely toward me, and the chips and the harbor—"it matters just as much to me."

There's a pleasant heat inside me that's a mixture of the cheap cider and the hot chips and something else too. But somewhere among the warmth, there's a sliver of ice, and I can feel it reaching out and turning everything else cold. Cat still hates me.

"So there was a fight at school." Alisha takes a long swig of cider.

"Really?" I say, not particularly interested. "Over what?"

"You." She looks at me sideways, putting her hand up to shield her eyes from the sun.

"What do you mean?"

"Robin came across a group of boys looking at the photos of you and totally flipped. I think he called them"—she pauses, screwing up her face as she tries to remember the exact words—"'out-of-control, sex-crazed Neanderthals with premature boners picking over the pictures like a bunch of pathetic, desperate vultures.' If I remember correctly."

I snort. "Was Simon there?"

"Oh yeah. He called Robin gay, said that was why he wasn't interested in looking at the pictures."

I wince. "What did Robin say?"

"Something about how limited your options must be when you're such a twat that real-life human girls aren't interested in coming within ten feet of you."

"Burn." In spite of everything, I find that I'm smiling. And Lish is smiling back at me, with a knowing look that makes me blush and grin even more.

She folds the last few cold chips into the greasy paper and scrambles to her feet, brushing gravel off her pants. "Come on." She reaches out her hand to pull me up, and I take it.

The sun's starting to sink into the sea as we zigzag our way back to the real world, and I wish we could stay out on the pier forever, and somehow capture the afternoon in a snow globe, always protected and perfect.

The first stars are starting to appear in the sky, which happens much earlier here than it ever used to in Birmingham. There seem to be so many more of them, as if the sky is bigger or the heavens are closer. A well-meaning great-aunt at Dad's funeral told me he was looking down at me now from among the stars, and, even though not believing in God has the unfortunate side effect that you can't really take refuge in the idea of your dead parent lounging happily on a cloud, sometimes I still let myself derive comfort from thinking that I'm somehow closer to him here than I was before.

"Lish," I say slowly as we wander along the harbor wall back toward the cottage. "Please don't think I'm completely insane, but…" I take a deep breath. "I've been having these really weird dreams."

She stops and raises an eyebrow at me. "What, like, *sexy* dreams?" she snorts.

"Never mind," I say, laughing and scuffing my toe along the cobbles and wondering whether Maggie once walked over these exact same stones.

Lish would probably think I was losing it anyway. So I keep my mouth shut and content myself with a massive hug goodbye.

THIRTY-THREE

"False tongue that lied. False tongue that lied."

The words stick in your throat like sawdust. Your eyes brim with bitter tears, but you are determined not to give those men the satisfaction of seeing them fall. They want you to hang your head in shame, and so you hold it high. You hold it so high your neck aches and it takes all the strength you have to keep your chin jutting proudly out.

The sackcloth shirt itches and irritates your skin as if a thousand ants are crawling over your back. Where it grazes your nipples, already sucked raw by the babe, they smart in agony. But the thought of her makes you feel stronger and you stand up straight. Child of rainbows with hair as red as flames. There is no shame in bringing her into this world.

"False tongue that lied."

You spit out the words, raging inside against the smug, contented faces of the kirk elders. As you stand, shivering slightly in the stone vestibule of the church, your neighbors shuffle past you for the Sunday service, some looking awkwardly down at their feet, some casting you gleeful glances, reveling in your shame. The sea breeze whips your hair around your face.

Stephen, the assistant priest, hovers in the doorway, his face flickering between pity and duty. He turns, half comically, between you and his master inside, as if he cannot choose between the two. A gust threatens to lift the sackcloth, exposing your shivering thigh, and he leaps forward, holds it gently down. His eyes meet yours and he smiles, a kind of pleading smile as if he's asking for forgiveness. You laugh a low laugh. As if you are in any position to forgive. There is a sharp throat-clearing, and the parson looms like a black crow in the doorway, eyes flashing, teeth gnashing, and his assistant scurries back inside like a church mouse, shepherded before him.

Then Jane is there, all pained eyes and creased brow, and it wasn't so hard until this moment, but her look of sympathy almost undoes you, and you have to swallow hard to keep the tears from spilling down your cheeks. She thrusts her soft gloved hand into yours as she passes and squeezes, hard, but her mother yanks her away by the elbow with a furious hissing in her ear and you are left alone again.

Your bare feet tremble against the cold stone floor.

And then it comes: the moment you have both dreaded and longed for. A clatter of hooves heralds his arrival, the only parishioner to travel far enough to need to ride to service, and the only one wealthy enough to own a horse. There's a swish of a fur cloak and you hear his confident footsteps. You fix your gaze proudly on the opposite wall, determined not to meet his eye.

"False tongue that lied."

He laughs.

Your cheeks flush with fury, and you look straight at him, in spite of yourself, straight into his cornflower-blue eyes that dance with amusement at your predicament. Funny. It's funny to him. A passing diversion. An amusing anecdote. Not a life transformed beyond recognition. Not an endless string of broken nights and exhausting days and whispers, whispers, whispers. Not friends lost and a family shamed and the burning sting of rejection by almost everyone you ever knew. Just a moment's chuckle in the doorway of a church.

You look at him then, and you see none of her. She is yours, all yours, with her crimson hair and her full pink mouth and the light dancing in her eyes like it sparkles off the top of the water. He sweeps past you in his furs and rich robes, his high brows raised in scorn, his lip curled in contempt and yet. And yet. You pity him. He cannot share her. And your own lip curls to meet him. His eyes flash then and his hand whips out and strikes you, hard, across the cheek. The shock is like electricity, and you gasp with it. And then you meet his eyes and smile again.

"False tongue that lied," you say, but this time you nod at him and the words are for him and your smile weaves a silken net out of them and casts it, effortlessly, in his direction.

The dream feels so real that it's a shock when my insistent phone alarm jerks me into Monday morning. My hands ache and it takes me a moment to realize they are clenched, tightly, into fists. I can feel the anger and frustration and the unfairness of my treatment, no, Maggie's treatment, like heat coursing through me. It takes me a few minutes to calm down, and try to step back into my own skin. I feel like someone has taken me by the arm and yanked me away from Maggie, and my mind is straining to go back. It's as if I'm abandoning her, just as she needs me most.

The visions (I can't call them dreams anymore, not when they feel like stepping into another world, more clear and crisp and real than any dream I've ever had) are taking over my nights. I'm consumed by them, almost eager to fall asleep to be reunited with Maggie and greedily drink in more of her story. At night, I hurtle through the terrifying ordeal of Maggie's world. By day, I hurtle through a terrifying ordeal of my own.

I still don't know what's happening, and I don't know if I even want to. I don't believe that Maggie was a witch, that she cursed her baby's father or put a memory spell on a silver necklace. Of course I don't. Those were the kind of stories that were told by people who wanted a reason to destroy her, and they don't have anything to do with who she really was. I should know.

But I can't deny that something strange and powerful is happening to me. And the initials in the necklace and the witches' marks... Is it possible that I could be living in Maggie's old house, wearing her necklace—maybe even somehow channeling her memories across time?

It sounds ridiculous. But there are details in the dreams that go far beyond what I've read in the library. And I knew she was Maggie before Glenn ever mentioned her name. I sigh and tuck the necklace gently under my shirt.

There's nothing I feel less like doing than going to school, but I don't think Mum's going to buy a faked sick day since I have no trace of a temperature. And I certainly have no intention of drawing more attention to myself by walking in late.

For a few glorious moments, I seem to blend into the green blur as the heaving mass of bodies in the corridor surges through the morning rush. For the first time in a week, it feels like maybe staring and whispering about me has lost its novelty. People seem to be discussing other things, talking about their weekends, bemoaning the misfortune of having double physics first thing on a Monday morning. Briefly, as I mentally run through the studying I did for today's chemistry test, I almost allow myself to relax.

Sodium, Potassium, Silver—valences of 1

Calcium, Zinc, Magnesium—valences of 2

Aluminum—valence of 3

I've turned the chemical symbols into a kind of chant to help me remember them, and I whisper it over and over in my head. *NaKAg, CaZnMg, Al. NaKAg, CaZnMg, Al.*

It's not quite a list, but it'll do.

Up ahead, the crowd seems to be slowing, and I can hear the buzz of talk growing louder. *NaKAg, CaZnMg, Al.* I turn the corner and stop dead.

It's leaning against my locker, full length. There's a small crowd gathered around it, swelling with every minute as more and more students push around the corner to see what all the fuss is about and join the watching ranks. People are laughing, chattering excitedly to each other, even taking photos. Over one shoulder I can already see an Instagram filter being applied to a photo of it. All I can think of is getting it out of there before more people see, before a teacher comes along the corridor, before someone tells my mum.

I push blindly forward through the crowd, hearing the din of voices sharply silenced by my presence. Finally, I'm free of them and I stand in front of it, alone, surrounded by a semicircle of students. I'm an island in a sea of shame.

The woman in my painting glares mockingly back at me. *SLUT* has been painted across her forehead in scarlet letters. My locker door all over again. The extended hand, which once looked playful and mysterious, now looks like a desperate attempt to hide her face in shame. Her once graceful dress has been slashed into ribbons. A sharp knife is still sticking grotesquely out of the center of the canvas and red paint trickles from the wound so it looks like the carcass of an ugly thing that has slowly bled to death.

A message has been scrawled in rainbow letters across the pretty purple sky:

You Can't Hide Your True Colors.

THIRTY-FOUR

INSIDE, I'M SCREAMING. OUTSIDE, I'M frozen. Maybe if I just stand here, silent and still for long enough, everybody will go away. Maybe if I stand just perfectly still, if I don't move a muscle, if I barely breathe, I will turn into stone and it will stop hurting so much. Maybe I should force my way back through the crowd and run as far and as fast as I can and never stop. My thoughts are flickering through my head too fast, like a movie on fast-forward. I can't get a grip on any of them long enough to decide what to do. I start breathing very quickly, and I'm feeling light-headed. I wonder if fainting in the middle of the school corridor—which I would ordinarily think of as the most embarrassing thing that could possibly happen to me—might actually be a relief in this particular situation.

Seconds stretch out seemingly forever while I stand there, frozen with shame and shock and indecision as the whispering starts up around me again. I wonder if I can speed up the whole fainting thing by holding my breath. I stop breathing and start to count in my head.

One, two, three—

"Anna?"

I accidentally take a gulp of air in surprise. So much for that plan.

It's Ms. Forsyth, looking at the canvas in evident horror. Around her, students are scattering, putting their heads down and walking away as if nothing had happened. She takes me by the arm, grabbing the canvas with her other hand, and leads me wordlessly into a nearby empty classroom, gesturing for me to sit at a desk in the front row before she perches awkwardly on the front of the teacher's desk.

I expect her to ask what on earth the painting is all about, but she doesn't. There's a long, awkward silence.

Eventually, Ms. Forsyth clears her throat. "Anna, I know that school can be a very complicated time in a young person's life."

I don't say anything, but inside I'm repeating a kind of mantra over and over and over: *Please don't let her have seen the photos, please don't let her have seen the photos, please don't let her have seen the photos...*

"Would you like to tell me what's been going on?"

I keep my eyes down, don't say anything.

She sighs. "Your absences haven't gone unnoticed, Anna. The school takes that kind of thing very seriously. As deputy head, it's my responsibility to investigate any unexplained nonattendance."

I feel my stomach turning cold. I knew this moment was

coming. I knew I couldn't just skip out and keep on getting away with it. But that doesn't make it feel any less terrifying.

Ms. Forsyth takes a deep breath. "Anna, I don't have a social-media presence, but Miss Evans and I have been discussing some"—she pauses—"*material* that has surfaced online, and which was brought to her attention."

I picture them, huddled together around a phone screen in the corner of the staff room, looking down at my stomach, my breasts, my nipples. Shame fizzes across my skin and rises from my pores like steam.

"Miss Evans and I are very aware of the enormous pressures that you girls are under." She gives what she obviously thinks is a reassuring and approachable smile. "It wasn't so long ago that we were in school ourselves, you know!"

Yeah, I think, *but you didn't have social media, did you?*

She waits, looking at me as if she thinks I'm suddenly going to open up and sob on her shoulder about how awful it's all been. As if hearing about her looking at those photos isn't making things significantly more awful.

"Anna, what I'm trying to say is, I'm sorry this is happening to you," she says, looking me in the eye. "I'd like to help, if there's anything I can do. It would help if you'd talk to me; tell me what's happening."

For a brief moment, I actually consider this. But what can she do? She can't control what people post. She might sound nice and comforting, but she can't actually change anything. And what if this is a trick, to get me to admit to the photos, admit to having sent them? "What if the school involves…"

"Your mum. She doesn't know, I presume?" she asks, her forehead furrowed with concern.

I shake my head, hoping, praying she isn't going to say what I think she's about to say.

"I really think talking to her would be a good idea, Anna. Talking things through with someone you trust, getting support—it can really help in this kind of situation."

But she doesn't know what she's talking about. She doesn't know what happened last time. Telling Mum didn't help, it just made everything even messier. She didn't help me sort things out; she decided we needed to run away. She promised me everything would be okay. That she'd just tell the new school about Dad and not mention any of the other stuff. She doesn't know anything about social media. She really thought we could just start fresh and leave it all behind us. And, after the way they'd treated me, she said my old school didn't deserve to know anything about where I went next, so she never told them. She thought we would be safe that way.

"Anna?" Ms. Forsyth is leaning forward, putting a warm, dry hand on my wrist, trying so hard, too hard, to help. I don't know how to explain it to her. She thinks it's just one page, one website. She has no idea it's everywhere.

"What do you think? Perhaps we could speak to your mum together?"

"No!" I shout, so suddenly that she jumps back in alarm. "I mean, I'm just not ready to talk to her about it yet."

For a moment, I think I've convinced her. But she frowns and her hand drops back to her side. "I'm so sorry, Anna, but the school has a duty to report something this serious to a parent or guardian.

And, as a teacher, it's then my responsibility to make sure the school leadership team is aware."

"Then let me break it to her myself," I blurt, desperately trying to buy time. "Please. Give me twenty-four hours, and I'll tell her, I promise."

She looks doubtful, but to my horror, my eyes are filling with tears and no matter how hard I try to swallow back the aching lump in my throat, it's pushing them out, forcing them to roll one after the other down my nose. I give an ugly sort of gulp and she quickly nods.

"All right, Anna. I'll give you twenty-four hours. But after that I will need to inform the relevant people. I know how difficult this is for you, but I really think that once things are out in the open, once you're able to talk about it, you'll see that it really does actually help."

I sniff and wipe my nose on my sleeve.

"Oh, and Anna?"

I look up.

"I'd advise you to dispose of that canvas as swiftly as possible."

THIRTY-FIVE

I LUG THE UNWIELDY WOODEN frame down the corridor, bumping my once-precious painting against walls and locker doors.

There's a buzzing in my pocket, and it takes me a moment to remember, with a lurch of guilt, that Mum has bought me yet another secondhand phone. It was sitting on my bed with a smiley-face Post-it stuck to the screen when I woke up this morning: *Same number. Love, Mum x.*

I can't walk into a classroom and face all those pairs of eyes. Eyes that have seen the photos. Eyes that have seen under my clothes. Eyes that will look straight through me at someone else they think is standing there. I start to panic.

There's a janitor's closet up ahead, and I slam the door open and collapse into the dark inside, bolting it behind me. It's cool and quiet and the smell of paint and cleaning materials is strangely soothing. I step on the middle of the wooden frame of the painting and pull up hard with my hands on either end, until it breaks awkwardly in two with a splintering and cracking of wood. At the back of the closet, there's a set of metal shelves crowded with turpentine and wood varnish, buckets and bleach, hammers and nails. I shove the painting behind the shelves, panting with the effort. It slides in along the wall and is swallowed by the darkness. Nobody would ever know it was there. I sink down onto an upturned bucket and rub my hands roughly over my face. I just want everything to stop. I want to disappear. I want to stay here, in the quiet, clean darkness, forever until everybody has forgotten that I even exist.

A church. Thick, lime-washed white walls. Rough, dark wood benches. Straw crackling underfoot, mixed with seagrass to sweeten the smell of the place. It doesn't work. The stink of sweat on skin, of scales under fingernails. The slap and crack of the waves pounding urgently against the cliff.

The stool feels hard and cold under your thighs, its three wooden legs wobbly, forcing your knees to tense and shift to keep you upright. You sit on a rough platform, a few feet above the congregation. Their hats quiver with disapproval and their eyes peer piously down at their own hands. Some avoid your gaze as if your shame could attach itself to them. Others sneer openly and murmur to their neighbors behind their hands. Their eyes rake from your hairline to your muddy, bare feet, disapproval in every look. You are not Maggie anymore, the girl they joked with as they bought their fish. You are the whore whose actions bring shame upon your family and your village. It is their duty to condemn and pity you. You must be punished until you are clean. They think half of your soul and half of their own.

The parson wheezes in the pulpit, sketching out your sins to the delight of the pews below. He calls you a "harlot" and a "scandalous limmer," and there is jeering and even applause. A gobbet of spit strikes your cheek, and you sit, shaking, as it drips foully down your face. You will not give them the satisfaction of wiping it away. You raise your eyes to the cross and think of your child. You wonder what kind of a God would judge you for giving life to her.

Your thighs ache. The list of your failings seems endless. You clench your fists until your nails cut painfully into your own flesh.

The sharp smell of turpentine brings me back to myself. The darkness presses in around me, and Maggie's anger beats in my chest. I'm running out of time. One day. That's all I've got left.

When I think of Mum, I panic. The choice is awful. The idea of telling her what's been happening, the idea of her eyes widening in horror at that picture all over again, of her reading the comments, hearing the words that have been put in my mouth… It's unbearable. Watching her world fall apart again, seeing the disappointment in her face as she realizes it wasn't just a one-off, something we can move away from and forget, that it's always going to be a part of who I am. Always going to follow us and ruin everything, no matter where we go. But then I imagine the school calling her in and telling her in detached, clinical detail, breaking her heart without me even there to tell her how sorry I am. And I know that's infinitely worse. I have to do it myself.

Suddenly it feels like the darkness is suffocating me. I scrabble at the door and it swings open, flooding me with a beam of bright fluorescent light from the corridor outside. There's a neat row of thin, half-moon-shaped cuts along the bottom of my palms. I stare at them like they belong to someone else.

I can't stay here. I can't go home.

I glance up and down the deserted corridor. Any second now, the bell is going to ring and students will flood the halls. If there's one upside to this situation, it's that I'm in so much trouble now that cutting one more afternoon of classes isn't likely to make much difference. I clutch at the necklace swinging gently underneath my school shirt. I have to know what happened to her.

Somewhere, deep down, some tiny part of me believes that Maggie chose to reach out, chose to somehow preserve her memories: chose *me*. If I'm the first person in four hundred years to hear her story, I owe it to her to find out the ending. And there's only one place left to look.

THIRTY-SIX

THE FIFE FAMILY HISTORY SOCIETY keeps its records at Cupar Library, according to Google. It doesn't take more than twenty-five minutes for the Edinburgh-bound X59 bus to deposit me outside the striking building. Made of honey-colored stone, the library boasts a square tower and beautiful fleur-de-lis-shaped windows that leave it looking like a cross between a castle and a church. Nestled between a café and a thrift store, it towers impressively above the uneven high street shops on either side.

I'm following the trail of bread crumbs Glenn has laid for me, but I'm not very confident I'm going to find anything. I've come up against so many dead ends and so many trails I don't know how to follow, it seems unlikely that I'll ever find out the whole truth of what really happened to Maggie. But this is the last place I can think of and I have to try.

The lady at the desk looks like she's thinking about asking me what I'm doing out of school in the middle of the day, but I say a silent prayer and she simply directs me to the family and local history room.

The man in charge of the archives wears a dark green corduroy suit with a flamboyantly patterned handkerchief sticking out of his top pocket. When I inquire about the kirk session records for St. Monans, he looks at me mournfully as if he feels personally responsible for the archives' failings. It seems Reverend Osbourne was right. "We don't have copies of the kirk records, unfortunately. They were all lost when the crypt and basement of the church were flooded." He looks genuinely mortified, but perks up when I tell him I'm interested in one particular person. "We have excellent genealogy databases; if you're looking to trace your ancestry, we can almost certainly help."

I hesitate and think about trying to explain the story, but it seems easier just to tell a white lie.

"Yes, I'm looking to trace an old family member who may have lived in St. Monans around 1650—her name was Margaret Morgan, but she was known as Maggie."

He disappears behind a towering pile of dusty books, and I can hear him tapping at a computer keyboard.

"Huh." He sounds surprised. There's a pause, then a few more taps as if he's double-checking something.

"It looks like you might be in luck." He emerges, beaming, from behind the books, dabbing at his perspiring forehead with the pocket handkerchief before tucking it carefully back into place.

"Margaret Morgan never married, but she had a daughter and the line continued through her. The family tree is incomplete, but it looks likely that her descendants can be traced to the area all the way down to the present day."

My heart leaps. It feels like Maggie is reaching out to me across time.

"It's a very curious thing," he continues, a slight frown puckering his forehead. "There are a few men in the genealogy, but, in general, the family all had daughters. Through every generation, the female line was incredibly strong. Almost no sons at all."

I feel a fizz of excitement in my stomach and a surge of pride. After everything Maggie went through, it seems fitting that she left a whole line of women behind her. I think of her fierce love for the baby she didn't choose to bear, and I know how much it would have meant to her to know her daughter lived and had a family that thrived for generations. I look at him expectantly, waiting for more, but he's beaming as if he's imparted the whole gift of his knowledge.

"But what about Maggie? Isn't there any information about what happened to her?"

He blinks and looks confused. "What happened to her?"

"She was accused of witchcraft," I half whisper as if I might absurdly protect Maggie's reputation all these centuries later by keeping it on the down-low.

"Witchcraft?" He looks startled. "I'm sorry, we don't seem to have any record of that here. I don't have a date or a cause of death, I'm afraid. The records are extremely sparse that far back."

I have to fight to stop myself from pounding the desk in frustration. I feel like sending the towers of old books toppling to the ground.

"Have you thought about looking into the kirk session minutes?" he asks, and I almost scream at him. "We know that the kirk records for much of Fife are very damaged and patchy for that period, but there should be something in there if there was a witchcraft case. The copies of what records there were are held locally I believe. In Largoward."

I swallow my rage and give him a feeble smile, nodding my thanks. After the way he reacted earlier, I'm afraid he'd burst into tears if I told him the minutes for that particular period have been lost for good.

As I leave the library, I feel my phone start to buzz and messages start popping up one after another. Most of them don't make any sense.

> Didn't realize you were a professional. Want to practice on me?
> Did you decide that slutting around in your own social circle was too low-key?

Then there's one from Lish.

> WHERE ARE YOU? Have you seen the video????

I feel the familiar dread rising in my chest and pull up the profile on my phone. It still hasn't been removed, although I've reported it in every possible way and even tried to send a message explaining it's an imposter account pretending to be me.

And there's a new post at the top of the timeline.

I feel my pulse start to quicken as I jab at the link with a sweaty finger.

Oh God, oh God, oh God. It's a porn site. Grainy images crowd the screen, women on their knees, women on their backs, women's faces covered in—Oh GOD.

I swipe down, frantically, whizzing past categories and choices—*MILF, busty blond, Asian temptress, Ebony and Ivory, hot teen*—

I freeze.

There's a girl on the screen performing a sex act on a bed.

It's me.

She's me.

It's not me.

I didn't do this.

She has my face.

Why does she have my face?

I can't breathe. I can't move. I can't take my eyes off the screen.

Her body writhes. My body. Not my body, though, it's not even close. She's thinner and taller, her hair is darker and straighter than mine, but there's my face, my face, my face.

I want to scream. I am gasping for breath, and I look wildly around the quiet high street as if somebody might come along who can somehow help me. It feels nightmarish to be looking down at this screen, feeling the video worm inside me, poisoning everything, when on the outside I'm standing on this completely ordinary pavement, a couple of doors down from the thrift store.

They've all seen this. They've watched it. They think it's me.

Fumbling, I switch back to the profile. The link has forty-three likes. Comments are streaming in underneath, appearing before my eyes. I lock the screen, but the phone keeps on buzzing in my hands like it's alive. I didn't do it. It isn't me.

Another message from Alisha.

Deepfake.

I stare at the screen.

??????

It's face-swapping technology. Lets you make it look like

someone's in a video when they're not. People have

been using it to photoshop celebrities' faces onto

porn clips. That's how they did it.

What do I do?

There's a pause before Alisha's next message comes through.

I don't know.

I look around the gray high street and feel at once completely free and utterly trapped. I could go anywhere. But I can't outrun this. A light drizzle has started to fall, and people pull up their coat collars as they walk past, their eyes sliding over me as if I'm not there. It's never felt like such a relief to be temporarily invisible. But I can't just stand here forever.

As soon as I spot the sign, I feel like someone is pointing me in the right direction. The one thing that has always calmed me down, no matter what. The place I go to hear myself think, to clear my head, to wash away tears. The only place I found momentary snatches of peace after Dad died.

The public pool is only a few minutes' walk away, and when I arrive, it's practically deserted. An uninterested girl in a tracksuit with her hair scraped back in a high ponytail hands over my change and a faded towel and points me toward the changing rooms.

Even the smell of chlorine and the wet tiles under my bare feet calm me down. It's like coming home, which is ironic, because even going home doesn't feel like coming home anymore.

There's one other swimmer laboriously pounding up and down the slow lane, and a janitor smearing a gray mop around at the other end of the pool, headphones over his ears. That's lucky, because I haven't got a swimsuit with me, so I slip into the pool as quickly as possible, hoping nobody pays close enough attention to realize I'm in my underwear.

The water receives me like a silky hug. The cold fluid slips over me like a balm, and I feel it rinsing away the dirt of the video, the shame of the painting, the frustration of the lost records. I feel free.

My arms slide powerfully through the surface, propelling me forward, and it's like I'm a seal that has been lumbering helplessly around on the shore, finally returning to my element. Here I'm safe. This is the one place I'm in control.

Maggie's necklace trails alongside me, glittering like treasure. The light pendant flutters and flashes, reflecting the light through the water.

I've always gone into a kind of trance when I swim. It's like my brain pauses and my body takes over. My breathing deepens and becomes as regular as a clock, air rushing out of my lungs and then swirling in as my face breaks the surface. In. Out. In. Out. In. Out. I don't need to think or try. I'm on autopilot. So, when the faded blue tiles rushing past my field of vision begin to blur and fade, I let it happen. I'm safe here.

The church is full of whispers. Neighbors and friends sit crushed in, wall to wall. The whole town has come, and girls you played at cooking with in the churchyard with a pie of mud and a stick to stir refuse to meet your eye. There is a strange, excited rumbling from the back of the crowd that develops into a kind of roar.

You do not understand why you are here. Somebody has roughly bound your hands behind your back, with rope that chafes and worries at your wrists. Your red hair tumbles before your eyes, and you shake it back impatiently.

Dead. Dead. Dead. There are so many whispers. Somebody is dead. But what has that to do with you? And why have they rushed you here, pulled by rough arms from your home while the babe wailed in your father's arms?

Even when you hear his name, you do not understand. Father of your child, lost to the waves, like so many other men before him in this tiny fishing village. Father of your child, lost at sea. Lost at sea. Lost.

You feel a dull ache, somewhere in the part of you that you still allow to feel. So there is no chance now of a different ending to your story. But what chance was there before? And why have they brought you here, to hear the news so publicly?

And then you make out a few words in the whispers and your blood turns cold.

"Witchcraft."

"No," you begin, but you choke on the words and nobody is listening to you anyway.

"The whore has sought her revenge," the pastor booms, his eyes glinting with a demonic energy, and the crowd bays at his feet like a pack of dogs.

"She waited for her chance!"

"Her punishment enraged her!"

"She could not bear to see him live!"

"The harlot must die!"

There is silence for a moment as the crowd catches its breath and yours is sucked clean out of your chest.

Then the voices begin to clamor again, and their excitement is rising, their faces turned hungrily toward you as if they would feast on you.

"I must protest." It is Stephen, the apprentice, his voice trembling, his face as white as chalk. He seems to quake under the disapproving glower of the pastor, but his face is set as he scrambles to his feet. "What evidence have we of wrongdoing? What possible proof of this most grievous sin?"

Your heart begins to beat again. There can be no proof. There cannot. This must be a nightmare; you will surely wake soon. You meet his eyes, and for a moment they steady you, willing you to keep your strength.

Somebody is shrieking in excitement, but your ears cannot or will not separate the words from the rest of the noise. And then you see it, borne toward you on a wave of eager hands. Blackened and twisted, its little face smeared in ash.

"A poppet!" they cry, and their voices are crazed now, and hoarse. A poppet bewitched to drown a man. And you think of your grandmother's stories about the Berwick witches who tried to kill the king, told to terrify on stormy nights while you huddled close to your brothers in bed. Your body ripples with fear.

"'Twas for my child," you beg, and it is strange because you did not know you were crying, but your cheeks are wet. "I could not form it right—"

"There is blood!" somebody screams, and the frenzy whips up higher still. "Blood on the cloth!"

"She will be tested!" the parson thunders with his fist raised to the heavens and his voice rumbling off the whitewashed walls as if God speaks through him to the people.

Hands are pulling at you now, pinching at your flesh and yanking your hair, and you stumble amid the crowd through the church and out, dragged backward by the mob to Inverie Burn where it burbles and rushes past the church toward the sea.

There's a place, hidden by a copse of trees, where the burn widens to a rushing pool and here they force you, sobbing now, your arms scratched and hair wild, into the seat of a rough-hewn wooden stool.

"Innocent, she drowns. Guilty, she floats. Innocent, she drowns. Guilty, she floats."

The crowd is chanting, their voices melting into one, as time slides into slow motion and your eyes scrabble frantically at the night sky.

Innocent drowns. Guilty floats. Innocent drowns. Guilty floats.

There is no space to speak, no time to breathe, no chance to think. Your wrists struggle frantically against their bonds and your skin crackles with fear as the stool extends over the surface of the water.

You open your mouth to shout your innocence again and the drop comes suddenly and brutally, without warning, smashing you into a confusion of water and pain, mud and cold and terror. The water floods into your mouth and pierces your chest. You splutter desperately, cough and claw toward the surface, but the twine still binds your hands and you are tethered to the stool. Your lungs burn and you begin to panic and twist, your hair like sodden ropes blinding you, fear searing through your body like acid. You will die.

But with a sickening thrust you feel the stool heave up, and your head breaks the surface as the water pours off your body in a surge, and the air floods into your lungs and burns them, and you cough and retch and gasp, and dimly you can hear the baying crowd, but you cannot speak before the water comes again and this time knocks you off the stool to whirl and tumble under the surface. Your knee cracks hard against a rock and sharp pain explodes behind it as you wrestle frantically with your ties, twisting your wrists against the twine that cuts into them like knives.

Your eyes are open, and the muddy water stings like sand, but you can sense as much as see the light above you, and you kick like a mad thing toward the surface, thinking only of your child as your muscles scream and your lungs threaten to explode. And then you're bobbing up again, your mouth half in, half out, gulping desperate breaths of air and water, half drowning as you try to breathe, your hands finally free, clawing at the bank, barely alive.

Alive enough.

GUILTY.

"Wait!" Stephen cries, but his voice is just one and they are so many. "This is too fast! We must pray on it."

But they shriek their satisfaction, arms reaching down like snakes to *drag you back into the mob and somewhere you can hear a voice begging, crying, and it sounds like yours, but the voice is very small and far away and it is swallowed by the crowd.*

I can't breathe. Water is filling me up from the inside out, and I choke, panicking. A pair of arms grabs me, roughly, under the armpits and drags me painfully out onto the side of the pool. I splutter painfully, retching chlorine into the plastic overflow grating.

"Are you all right, love?"

The janitor looks shaken, his face white, his mop abandoned, and the bucket kicked over in his haste to reach me.

"You looked like you were having some kind of fit. I thought you were going to drown." He's still holding on under my armpits as if he's worried I might slide back into the pool again if he lets go. "You looked like you took a nasty knock against the bottom of the shallow end." He nods toward my knee, where a deep purple bruise is forming.

I cough again and again, forcing droplets painfully out of my windpipe.

"I'm fine," I wheeze, pulling myself to sit upright, painfully aware of his eyes traveling farther up my legs to my underpants and bra, flushing as he realizes I'm not even wearing swimwear.

"Is everything okay?" he asks, suddenly looking as suspicious as he is concerned, and I swiftly force my aching legs to stand and thank him again before hurrying back into the changing rooms.

My mind is racing. The visions are getting stronger. I felt Maggie's panic like it was my own, felt her chest screaming for oxygen. If that janitor hadn't been there… Suddenly it occurs to me that I have no control over this. I don't choose when to visit Maggie in my dreams, and I don't decide when to return. Maggie's world is becoming clearer and bolder. What if my own starts to fade away? What if I can't come back?

I stand underneath the steaming shower and let the hot water soothe my aching muscles. I realize I'm afraid to find out what happens next.

THIRTY-SEVEN

I WALK THROUGH THE DOOR of my bedroom in a trance, barely remembering how I got here. Mum isn't home, and the laptop light is blinking at me.

I hold out for all of eight minutes before turning it on. I can't bring myself to look at the video again. But I'm relieved to see that not much seems to have changed. There are no new posts and even the number of comments seems to have slowed down.

I'm about to close all the windows when I notice the little red indicator at the top of my real Facebook profile. One new friend request. I click on it more out of habit than anything else. And then it's like time stops. My whole body feels as if it's stuck. I have to physically remind myself to breathe.

It's Dad.

My dad.

His picture. His name.

I draw a ragged breath and click on the profile. His face stares back at me. It's the picture they printed in the local paper with his obituary. *Local heart surgeon loses cancer battle.* His warm brown eyes, creased a little at the corners like somebody's just told a joke and he's halfway to laughing. His dark blue scrub cap in his hand. Blond hair slightly messy where he's taken it off. His ears. His chin. My chin.

They've filled in the location information so that at the top of his profile, where it would normally say Lives in: London or wherever, his says: Lives in: Hell.

I read on, even though the screen is blurring, even though everything inside me knows I shouldn't look.

So ashamed of my skank daughter. I'm glad I'm dead so I
  don't have to deal with people knowing I'm her dad.

It feels like every bone, every piece of muscle, every atom inside me is dissolving. Nothing has ever made me feel like this before.

I don't know how much time passes. I'm still staring at the screen when I hear the front door creak. Every thought of breaking the news to Mum has gone out of my head. I have to protect her from this. I'm shaking. Mascara has run down my cheeks until there's more black under my chin than on my eyelashes. I crack the door open and try to control my voice.

"Mum, I'm upstairs—I'm feeling really sick, so I'm just going to try and sleep."

"Oh, love, did you get sent home early?"

I can hear her tread as she climbs the first few stairs. Her voice is full of concern.

"Yeah, it's okay. I think I've just eaten something funny. I just need to sleep it off."

"Shall I bring you up some dry toast?"

"No thanks, I can't stomach anything—I've got a bottle of water."

"All right, darling, try and get some rest."

I ease the door closed again and bury myself under the duvet. But I take my phone with me and sleep doesn't come. Instead, my worst nightmares are coming true around me, and I'm powerless to wake up.

I log in to Snapchat and watch helplessly as the rumors spread. There's a group story with hundreds of snaps added by students in my class, some of them screen grabs of the fake profile, some of them photos of me, taken in class without me noticing, edited to circle my breasts or write *SLUT* across my forehead.

There are screen grabs of the porn clip, slightly blurred as if taken while it was playing, which makes it look even more realistically like the woman on the bed is really me. There are comments and jokes and highlights. Someone has even been through the porn video frame by frame, taking a thousand photos and adding a different filter to my face in each one. They've each been shared as individual snaps. Me on my back with sparkles all around me. Me looking up at the camera with huge fake eyelashes. Me doing it doggy style with a dog filter over my face. And, until twenty-four hours goes by without someone commenting, the story will run and run. It updates as I watch and I can't tear my eyes away. Every time I think there can't possibly be another new way to call me a whore, someone surprises me.

Once I've started looking, I can't stop. It's like I've been picking at the edge of a scab for days, and suddenly I've started ripping great pieces off more and more obsessively, no matter how painful it is. I'm flicking between different screens on my phone, and my laptop has four windows open, running a sordid revolving show of all the profiles, all the websites, all the photos, the porn site, and the anonymous Q-and-A profile.

There are pings and buzzes and flashing lights every few minutes, and the later it gets, the more the activity whirrs toward a frenzy. Sleep seems like a distant dream. I'm being sucked into the vortex, and the more I look, the faster it feels like I'm spinning.

Slut

A text of a photograph of me from several years ago, at Halloween, dressed as a cat, carrying a sign that said TRICK-OR-TREAT. Except the sign has been edited to read WANT TO SEE MY PUSSY? I turn the lights out and bury my head under the pillow.

My eyelids start to feel heavy, but then—

Whore

Another anonymous question. Have I screwed as many girls as guys, and would I like to expand my adult-movie repertoire?

I thrash in the bed, desperate to drown out the noise. I try to breathe slowly in and out, feel myself beginning to drift toward sleep...

Tramp

The profile of my dad adding a new picture, the same one as before, but with large cartoon tears crudely photoshopped falling down his cheeks. A speech bubble protrudes from its mouth. "Where did I go wrong to raise such a loose slut?"

I'm pacing the room now, frantically humming under my breath.

Thot

Tiredness is like a blanket around me, pulling me down, but every time my body is ready to succumb, there's something else.

A new snap featuring my naked breasts, an obscene cartoon nose scrawled below them so they look like eyes on a grotesque face.

Easy

By five in the morning, I think I'm going mad. My hair is matted and my eyes are red. My face is puffy in the mirror, and I don't recognize the haunted eyes that stare back at me. I have abandoned all hope of sleep. My phone has run out of battery and finally, blessedly, gone black. The sun is peeping above the horizon, its pale pink light creeping between the gaps in the curtain and filling the room with an ethereal glow. There is quiet. I sit on the bed and look down at my hands. Time suddenly stretches out in front of me. I'll never be able to change what has happened. Everybody who has seen it will have seen it forever. I can never change that.

I feel my body begin to slump, and I no longer have the strength to hold it up. In the rosy light of dawn, my eyelids finally flutter closed.

You huddle on a cold stone floor, every part of your body shaking uncontrollably. You are so cold you feel like part of the stone, as if you have been here in this tiny cell for a hundred years. Muddy water still drips from your hair and your lips have gone numb. You cannot stop shaking.

You have never felt so tired. They will not let you sleep.

At first, you screamed your innocence, beating at the bars in the door. Then they forced it onto your face, a monstrous mask of metal that pinched and bit at your flesh. The blade, cold and hard, protruding into your mouth, hard against your tongue, slashing at your every sound. You hated them for turning your screams into whimpers. You felt your energy begin to drain away.

That was hours ago. Now you start to see colors and shapes swimming in front of your eyes. It's difficult to focus. You think Jane was here, that she pressed her fingers urgently through the bars, weeping, and promised to take care of your child, but it is hard to remember and it may have been a dream.

The long, mournful face of the assistant priest, Stephen, surfaces. He is saying something about confessing, about forgiveness and mercy, but you do not understand. How can you confess to something you did not do? Admit something you never dreamed of? He speaks loudly, insistently, but his words are like raindrops pattering down around you without sinking in, and you gently turn your face away. You are so tired. If you could just rest, perhaps you would wake up and find that this was all a terrible dream. If you could just sleep, you feel sure you could explain.

You lay your pounding head against the damp stone wall and try to close your eyes. A sharp pain jolts them open. You look down, uncomprehending. A thin red line of blood trickles from your calf to mingle with the moisture on the wet, filthy floor. A thick needle, attached to a long stick, protrudes through the bars.

"You will not escape in sleep, witch," hisses a voice. You cannot see its owner. He stabs you again, the needle pricking and biting at your flesh. Your limbs are heavy, clumsy with sleep and numb with cold. You stumble away from the sharp pains, but they prod at you over and over. There is little room to escape. The stone walls press in on you relentlessly. The cold feels as though it is eating at your flesh. The little rivers of blood are multiplying, trickling down your arms, your hands, your legs. You are leaking. Your last reserves of energy are ebbing out with your blood. If you could just sleep for a moment.

Your eyes drift closed. Another pain. You groan in frustration, jerking awake. You try to beg for time, for peace, for just a few moments' rest. Your words are no longer working. What comes out is a stream of need. You mumble baby and guilt and alive and alone and outcast. You slur and shake your head. Try again. Your teeth are chattering. You cannot feel your feet. There is another line of blood. You look at it in quiet surprise. You did not feel it. A voice outside, raised in excitement. A string of shouts you cannot sort into syllables. You watch the blood snake gently between your toes. Hands grasp your foot, prodding at the cut. You are numb. You feel nothing. Your eyes roll back into your head and you slip gratefully into glorious darkness.

THIRTY-EIGHT

I BLINK GROGGILY AND RAISE a hand against the sunlight streaming onto the bed. For a moment, I feel my shoulders against the cold, hard floor of the cell, the bars of sunlight like the metal bars containing me. My mouth feels furry, and I swallow uncomfortably. I grope for my watch, trying to find my bearings. It's 7:00 a.m. I've only been asleep for a couple of hours. My head swirls with Maggie. The cold. The bridle. Waking the witch. It feels like a great effort to pull myself back into the present, to leave Maggie behind. My head throbs painfully.

My outstretched arm falls onto the still-open laptop. Sideways, through half-open eyelids, I see Glenn's name and *URGENT,* and I scramble to prop myself on my elbows.

I scan the first line or two of the email.

Diary—extremely rare—very exciting—answers to your questions about Margaret Morgan.

"How are you feeling, darling?"

Mum walks in, concentrating on not spilling a full cup of tea, which she carefully sets down on the bedside table. She leans over to place a cool, dry palm on my forehead and I remember my lie about feeling unwell. Suddenly it all rushes back over me. Mum. School. The truth.

"Not hot at least. But I wonder if we should make a doctor's appointment, just in case."

"It's okay." I catch her hand and pull her down to sit beside me on the bed. She strokes back my hair, and I wish I could just wait in this moment forever, feeling the comfort of her hand caressing me. I'm six years old again, puking into a plastic bowl, her steady hand holding back my hair. I'm eight, her gentle fingers cooling my feverish cheeks. I'm twelve, her smile reassuring on the pillow next to me while I fitfully sleep off the flu.

"What is it, love?"

I wait for a very long time. I'm afraid that when I open my mouth, my stomach will come out. I'm afraid that once I start talking, I won't ever stop. I'm afraid of what will happen to her face, and to her eyes. I'm afraid of the pain I know I'm about to cause her.

I don't have any choice.

"Mum, you have to come into school with me today." It comes out as a whisper.

"Oh, Anna, I need to tell work in advance if I'm taking time off. Is it a swimming match? I might have to come to the next one instead—"

"No," I say, in a tiny voice that ends in a sob.

She leans forward and puts her arms round me, and I smell her clean vanilla smell.

"What is it?"

And then I open my mouth, and it feels like my stomach does pour out, fast, all spewing and in the wrong order, a canvas mixed up with condoms and Cat and porn and phones and why don't you kill yourself, whore? Everything comes tumbling out in a rush. Everything except Dad. I can't do that to her. I won't ever.

I can't look at her while the words spill out of my mouth like water, so I twist my hands into the duvet and stare down at them as if my life depends on it. And, though I can't raise my eyes to her face, her hands are next to mine so I watch them as I talk and then they're on mine and holding them and even though the knuckles turn whiter and whiter, she doesn't let go.

When I finally stop talking, we both sit there, just breathing fast together as the sun creeps up our necks.

"Why didn't you tell me?" Her voice is croaky, and I can tell she's trying not to cry.

"How could I? You wanted this fresh start to work so badly." I look up at her briefly. A look of hurt flashes across her face and she looks like she's about to object, but she doesn't say anything.

"You've been trying so hard to make everything okay, Mum. For a long time now. After Dad—" I break off, trying to find the right words. "I think you wanted me to be okay so badly, you pretended you weren't broken either. But it made me feel like I couldn't show any cracks. I know you were trying to be strong for me, I know that. But it was too much. Too much pressure to pretend that everything was fine because you were doing such a good job of acting fine, and I didn't want to let the team down."

I risk another glance, and two fat tears are rolling down either side of Mum's nose, into the corners of her mouth. But she's nodding. And I feel the most enormous burst of relief. It's like there's been a fist in my chest, gripping my heart and my lungs, and suddenly, unexpectedly, it's let go. Suddenly I can breathe again.

"I'm so sorry, love. I just wanted to help you to move on."

"I know you did. I know. But I missed Dad. I missed him so much, and sometimes I wanted to be able to talk about him, without being all phony and pretending everything was fine. Being fine all the time was exhausting."

"I miss him too. Every day."

Just hearing her say it is a massive, massive relief. She sighs and wipes one of the tears away with the back of her hand.

"And when I brought you all the way up here…" She looks at me, trails off, inviting me to finish the sentence. She's giving me room to tell her the truth and it feels so freeing.

"It felt like you needed to fix it so badly."

She's nodding. "Of course I did. I couldn't bear to see you going through that. I just wanted to make it stop."

"But it made me feel—" I pause. "So ruined." I've never said it out loud, and I don't think I even completely knew it until I heard it in my own voice. "Like there was something so rotten about me that it was unfixable. We had to run away and pretend to be other people just to escape me."

"Oh, Anna. That's never what I wanted. You're perfect." She's got her hands on either side of my face, and she's looking me straight in the eyes like she wants to burn her words into my brain until I believe them. "My perfect girl. You're not the rotten one. I thought it was the best thing for you."

"I know. I get that. But when you uprooted your own life so I could get away from mine, it made me so terrified of letting you down, I felt like I couldn't even breathe."

"You could never let me down," she protests.

"Of course I could! You wanted me to be okay so badly, you couldn't let me not be okay. You'd have seen it as your own failure."

She shakes her head, but she's staring out of the window like she's seeing the garden for the first time, and I think maybe she's starting to get it.

"When your dad died"—she looks at me, then back out of the window, tears pooling again in the corners of her eyes, but she swallows and they don't fall—"I just wanted to pull you into my lap and never, ever let you go again. I wanted to wrap you up and keep you safe and never let you go outside. I wanted to put you back inside me where I could keep you safe forever. And then..." She falters, like she doesn't know how to say it.

"And then I got hurt."

She nods. "And I needed to make you safe again."

"So we ran away." She nods again.

"But it wasn't what I needed."

Wordlessly, she lies down, pulling me next to her on the bed and hugging me tight. We lie there like that for what feels like a long time.

"It just doesn't add up," I murmur, finally able to say it out loud instead of whirring around and around in my head. "How did they find me?"

"Oh."

Mum sits up so suddenly, she practically sends me flying off the bed.

"What?" I yank myself back from the brink.

"Oh, Anna."

"Mum, *what?*"

She has her hand over her mouth and her eyes are horrified. "I've been talking to Pat."

This takes me completely by surprise. Pat is Suzanne's mum. She and Mum were really close before everything that happened, but their friendship turned frosty when Suzanne and the others started distancing themselves from me after the photos first went round. I remember a night when I could hear Mum downstairs, shouting down the phone after she thought I'd gone to bed. ("Well, *talk* to her, Pat, you're her mother, for Christ's sake." And then a long pause. And then, "How dare you? My daughter does not pose a *risk* to yours. How dare you?" And then a sudden crash as the phone went down in the receiver.) And, when the girls started to join in the slut-shaming and the bullying, Mum and Pat broke off contact altogether. At least I thought they had.

"It was just a couple of phone calls," Mum is saying apologetically. "She got in touch out of the blue, and she was mortified about everything that happened, asking how we were and saying there wasn't any need for all this cloak-and-dagger secrecy."

Her eyes are glinting with anger.

"I told her a bit about where we were, how you were getting on—" She spreads her fingers. "It was before I'd made any friends at my new job. I didn't have anyone else to talk to. But…"

Mum watches me working it out, guilt written across her face.

"And you told her how I was," I say slowly, "including stuff about my new school and my friends?"

She nods, looking horribly guilty.

"Did you mention Cat by any chance? Was there anything—" I trail off. I can't imagine any possible way that Mum could have known. Unless...

"The kitchen window." She looks absolutely miserable. "It was open that night, when you were in the garden with the girls."

"Mum, how could you?"

"I wasn't listening in on purpose, Anna, I *swear*. I just opened it to let the steam out as I did the dishes and I overheard. I should have talked to you about it. I would have, except"—she looks wretched—"I was so happy you'd finally brought some friends home. I didn't want you to feel like you couldn't do that again."

"But what on earth made you tell Pat, Mum?" I still don't understand. I'm still grappling to catch up, to work out how this could have happened.

"It's what mums do," she says simply, spreading her hands out. "When we're worried about you, we talk."

"Worried?"

"Oh, come on, Anna. Overhearing my teenage daughter talking to her friends about abortion. Of course I was worried." She looks at me, appealing to me to understand. "I know those girls are wonderful friends now, but you have to remember, you hadn't known Lish and Cat for very long at the time. For all I knew, they could have been really bad news..." She trails off, looking mortified, then her face hardens and she hisses: "I cannot *believe* she passed

283

all that on to Suzanne." Mum looks like she's ready to strangle Pat with her bare hands, and it occurs to me it's quite lucky that we're hundreds of miles away. Lucky for Pat, that is.

"I can't believe Suzanne passed it all on to Chris and his friends," I say flatly. And perhaps for the first time, I truly accept that our friendship is over. I know Suzanne didn't create the fake accounts. She wouldn't have gone that far. And I know her well enough to know she would never have made that fake profile of my dad. But she still chose to tell Chris about my new school, about Cat, knowing he could use it to hurt me.

Mum is halfway to her feet before I grab her hand to stop her, already knowing with complete certainty that she's heading for the phone.

"Don't, Mum. It doesn't matter. Looking backward isn't going to help." And, as I say it, I realize it's true. The thought of Suzanne and Prav talking about Cat, turning over her most precious, painful secret in their hands like a bauble and then tossing it carelessly to Chris, makes my blood boil. I feel a wave of protective rage wash over me, and I know my loyalties have changed. I always thought that losing friends was a bad thing, that it would make me smaller and weaker. But now I know I don't need to hear from Prav or Suzanne again. I can leave them behind. And it doesn't make me weaker. It makes me so much stronger.

"I need to fight this myself. Somehow." I give a shaky laugh and add, "I have no idea how."

Mum is blowing her nose like a trumpet, and even though the tip is red and her cheeks are all blotchy, she has this look in her eye like the time a boy stole my lunch box when I was six and she strode into the playground and told him if he ever bullied me again, she would dip his feet in honey and tie him to a beehive.

"Well, the first thing we're going to do," she say grimly, "is go into that school and set a few things straight."

I hesitate. "There's something I have to do first. It's for my history project, and it really, really matters to me."

Mum gives me a long, hard look, and nods. "Tomorrow then. I'll call the school and arrange to come in during my morning break."

I give her one last massive hug, pull on a pair of jeans, and set off at a run toward Glenn's house.

THIRTY-NINE

"I'M NOT SURE HOW TO say this," Glenn murmurs twenty minutes later as I sit at his table, eagerly eyeing the old diary in front of him. For a horrible moment, I think he's going to tell me he hasn't been able to translate it after all.

"Was it not in Latin, then?"

"Oh no, it was quite easy to translate, for the most part. It's not that. It's just…" He takes a swig of coffee and pulls at his sideburns as if he's trying to buy himself time. "It might be difficult for you to hear what Stephen Browne has to say."

I feel strangely calm. After last night, I think I already know what's coming. But I have to know the whole story. Somehow, I owe it to her.

"Did he know Maggie?"

He nods. "It seems that Browne joined the parish as a parson's apprentice around the time of Maggie's pregnancy. Initially, he writes about his excitement at being assigned to his first congregation. He was very young and idealistic. Full of dreams about doing God's work."

"But it didn't turn out like that." I say it without meaning to, before I even think. Glenn shoots me a look of mild surprise.

"No," he says eventually. "It didn't. Though Stephen Browne was uncomfortable with the declaration of Maggie as a harlot and her punishment in front of the congregation, he writes in the diary that it isn't his place to interfere. Remember, this was his first-ever church placement, and from what he writes, the parson was a fearsome man who warned him to stay in line or risk being dismissed."

I'm gripping my mug of tea very tightly.

"Though he felt conflicted about his failure to intervene, he held his tongue, until some months later the aristocrat who had fathered Maggie's child was lost at sea in a tragic boat accident. Fired up by the parson and half-delusional with the excitement of witch hunting that was sweeping the country, a handful of kirk session elders and a mob of villagers dragged Maggie from her home and into an improvised trial."

I nod, turning Maggie's necklace over and over in my fingers. "Why didn't he do something to save her?"

"He tried," Glenn says, looking genuinely sad. "He did speak out on her behalf at that point at least. But by then—"

"It was too late."

"Yes. The parishioners were whipped into a frenzy, obsessed with seeing justice done, and convinced there was a witch in their midst. It seems some kind of doll was found to have been burned at Maggie's home, and that effectively sealed her fate. There was very little Stephen Browne could do to stop it."

"So they found her guilty?"

"Yes."

I whisper the question that I've yearned to have answered for weeks now and, even though I'm finally about to hear the answer, I dread it with every atom of my body.

"What did they do to her?"

Glenn looks at me as if he's trying to work out whether or not he ought to say. I gaze back at him fiercely, trying to look like someone who has it together and is definitely not about to burst into tears (as well as someone who has not already been in tears for a considerable amount of time today already).

"They burned her at the stake."

Everything goes flat. Even though I strongly suspected, some tiny part of me had hoped for a reprieve—wanted to believe that she'd been banished or something, never to return. My whole body feels heavy, dragging me down toward the ground.

"Stephen Browne was consumed by guilt," Glenn goes on, interrupting my thoughts, and I look stupidly at him, trying to process the idea that there is more to the story beyond this horribly final shock.

"Afterward, he spent months praying, trying to rid himself of the idea that it was his fault Maggie was dead. He couldn't bear that he might be to blame for what had happened to her, and, unusually for that time, he was obsessed with the idea that future generations would see the folly and evil of executing women for witchcraft."

"He didn't believe in it?" I ask slowly.

"No, he did not. In fact, he became so angry about the whole thing that he destroyed a great swathe of the church records, burning everything associated with Maggie's case."

"The missing kirk session records," I murmur.

"Whether he wanted to protect her reputation for future generations or erase his own part in the whole sorry tale isn't completely clear from his diary. I'm not even sure if he knew himself. But he left the Church after that."

"St. Monans Church?"

"No, the Church of Scotland. Changed course altogether and abandoned training for the priesthood."

"What happened to him afterward?"

"I don't know," Glenn says with a shrug. "The diary doesn't go on beyond that point."

I feel numb. Glenn seems to understand the enormity of what he's shared. He doesn't rush me to speak before I'm ready. We sit in silence for a little while.

"I think I might be living in Maggie's old house," I say at last, and his eyebrows jump about two inches.

"It's one of the really old fishermen's cottages down by the harbor, and I've found these marks around the doorway." I pull a piece of paper across the table and sketch out an imitation of the witches' marks. He studies them with great interest.

"Well—" He breaks off. I nod encouragingly. "This is no more than a guess, but the case would have been a huge scandal in the village—everyone would have gossiped about it. Whoever moved into Maggie's house after her father and brothers had moved on would have been terrified about the prospect of her ghost returning for revenge." He looks up and adds, "People were incredibly superstitious in those days, you see."

"No kidding."

"You have to remember that Maggie was seen as a powerful witch—one with the ability to kill a man—and as such she would have been feared, even after her death. Especially because witches weren't granted Christian burial...in fact..." He pauses, looking at me carefully as if he's somehow weighing me up, trying to work out whether to continue or not.

"What?"

"Well, there was a small loft room built into the spire of many churches during that period, including St. Monans Old Kirk. It was called the Brunt Laft, and its sides were open to the weather." He eyes me cautiously. "When a witch was burned at the stake, her ashes were deposited in the Brunt Laft afterward for the winds to disperse." He sighs heavily. "In those days, it would have been seen as a great punishment, even after death."

My throat aches. Poor Maggie. But then I picture her in my mind's eye, running breathless across the grassy hill in the sunshine, and I wonder whether maybe, for her, it wouldn't have been the punishment they thought. I take comfort in the idea.

Glenn is still talking. "So my best guess would be that the eventual new owners of her home would have taken every possible precaution—"

"To prevent her spirit from returning? Which might explain the witches' marks?"

"Exactly." Glenn beams with pride. "You've really picked up

a feel for the historical period, Anna. I think you're going to get a fantastic result." I look at him blankly. "On your project?"

"Oh. Thanks."

He peers at me closely, and it looks as if he's going to say something else, but he seems to think better of it at the last minute.

"Mr. Sinclair, could I ask you one last question?"

"Of course."

"I found a necklace...this necklace"—I slip it over my head and hold it out in the palm of my hand—"in my attic."

Glenn leans forward with interest. "May I?"

I feel a childish urge to clasp my fingers tight and pull my hand away, as if I'm betraying Maggie by letting anyone else handle the necklace. I force myself to let him take it. He runs his fingers over the same initials I've traced a hundred times.

"I know this sounds improbable, but I think the markings read 'MM,' and I was wondering if it might be Maggie's."

He rummages among a messy pile of documents at the end of the table and pulls out a small magnifying glass, peering through it at the pendant.

Impulsively, I press on, finding myself asking the question I hadn't intended to say out loud.

"I know how this sounds, but..." I take a deep breath. "I've been having these dreams." Glenn looks up at me but doesn't interrupt. "Really vivid dreams. About Maggie."

"Well, that's understandable. It's a fascinating story."

"No," I say quickly, shaking my head. "It feels like more than that. Like..." I trail off, unsure of how to say what I want to say without prompting Glenn to examine me for a serious head injury.

"I read something in a library book about people believing that witches could somehow transfer their feelings or memories into a special object and it makes no sense, because Maggie wasn't even a witch, and I'm probably just imagining things, but..." I trail off. "Do you think that's possible?" I whisper.

"Do you believe in God?" Glenn asks.

The question takes me by surprise. I hesitate, then shake my head uncertainly. "I don't think so. At the moment."

"Nor do I," he says. "But I don't know for sure. All I know is that I haven't experienced him directly."

I'm not sure what he's getting at.

"Just because people believe different things, it doesn't necessarily mean somebody is right and somebody is wrong. They've just had different experiences. Who am I to say that something doesn't exist simply because it hasn't personally revealed itself to me?"

It's a generous answer. He hands the necklace back, and I fasten it wordlessly around my neck again, smiling.

"Is there any other reason you've been thinking a lot about Maggie?" he asks, and I don't answer.

"This isn't the first time you've arrived during school hours," he says as gently as he can.

"It's...complicated." There's no way I want Glenn to know the whole sordid story. A weird part of me feels this huge desire to impress him, like somehow I want to make him proud of me. He thinks I'm a good historian. I don't want him to see me as the girl whose tits are plastered all over the internet. "I guess you could say I've been identifying with Maggie." I try to give a light laugh and find an unexpected lump in my throat instead.

"I've been using a wheelchair since I was eight years old," Glenn says suddenly, and when I look up, surprised, he's giving me his crinkly smile.

"But, when I was at university in my early twenties, I used to get a friend of mine who was a medical student to put my leg in a plaster cast up to the hip."

This is so unexpected, I burst out laughing, and Glenn chuckles too.

"Why?" I ask. "Was your leg painful?"

He shakes his head. "No. But I wanted people to think of me as a normal person who had just broken a leg, instead of a disabled person."

"What difference would that make?"

He smiles. "Quite a lot actually."

"Why?"

"Because suddenly they saw me as a person instead of a wheelchair."

"Oh."

He laughs. "It's a trick I grew out of as I grew into myself. But I just thought..." He looks at me carefully as if he's trying to find the right words. "It's worth knowing that sometimes people see you as a symbol of something, instead of a person. And, when they do, it reflects on them, not on you."

I feel a sudden huge urge to hug him. But instead, I smile, and thank him very much indeed for his help.

As I leave Glenn's house for the last time, I think about Maggie, and about her daughter.

I've read something, in one of my research books, a saying that goes: "We are the granddaughters of the witches you could not burn."

I think about Maggie, about the necklace, about her baby, about walking in her shoes. I feel like a little piece of her is inside me now, holding me up, helping me to stand straighter. And I whisper to myself: "We are the granddaughters of the witches you burned. And we're not putting up with it anymore."

FORTY

VERY SLOWLY, THINGS INSIDE MY head are shifting into different places. I know I need to go home, that Mum and I have a lot more talking to do. But there's one more thing I have to do first.

There's no sign of the gardener or anybody else. The grass is neatly trimmed and a few half-dead flowers stuck into little pots at the bases of the gravestones wave in the wind. I stand at the top of the cliff and look out at the restless sea. And this time Maggie's world slips effortlessly into mine.

Everything is moving fast, too fast, and the moon is red and the crowd jostles as you're dragged along the stony ground outside the church and everyone is shouting and there's wood. What wood? Why are they tying you to the wood? And Jane is there and she has your baby, has your heart outside your body, and you reach out toward her with your final strength, and she stretches and your fingertips touch, and you press your necklace into Jane's hand, and you see her slip it around the baby's chubby neck.

You hear crackling loud in your ears, and your brain strains to process what is happening. Their faces—Suddenly you are overwhelmed by rage and frustration and the unfairness of it, but it's getting harder to breathe.

The flames are beautiful and sear with pain. They lick you with tongues like blades, and you are skin and blood and fire and all your body's screaming.

Your eyes frantically search the crowd and find Stephen, his stricken face, and he cannot meet your eyes, but quickly looks away, and you see his suffering too, but you cannot care, there isn't time, and then you find her, tiny in the crowd, innocent in the melee, and you drink her in with your eyes until she fills you up and time stands still for just long enough.

And then Jane wraps a cloak around her, and she meets your gaze with terrible pain in her wet eyes, and you force yourself to nod although your throat is bursting, and she turns and takes her, and it's right, but it breaks you and the sobs come, but with each one that shakes your body, you picture the life she'll have with Jane and she'll be safe and fed, and it lets you stand a little straighter because it's all that really matters now.

Smoke chokes you and you cannot breathe. Your chest screams. Your throat is fire. Your eyes stream. There are only moments left now. And suddenly you feel the sharpest sadness for the things you didn't know you loved. You want to feel the water warm on your skin in the tub before the fire one more time. You need to taste the crispness of a season's first apple as the juice runs between your fingers. You cry for the smell of autumn air and the feel of grass under bare feet and the roughness of bark under your hands. You stand among the bright halo of your own hair and you are ravenous for the whole sky and you raise your eyes to it and it is as black as pitch, but the stars are shining.

My cheeks are glassy with tears and the wind whirls my hair around my face like a wild thing. I feel a heavy sense of grief and, somewhere underneath, a deep, still peace. It's over now. Very gently, I lift the silver chain over my head and let it pool in the palm of my hand like a spool of thread. I don't know how it found its way back to Maggie's house. Perhaps her daughter hid it there, in later years. Perhaps it was handed down through the family, and then forgotten. It doesn't matter. I know that Maggie doesn't need me anymore. She has sent her message and now she's free.

I stand there for a very long time, feeling the tears dry on my face as the waves pound the cliff and the wind moans around the church. And then, very gently, I let the necklace slide like water through my fingers to the sea below.

FORTY-ONE

WAITING OUTSIDE THE HEAD OF school's office the next morning is one of the most nerve-racking moments of my life.

It's second period and everyone else is in class, but I'm waiting for Mum to arrive, staring at the shiny door with its brass HEADMASTER plaque, wondering what's going to happen. I'm trying desperately not to think about last time, not to feel a horrible sense of déjà vu. If we have to leave here, I don't know where there is left to run to.

As I sit there, lost in my thoughts, a familiar scruffy jacket rounds the corner of the corridor.

"Hey, Robin!" I call, and he stops, peering at me around a pile of books, panting as he rushes to yet another lesson five minutes late.

He doesn't exactly look thrilled to see me, and he approaches cautiously, as if he's not sure if I'm going to explode at him again. I guess I can't blame him.

"Hi."

"Hi."

Suddenly I have no idea what to say. "So," I say slowly. "I owe you a thank-you."

"Oh yeah. For fixing your terrible algebra? I knew you'd thank me eventually."

"Yeah, no. For the…the other thing."

He shrugs. "They had it coming." He smiles and that dimple appears next to the edge of his mouth. "You were having a pretty bad day the last time we spoke, huh?"

"You could say that, yeah. But I didn't mean to take it out on you."

"I figured."

"It was like when you're trying really hard not to cry, and then someone comes and starts being all nice to you and you hate them for it because it makes the tears come."

"I know."

Suddenly I'm very aware of how quiet and empty the corridor is.

"How are you, anyway?" He looks at me, and it's like he can see into my head. Immediately, the picture pops up in my mind's eye, stubborn and vivid. I blush. I hate the idea of him thinking about it. I hate the idea of it living on in his mind.

"I'm fine." *I'm not.* "Things are okay." *They're not.* The reality hangs between us, but he doesn't challenge me.

He takes a step forward and looks me right in the eyes, his face just inches away from mine, almost challenging me to tell him to back off. I don't. I try not to breathe too loudly and wonder if he can smell my breath.

"I never looked at the photos, Anna."

"What?"

"I'm not very big on social media." He gives his easy, lopsided smile. "I heard about it, but I didn't see them."

"And you didn't go looking?"

"No, I didn't."

"Well, you're the only one." I say it harshly, almost accusingly, like I'm throwing the words at him to see if they'll push him away. But he just keeps standing right there in front of me.

"I don't care."

"Why not?"

"I'm not a Tralfamadorian."

It's so unexpected, I laugh out loud. Tralfamadorians are the aliens from *Slaughterhouse-Five*, who see every moment in history at the same time, so when they look at a person they see their past and present and future selves all at once. I think I know exactly what he means, but I wait, hoping he'll explain it anyway.

"When I look at you, I'm not seeing everything that's ever happened to you. I'm just looking at you. Now."

"Not looking at old pictures?"

He's so close, I could count his eyelashes.

"Nope."

"What about seeing the future?"

He smiles and leans forward so that his lips brush my ear.

"Just this moment. Right now."

And, right now, that's all I need to hear.

FORTY-TWO

"NO," SAYS MUM FIRMLY, AND I'm not the only one in the room whose head swivels toward her in surprise.

We're sitting on two hard, uninviting wooden chairs in Greaves's office, the headmaster in a leather seat behind his desk.

"I'm sorry, Mr. Greaves," Mum continues, in a steely voice I have rarely ever heard, "but my daughter will not be forced to stay away from school because of somebody else's bad behavior. She has done nothing wrong. What I would like to know is what measures this school will be taking to tackle those who have been hounding her."

Mr. Greaves smiles uncomfortably and glances around the room as if he's looking for support.

"Well, Mrs. Reeves," he begins, speaking slowly and clearly as if Mum is stupid, which does nothing to calm down the vein that's gently starting to twitch in the side of her neck. "I do appreciate that you're concerned for your daughter's well-being, but we must face the facts." He gives a silly little smile and a half shrug as if to show how helpless he is in the situation, and I almost feel sorry for him because he doesn't seem to have realized that there is no arguing with Mum when her mouth is set in a straight line and the white dents are showing on the sides of her nose.

"We do have to take into account Anna's—ah—choices…" He says it delicately, looking over my head as if he thinks he's doing me a favor by not being more specific. As if we don't all know exactly what we're here about.

"We have always made it very clear at St. Margaret's that we are happy to support our students when they experience difficult times. But we also make it extremely clear what we expect from them. I am truly sorry that Anna was placed in a situation in which she presumably felt she had no choice but to create these images. But their creation and distribution is nonetheless a very serious act, and one which the school has no choice but to take seriously.

"It's a shame that Anna didn't feel able to confide in a member of the school staff sooner. Please rest assured that now the situation has been brought to our attention, we will be thoroughly investigating the circumstances that led to these events and any student who was involved in unkind behavior will be punished accordingly."

He pauses, wiping the sweat from his top lip.

"However, we cannot discount the undeniable part that Anna played in this. She made a choice that has had very serious consequences, and for her own sake and that of the other students, it is very important that she learns to take responsibility for those consequences."

"Responsibility?" Mum asks, so softly that I'm not sure Greaves even hears her.

"It is my hope," Greaves continues, "that dealing with this in a strict, zero-tolerance manner may in fact be greatly beneficial to our female students, by helping to avoid these—ah—very unfortunate situations arising in the future."

He spreads his hands expansively as if to communicate the favor he is distributing to the girls of St. Margaret's.

"I must be frank with you, Mrs. Reeves. In light of Anna's actions, and our need to send a very clear message about this type of behavior, the school feels that it might simply be best for all involved if she were to continue her education elsewhere after the midterm break."

I feel my stomach sink toward my shoes. Start again.

Move again. Run again.

"No," Mum says again, and this time a little bit of spittle flies out of her mouth and lands on Greaves's forehead. He freezes, his eyes darting back and forth as if he wants to wipe it off, but doesn't dare.

"I'm not sure I quite understand your position," Mr. Greaves says politely as if this is just a silly misunderstanding.

"I'm not at all sure I understand yours," Mum replies evenly and, even though I can't see how she can possibly turn this around, I want to cheer.

Mum pauses, and he clears his throat as if he's about to have another go at explaining how I need to leave before I infect the other students. But Mum holds up a hand, and the words die in his throat.

Her voice is even lower and quieter. "Let me just make sure I have got this exactly right. My daughter"—Mum's voice is almost quivering—"while in your care, has been subjected to an extended campaign of misogynistic bullying and abuse, some of it bordering on illegal. It has involved numerous pupils at your school creating fake pornography using her image and sharing nude photographs of an underage girl without her consent."

She looks at him as if she's daring him to interrupt or disagree.

"My daughter, on the other hand, has done absolutely nothing wrong since starting at your school. The photograph you have accused her of spreading was taken, privately, over a year ago, and shared without her knowledge or consent. Its resurfacing is in no way her fault or choice. Indeed, it has made her life an absolute misery."

She's standing up now, towering over Greaves's desk.

"I must have misheard because it sounded to me for a moment like you were threatening to expel Anna, while so far having utterly failed to discipline the students responsible for her suffering."

The headmaster is opening and closing his mouth weakly like a fish.

"Please try to understand," he says, and he's almost pleading with Mum like a schoolboy now, their positions reversed. "Put yourself in my shoes. Social media has created a plague of new problems, and we're just trying to catch up. The situations it has created for these young girls are dreadful, and we simply have to stamp it out. Yes, we are aware that boys are often involved, but ultimately these are young women with their own minds and choices, and we simply have to make it clear that girls who choose to share these images are doing themselves a huge disservice and will face consequences. How else are we supposed to stop it happening?"

"No," says Mum for the third time, and I almost burst into spontaneous applause. "Boys are responsible for their own behavior. They are quite capable of controlling themselves. The school should make this very clear to them." I'm singing inside, every part of me fizzing with Mum's rage and righteousness.

"Here's what's going to happen. You are going to investigate the bullying that has been going on, fully punish those responsible, and take action to ensure these social-media pages and obscene materials are removed from the internet immediately."

She pauses and casts a scathing glance at Greaves, whose hands are hanging slackly by his sides as if he doesn't know what to do with them.

"You will train your staff in dealing with these cases so that future victims are not blamed and shamed for their own abuse."

Greaves has gone an ugly shade of pink. But Mum hasn't quite finished.

"If you are extraordinarily lucky, I will choose not to sue this school for the harassment and abuse of my daughter, which, by the way, breach her human rights under the Equality Act to an education free from harassment and discrimination on the grounds of her sex."

Without waiting for a response, Mum starts gathering her bag and keys from the floor and swipes her coat off the back of the chair. Then, as an afterthought, she adds: "She will be in class tomorrow morning as usual."

With that, she sort of rises from her chair as if her anger is carrying her on a wave, and I swear the office door swings open in front of her outstretched hand before she even touches it. She doesn't even look at me. I hesitate for a second and glance at Greaves, but he's staring after her, openmouthed, so I let myself be swept along in her wake and don't bother to stop the door slamming behind me.

I want to punch the air and hug her, but Mum's still breathing heavily, and she's moving so fast it's all I can do to hurry along at her heels. I'm struggling to compute what has just happened.

Then we're in the car, and Mum's hands are gripping the steering wheel, and she's driving steadily and looking straight ahead, and she still has that weird, steely look on her face, and we pull into the traffic in silence.

After about five minutes, without warning, she suddenly veers into a turnabout, screeches to a halt, slumps over the steering wheel, and bursts into tears.

"Mum? You. Were. Amazing." I put a tentative hand out and pat her shoulder, and she wipes the tears from her eyes with both hands and gives me a weak smile.

"I should have done it sooner. I should have done it last time. But I just wasn't prepared. I never thought something like this would happen, and I was in such a state, it all just felt so overwhelming, and I couldn't see through the fog." She runs out of breath and draws another huge, shuddering gulp of air. "Running just seemed like the only real option. But it wasn't. It wasn't right."

I smile at her. "It's enough that you did it now. It was *brilliant.*"

FORTY-THREE

THAT NIGHT, I SLEEP A dreamless sleep for the first time in weeks.

When I open my eyes the next morning, there are two cats sitting on the end of my bed.

"Hi," says Cat, stroking Cosmo gently under the chin.

"Hi," I say. "What time is it?"

"Just before six a.m. Your mum came around early this morning and told me everything. I mean, *really* early."

"And you let her?"

"Well, it's not so easy to shout at a grown-up and storm off." She gives a teeny, tentative smile.

"Are you really here? Am I still asleep?" I make a big show of pinching myself, and she rolls her eyes and throws a pillow at my head.

I pull my knees up to my chest, still snuggled under the duvet. Cat swings her legs in under the duvet at the other end of the bed, and we sit, looking at each other.

"So," I say eventually. "I *told* you I would never do that to you." I don't know what's wrong with me, why I sound so accusing. Until this moment, I thought Cat being my friend again was what I wanted more than anything. But, now that she's here, I'm suddenly finding it hard not to be mad at her for how long it's taken. Why didn't she believe me before?

"I'm sorry. It just felt impossible. There was no way anyone else could have known. I never even told Toby. And I knew Alisha would never lie to me."

A small, begrudging part of me does understand that. Their friendship goes back years and years, even though it feels like a bruise to remember that I'm still catching up.

"I get that. I just wish you'd have given me the benefit of the doubt too."

"I know. Next time I will. Not that there's going to be a next time, I hope." She smiles grimly. "It was just such a shock. One minute we were standing there on the pier, everyone's phones buzzing, people talking about you. It all happened so fast. It was hard to know what was going on. Then suddenly people started looking at me, whispering behind their hands, laughing..."

She pauses and takes a shuddering breath. "Those next few days were some of the worst of my life. It was like I'd been labeled, like I could never escape it. Like nothing I ever do in the future will be able to erase this. It'll always be who I am."

"I know the feeling."

"I know." She looks apologetic. "I know you've been going through something so similar. I know it's stupid that I didn't realize sooner you wouldn't have put yourself through all that. But I couldn't think straight at the time. It was like—"

"Like a million people were shouting inside your head every second, even when you were alone in your bedroom?"

"Yeah. Like that. I'm sorry, Anna."

"I'm sorry too. I'm sorry my mum was listening to us. I'm sorry my messed-up past sucked you into the chaos too."

"It's worth it."

I look at her quizzically, not sure I understand.

"It's worth dealing with your messed-up past if it means getting to have you as a friend."

My hand reaches out by itself and grabs hers. And then I'm holding her other hand too.

As I pull her into a massive hug, the door opens, and there's a screech and a whirl of braids flying through the air, and Cosmo darts under the bed, and suddenly Alisha and Cat and I are all tangled up in my duvet, and everybody's talking at once and I feel happy, really happy, for the first time in weeks.

"What are you doing here? It's six thirty in the morning!"

"Cat texted me. My big brother just got his license and he's desperate to drive anywhere right now, so I woke him up and paid him to bring me over."

I look at them both beaming at each other, and my cheeks feel weird and I remember that this is what smiling feels like.

But then there's a little *ping* and we all look over at the laptop squatting on my desk like an evil goblin. I sigh heavily and reach over to pull it onto my lap, and Alisha and Cat rest their chins on each of my shoulders as I wearily open the window.

There once was a young girl from Fife

Who wanted to ruin her life

So she posted her twat

All over Snapchat

Now she'll never be anyone's wife

I sigh and close the screen, and we all sit huddled together while Cat and Lish rub my back and say nice things. Cat makes a weak joke about how shit their poetry is and says she doesn't want to be anyone's wife anyway and is that the worst threat they can come up with, and Lish murmurs something about how it's going to get better, and they'll run out of steam eventually. But we all know that's not how it works. It might get a bit better after a while. But I'll still always be *that girl*. The taunts won't go away, not completely. It'll always be waiting just beneath the surface, any time anyone wants a stick to beat me with. It's there online, waiting for new people to find when I meet them. The whispers won't die. The insults will never stop. You don't exactly bounce back from being branded the class slut.

"Basically," Lish muses, "we need something to break the spell."

Cat sits up and crosses her legs. "Go on."

"We've got to somehow snap them out of it. It's like a group mindset, right? They all think the same thing. But what if we could get them to see it differently?"

"Right," Cat jumps in eagerly. "Like everyone just thinks the same thing because that's the way it's always been."

"Exactly." Lish grins. "Peer pressure is a powerful and ancient force."

I look skeptical.

"You can raise your eyebrows all you like, but in Strasbourg in 1518 a group of about four hundred people all started dancing obsessively together, and they were so worked up into a frenzy by one another that they didn't stop for months! It was called the dancing plague!"

She pauses dramatically, and Cat and I look at each other and crack up.

"*It's true!*"

"Okay, Professor Alisha," Cat says, wiping tears from her eyes, "what did they do to stop it?"

Alisha's face falls. "Oh. Well, most of them just died of heart attacks or heatstroke in the end."

"Great plan, Lish. Really top-notch. Just wait till they all drop dead."

We all subside into thoughtful silence.

"You could do that thing," Alisha says, "where you write a letter to everyone who's bullied you and then burn them."

"Sure, but then what would she do with all the letters?" Cat jokes.

We lapse into silence again.

Suddenly I turn to them both with a grave expression. "You guys, since we're being all open and honest about everything, I have a confession to make."

"Oh God," says Alisha, "what now?"

I try to keep a straight face. They both look worried.

"I ate the school stew. And…I kind of liked it."

Alisha shakes her head sorrowfully. "I knew it was too good to last." She starts pretending to pack up her things. "It was nice knowing you, Anna."

Cat starts singing under her breath to the tune of "I kissed a girl and I liked it." "I ate the stew and I *liiiiiked* it…"

Ping.

Our heads all swivel toward the laptop. This time I don't even open the screen.

FORTY-FOUR

WALKING INTO THE CAFETERIA WITH Lish and Cat by my side is a million times better than the torture of the last few weeks. But the whispering doesn't stop. And it still hurts.

Catherine of Aragon. Anne Boleyn. Jane Seymour. Anne of Cleves. Katherine Howard. Catherine Parr.

Ignore it. Ignore it. Ignore it.

Divorced, beheaded, died, divorced, beheaded, survived.

Now that I come to think of it, listing Henry the Eighth's wives to try to drown out the noise wasn't exactly a good omen. But I had to learn them for a history test anyway, and at least it's doing its job of keeping my brain occupied. But then we sit at our usual table, and someone hisses something and I've had it. I've just had enough.

Everything in me strains to run away—just to sprint out of the door and run and run—but I know that if I give in to that urge, I'll never stop. And I'm so tired. I need to stop running now.

So I let the whispers envelop me like a gentle tide, and instead of fighting, I drift with them, into the center of the room, and I'm climbing on a plastic chair, and I can see Cat and Alisha looking at me in confusion and then looking at each other in horror, their eyes telegraphing "What on earth is she doing? This is social suicide!" And now I'm standing on a table like some kind of absurd, terrified street-corner preacher. And I wait.

It doesn't take long for the first shout to come.

"Planning to treat us to a pole dance, Reeves?"

Anxiety and shame start to flicker up my legs. And the laughter starts. The heat quickly reaches my stomach, and I can feel sweat standing out under my hairline and starting to trickle uncomfortably down my back.

But I answer. Just the truth.

"No."

They laugh more then, and the comments ripple, and suddenly I wonder if this was a terrible idea.

"She needs to get a better view to spot the last guys in Fife she hasn't shagged yet."

I see Alisha and Cat wince and clasp each other's hands, and I feel the heat creeping up toward my chin. But somehow, I force myself to open my mouth, though my throat is so hot and dry that my voice is just a croak.

"You're all talking about me anyway. I might as well answer."

There's another ripple of snickering, and I can see people

rolling their eyes and whispering behind their hands, and I almost just jump off the table and run because what on earth am I doing and how much longer can I take this?

But then, through the haze, I see Cat and she catches my eye and smiles like she's proud of me, and I remember I'm doing it for her too, and for other girls as well, and I lock my eyes on hers and try to breathe in a little air though the oxygen is being sucked out of the hot room.

"What is this, a public slutpology?" someone yells, and laughter fills the cafeteria.

I think of Maggie. The dreams flash like pictures through my head, and I remember her fear and her confusion and shame and the way she was punished for everybody else's ideas about her, instead of who she really was, and I think of her child and I think of her courage, and I feel a rage and a hotness burn from inside me as well as out. And slowly I tell the truth.

"It's not an apology because I'm not sorry. I'm not sorry I took the photo. I'm sorry it was taken from me."

My lungs are struggling, and it feels like the heat is consuming me, burning me all over with shame. I think I'm going to faint. I stumble, and in slow motion as if I'm watching from above, I see myself start to fall.

And then a miracle happens.

I stumble, but I catch myself. And, as I resurface into the crackling heat of the stares and the hate and disgust, I see Cat and Lish standing quietly behind me. And next to them is Emily Winters. She looks steadily back at me and nods. So, with the last strength I can summon, I keep going.

"I'm not sorry I took it. I'm sorry it was taken from me."

Someone hisses, "*Shame*," and the hissing is like a snake and like steam, and it's hot, hot, hot all around me until my eyes hurt, but I have to keep going or I'm going to dissolve, and so I gather every scrap of energy and I force myself to keep talking.

"I'm not ashamed of my body. I'm ashamed of the way my body was treated by everybody else. I'm not embarrassed because it's sexual. I'm embarrassed because it's being used in a way I didn't agree to."

Like a mirage, as I'm speaking, I can see somebody else standing up too. It's Lola. And she's moving through the tables and standing silently next to Emily. And it's the strangest thing, but suddenly the air feels a little cooler, and I find that I am beginning to breathe.

Someone coughs loudly and deliberately, only half muting the word "slut."

"Tell me what one is and I'll tell you if I am."

Just for a moment, there's silence for the first time, before laughter breaks out again and someone whistles. But the atmosphere has shifted. People are looking at one another; one or two are frowning. They're less certain. The heat is rippling on my arms the way the sky shimmers at the end of a summer's day when the sun has lost its fire. And somebody else is standing up.

"Does a slut like sex? I don't know. I haven't had sex yet." There are a few mocking howls and people nudge their friends, but others don't seem to know where to look, and my vision is beginning to clear.

And I can see another girl, and then another, and even a few boys standing up hesitantly and moving to stand silently with the others. I see Robin, his eyes twinkling at me, and Martin is standing next to him, looking nervously at the other boys, but holding his ground nonetheless. Lola and Emily have linked their arms behind me like a kind of shield, and Simon is looking from one to the other, and I swear I actually see his pupils dilating.

"But if I did have sex, I don't think it would change who I am." I wait for a moment, and I realize that there are more of them now, standing behind me, and this time for the first time, nobody shouts, so I keep going. "No more than having an abortion would change who I am. Or breaking up with someone, or having sex with someone who used to date someone else. You can never fully know what someone else is going through. There's no one type of person who does any one of those things. We're all still just people.

"Does a slut kiss boys? Because I have, and I probably will again. But so have lots of you. You can call me a prude, and you can call me a whore, but really you're just calling me a girl. I am a girl. But those other things are yours. They're in your minds, not mine."

There's a long silence this time, and someone throws a scrunched-up ball of paper, which patters harmlessly against my leg and drops foolishly to the floor. And this time nobody laughs.

"Is it a body that makes a slut? A body that's seen? Then I'm guilty. But it's just a piece of flesh, like yours and everybody else's. It doesn't make me good, or bad, or loose, or tight, or valueless. It's just a stomach. Just a breast. Just a calf."

Silence.

"It's you who've made me a slut. All of you. I didn't have to do anything at all."

The flames have gone. I feel coolness washing over me like a balm, and suddenly, for the first time in weeks, I feel peaceful. I'm very tired now. I look at Cat and Alisha, and they each reach a hand up toward me and it's time.

So I climb down from the table and I take their hands, and we walk out together into the fresh air.

EPILOGUE

THINGS GET BETTER. SLOWLY. IT'S not like magic, but it heals.

Mum and I are hesitant with each other, testing out our renewed closeness, relearning each other day by day. Robin comes over for dinner, and she nearly manages to play it cool... Of course, she almost knocks all the wind out of him with a massive bear hug as he leaves, but he just raises his eyebrows and smiles that dimpled smile at me over her shoulder.

I think about Maggie constantly. I spend most of spring break writing up my project, trying to separate the facts I can trace back to books from the dreams I can't explain.

I lie awake at night, counting the beams in my bedroom ceiling and wondering if she counted them too. I walk along the cliff path on a calm, dry day and think of her battling against the storm to confront the man who hurt her so badly. I stand at the very edge of the cliff, the church looming behind me, and look out at the waves. There's nothing left to mark the spot where Maggie died. I think about her life dissolving into the wind.

But I know Maggie lived. I know how she died. And that's enough. She won't be forgotten.

We spend our break outdoors as the weather slowly gets warmer, lounging on the grass in Cat's garden, eating ice pops and proofreading one another's history projects.

The sun shines down at us through the leaves, and we've all rolled up our jeans and stuck our legs out, dipping them into its golden dye. There's just one late spring day left before school starts again. I lie on my back, staring up at the pattern the leaves make against the sky, and realizing that I never felt this comfortable before, even with my so-called best friends back in Birmingham. There was always that tiny part of me worrying what they were thinking of me, second-guessing them. With Cat and Alisha, it doesn't even cross my mind.

"It's going to be different," Alisha says, propping herself up on her elbows and looking at me as if she can read my mind. "Better. People will have moved on."

I try to smile. "Yeah." I glance over at Cat, who is chewing on a piece of grass, frowning at her laptop.

"A lot of it's still there, though. Waiting for people to find. It bothers me that that's the version of me that's out there online. That I can't take it back."

I pick at the bark on the tree trunk behind my head.

"Maybe I should just get really radical plastic surgery so nobody recognizes me," I say gloomily.

Cat and Alisha exchange a look which they clearly think is surreptitious, but I catch it.

"Don't pity me," I tell them grumpily.

"What you really need," Alisha says slowly, "is something else that takes over—drowns out the stuff that's already online and pushes it down the search listings. Something that puts it all to bed, once and for all."

"Oh yeah. If only it were that simple."

Suddenly her eyes widen, and she grabs Cat and starts whispering urgently into her ear. Cat's mouth twitches in surprise, and she seems to sparkle with excitement.

"Yes!"

"What?"

They're both grinning at me like Cheshire cats and, even though I cannot imagine they could possibly have thought of something that can ever begin to fix this mess, I can't help grinning back.

Five minutes later, I'm lying on top of Cat's duvet in my underwear.

Cat pokes her tongue out of the corner of her mouth with concentration as she peers at the sharpened eyeliner in her hand. "Hold still," she barks.

I try to slow down my breathing so my stomach won't jiggle so much, but it's hard when it feels like a band of butterflies is dancing under my ribs.

"Sorry, it tickles. And I'm nervous."

She frowns and uses her thumb to smudge out a small mistake on my shoulder.

When my front is finished, I try to get up. But Lish and Cat are whispering to each other, and they pull me back and smush me down face-first on the bed, and the tickling starts on my back as well.

"Uh, guys?" I say, my voice muffled. "I'm not sure that's really necessary. I think the front is enough."

"Shh," Lish hisses firmly, squashing my face back down so I get a mouthful of pillow. I obediently subside.

Ten minutes later, I stand nervously in front of the mirror, my eyes closed. I hear the camera shutter click and Lish gasps.

"Oh my gosh. You need to see this."

I pull on Cat's dressing gown and join her, leaning over Cat's shoulder.

I'm standing, staring straight at the camera. The light from the window outlines me so I'm almost glowing.

In beautiful, scrawling calligraphy, they have covered my entire torso with words. Words snake round my belly button and curve into my hip. They entwine my collarbone and interlace my ribs. Cat ran out of black eyeliner, so they moved on to green and then blue and then different colored lip liners and glitter pencils. It's like I'm wearing a fine rainbow net of words. I think of Maggie.

My body is a canvas of quotes. They are all real. And they are all signed.

How baggy is your vagina now anyway?
Simon Stewart, May 5

Slut is probably disease-ridden
Mark Chambers, May 3

Fucking whore, why don't you kill yourself?
Anon., May 1

Cat really is a brilliant photographer. She's captured me slightly turned away from the camera, my eyes slanting almost closed, my hair cascading down my back, the dying sun turning my curls bronze. I look powerful. I look defiant. I look beautiful.

I'm ready. I smile at them and swallow the lump in my throat. "Let's do this."

"Wait," Cat says. "You haven't seen the second photo." She taps a key, the screen changes, and I'm looking at my own back.

I'm holding my hair out of the way, but one curl has escaped, tumbling loosely down my shoulder. From the nape of my neck to the dimple at the base of my spine, there are words. But this time they aren't quotes. They're something else.

Kind.
Thoughtful.
Loyal.
Funny.

I look at my friends in confusion.

"If we're going to show everyone what people have called you," Lish says steadily, looking me straight in the eye, "we thought we should also show them who you really are."

My eyes are swimming. They're both grinning at me. I look back and read some more.

323

Procrastinator.

Old movie fanatic.

List-maker.

Beef-stew lover.

Occasional dork.

"That last one was me," Cat admits, and I do an ugly snort sob and bury my face in her armpit.

I'm ready.

We upload the photos and write a simple message with the link on the fake Anna's original account. "Want to really see me? All of me? Here I am." Then, all three of our hands on the mouse, we click post.

AUTHOR'S NOTE

IF YOU HAVE BEEN AFFECTED by any of the issues in this book, you are not alone. In fact, almost everything that happens to Anna is based on the real-life experiences of students I have worked with in schools, or young people who have contacted me online. This will come as a shock to some readers, but for thousands of girls, I know these issues are a daily reality.

I want you to know that change is coming. Every week I meet young people across the country who are taking action, determined to make things change. From launching a campaign to starting their own feminist societies, a generation of girls is taking matters into their own hands and fighting back, just like Anna and her friends.

And for the days when you might not feel able to fight back (we all have days like those), help is out there. The following organizations provide information, confidential support, and a listening ear when you might need it the most. Don't be afraid to reach out for help. You are not alone, you are not to blame, and you deserve to feel better.

rapecrisis.org

samaritans.org

stopbullying.gov

suicidepreventionlifeline.org

cybercivilrights.org/ccri-crisis-helpline

teenlineonline.org

yourlifeyourvoice.org

nationaleatingdisorders.org

helpguide.org

plannedparenthood.org

nami.org

jedfoundation.org

DISCUSSION QUESTIONS AND CONVERSATION STARTERS

1. Maggie's story, though four hundred years old, has been handed down for centuries through local accounts and area folklore. Anna's story is based on the real-life experiences of thousands of teenage girls. What are the main similarities and differences between their stories?

2. Have things changed for young women in those four hundred years?

3. How do you feel about the conversation between Anna and Emily Winters? How do you think both girls feel afterward?

4. How well do you think Ms. Forsyth and Miss Evans handle the information they learn about Anna online? Is there anything they could have done differently to better support her?

5. When Robin tries to stand up for Anna, he experiences homophobic bullying from some of the other boys. What pressures do the young men in the novel face, from one another and from outside?

6. What do you think Anna's mother is thinking and feeling when they arrive in St. Monans?

7. How would you describe Anna's relationship with her mother? Does it change over the course of the novel?

8. Why do you think Headmaster Greaves reacts the way he does to Anna's situation?

9. How would you describe Alisha's character? What do you think about the way she defines true love in her conversation with Anna on the pier?

10. Alisha and Cat are very different but are extremely close friends. What do you think makes their relationship so strong?

11. How do you think Anna's old friends back in Birmingham feel now that she is gone? Do you think the way they feel about Anna will change as they grow older?

12. Both Anna and Cat experience backlash for making decisions about their own bodies. In what ways are girls' bodies policed in the novel and in real life?

ACKNOWLEDGMENTS

In writing this book I have been indebted to many wonderful writers for their fascinating exploration of the topic of witchcraft and witch trials, in Scotland and more widely. Like Anna, I was surprised and thrilled to discover how many books documented the unfolding of this craze, into which I was able to delve for hidden gems of historical information. These include *An Abundance of Witches: The Great Scottish Witch-Hunt* (PG Maxwell-Stuart), *Witch-Hunting in Scotland: Law, Politics and Religion* (Brian P. Levack), *The Scottish Witch-Hunt in Context* (Julian Goodare), *The Witch Hunts* (Robert Thurston), *Witch Hunt: A True Story* (Isabel Adam), *The Witches of Fife* (Stuart MacDonald), *An Historical Account of St. Monance, Fife-Shire, Ancient and Modern* (John Jack), and *Scottish Witches* (Charles W. Cameron). I am particularly grateful to genealogist and local history researcher Bruce Bishop for his wonderful book, *Witchcraft Trials in Elgin, Morayshire*, and for his exhaustive help in researching the St. Monans kirk session records and St. Andrews presbytery minutes, searching for the elusive Maggie.

I am hugely grateful to Georgia Garrett, Madeleine Dunnigan, and the whole wonderful team at Rogers, Coleridge and White.

I have been so lucky to work with the most brilliant team at Simon & Schuster UK, who loved and cared about Anna and Maggie as much as I did from the very start. In particular, my fantastic, encouraging editor, Lucy Rogers, who supported and guided me every step of the way on this exciting journey. And of course the whole publishing dream team who made this book a reality, including Jane Griffiths, Alex Maramenides, Sarah Macmillan, Eve Wersocki-Morris, Laura Hough, and Stephanie Purcell. Special thanks to the super talented Jenny Richards and Helen Crawford-White for the gorgeous cover design and the eagle-eyed Jenny Glencross, Jane Tait, and Sally Critchlow for their superb copyediting.

Thank you so much to my early readers Lucy, Hayley, Aileen, and Emma for their thoughtful feedback and encouragement, and a big thank-you to the students of Bablake school. Very special thanks to Ellie, my earliest young reader, who is one of my biggest inspirations, and who is so special because she is always herself in a world which tells girls they should try to be somebody else. And to Abbie Bergstrom, for her infectious enthusiasm, drive and support, and for being such a brilliant cheerleader to other women.

Finally, thank you to my family and friends, for their endless love and encouragement, and to Nick, whose second shifts made this book possible.

ABOUT THE AUTHOR

LAURA BATES is a UK-based author and the founder of the Everyday Sexism Project, a crowdsourced collection of stories from women around the world about their experiences with gender inequality. Laura has received the 2015 British Empire Medal in the Queen's Birthday Honours; has been named in the BBC Woman's Hour Power List 2014 Game Changers; and in 2013 she won *Cosmopolitan*'s Ultimate Woman of the Year Award. She was also named in CNN's 10 Visionary Women List. Follow her efforts on Twitter @everydaysexism.